The Camel Bookmobile

ALSO BY MASHA HAMILTON

Staircase of a Thousand Steps
The Distance Between Us

The
Camel Bookmobile

Masha Hamilton

HARPER PERENNIAL

NEW YORK • LONDON • TORONTO • SYDNEY • NEW DELHI • AUCKLAND

HARPER ● PERENNIAL

A hardcover edition of this book was published in 2007 by HarperCollins Publishers.

P.S.™ is a trademark of HarperCollins Publishers.

FIRST HARPER PERENNIAL EDITION PUBLISHED 2008.

Designed by Kara Strubel

The Library of Congress has catalogued the hardcover edition as follows:
Hamilton, Masha.
    The camel bookmobile / Masha Hamilton.—1st ed.
        p.   cm.
    ISBN: 978-0-06-117348-6
    ISBN-10: 0-06-117348-7
    1. Librarians—Fiction.   2. Bookmobiles—Fiction.   3. Books and reading—Fiction.   4. Americans—Africa—Fiction.   I. Title.
    PS3558.A44338C36   2007
    813'.6—dc22   2006041316

ISBN 978-0-06-117349-3 (pbk.)

08   09   10   11   12   ID/RRD   10   9   8   7   6   5   4   3   2   1

*For the inspiring librarians who help keep the real
Camel Bookmobile running into the African bush,
and who are dedicated to decreasing an illiteracy rate of
more than 80 percent: Rashid M. Farah,
Nimo Issack, Kaltuma Bonaya, and Joseph Otieno.
Thank you for the time my daughter and I
shared with you.*

The Camel Bookmobile

Scar Boy

THE CHILD, WIDE-LEGGED ON THE GROUND, LICKED DUST off his fist and tried to pretend he was tasting camel milk. Nearby, his father spoke to a thorny acacia while his older brother hurled rocks at a termite mound. Neither paid him any attention, but this didn't change the fact that for the child, the three of them existed as a single entity. It was as if he drank dust, beseeched a tree, and threw stones all at once. He took this oneness for granted. Separate was a concept he was too young to recognize. Nor did he know of change, or fear, or the punishment of drought. All of life still felt predictable, and forever, and safe.

Now, for instance, this child-father-brother unit was enveloped in the reliable collapse of day, when the breeze stiffened, color drained from the sky, and shadows tinted three sets of cheeks simultaneously. The child welcomed this phase. The texture of the graying light transformed faces. It made people, he would later think, resemble charcoal portraits.

Something disturbed this particular dusk, though, tugging his attention away from the intimate comfort of his tongue on his skin and the dust's piquant flavor. Out of the gloom of nearby bushes rose a rigid, narrow object, standing frozen but quivering. This was odd. Everything in his experience either walked or dashed or flew or was blown by the wind or planted in the ground—in other words, it plainly moved or, less frequently, it didn't. What could he make of this harsh immobile shuddering, this tense and stubborn suggestion of flexibility? He crawled closer, then sat back to look again.

From this perspective, he spotted another object, small and round against the other's long narrowness. It was the color of a flame.

In fact, there were two.

Aha, he thought with satisfaction, the puzzle starting to shift into place. Eyes. Eyes, of course, moved and stayed still at once and could flicker like firelight. So the object must be human. Or maybe animal. Or maybe an ancestral ghost.

Whatever it was, he understood from somewhere, an inherited memory or intuition, that he needed all of himself to meet it. So he called to his other parts, his father-brother. "Here I am," he said, a gentle reminder. Even as he spoke, he didn't look away from the eyes and the rigid tail, and so he saw the object begin to grow larger. And then it lunged. It joined him, as if it too wanted to be part of the son-father-brother entity.

He was unaware of pain. Instead, the moment seemed unreal and confusing, like drifting off to sleep in the midst of one of his father's sung tales and losing track of the story. What had already happened? What was happening still? He would have to ask his father in the morning.

Only one part remained distinct: the sound that would echo in his mind until death. The wet, high-pitched ripping of his three-year-old flesh as the spotted hyena, never a kind beast and now mad with hunger, dove onto his leg, chomped at his waist, and then reached his face and gnawed, grunting with pleasure.

Later he would hear how his father turned, killed the beast with a miraculously aimed knife, scooped his son into his arms, and began running, the child's blood weeping down the father's arms. He would learn that all this took less than five meditative breaths—but he would never quite believe it. In his memory, the crunching of bone and tearing of flesh stretched over a decade of sundowns and sunups, disrupting all patterns, making everything separate and fearful and dusty and fleeting forever.

Part One

Mosquitoes' lives may be ephemeral, their deaths almost always brutal. But during their transitory span, absolutely nothing will stand in the way of their two formidable guiding desires: to soak up human lifeblood, and to reproduce.

—*A Mosquito's Life*, J. R. Churin, 1929

The American

FIONA SWEENEY SHOVED A PAIR OF ROLLED-UP JEANS INTO THE corner of her purple duffel bag. Outside her bedroom window, a siren's wail sliced through the white noise of a wet snowfall. Those eerie man-made moans were part of New York City's wallpaper, a signal of trouble commonplace enough to pass unnoticed. But Fi registered this one, maybe because she knew she wouldn't be hearing sirens for a while.

She turned her attention back to her bag, which still had space. What else should she take? Lifting a framed snapshot, she examined her mother as a young woman, wading into a stream, wearing rubber boots and carrying a fishing pole. Fi cherished the photograph; in real life, she'd never known her mother to be that carefree. The mother Fi had known wouldn't want to go to Africa. In fact, she wouldn't want Fi to go. Fi put the picture facedown and scanned the room, her attention drawn to a worn volume of Irish poetry by her bedside. She tucked it in.

"How about the netting?" Chris called from the living room where he sat with Devi.

"Already in," Fi answered.

"And repellent?" asked Devi.

"Yes, yes." Fi waved her hand as though shooing away a gnat—a gesture that Chris and Devi couldn't see from the other room. "Should have kept my mouth shut," she murmured.

Early on in her research about Kenya, she'd discovered that the country's annual death toll from malaria was in the tens of thousands. She had pills; she had repellents; logically, she knew she'd be fine. Still, a figure that high jolted her. She became slightly obsessed and—here's the rub—discussed it with Chris and Devi. *Mbu*—mosquito—had been the first Swahili word she'd learned. Sometimes the insects even dive-bombed into her nightmares. Eventually, mosquitoes became a metaphor for everything she feared about this trip: all the stories she'd read about a violent and chaotic continent, plus the jitters that come with the unknown.

And what wasn't unknown? All she knew for sure, in fact, was why she was going. Fi's mom had never been a big talker, but she'd been a hero, raising four kids alone. Now it was Fi's turn to do something worthwhile.

"Fi." Chris, at the door of the bedroom, waved in the air the paper on which he'd written a list of all the items he thought she should bring and might forget. Money belt. Hat. Granola bars. "Have you been using this?" he asked half-mockingly in the tone of a teacher.

"I hate lists," Fi said.

He studied her a second. "OK," he said. "Then, what do you say, take a break?"

"Yeah, c'mon, Fi. We don't want to down all your wine

by ourselves," Devi called from the living room, where an Enya CD played low.

Pulling back her dark, frizzy hair and securing it with a clip, Fi moved to the living room and plopped onto the floor across from Devi, who sprawled in a long skirt on the couch. Chris poured Fi a glass of cabernet and sat in the chair nearest her. If they reached out, the three of them could hold hands. Fi felt connected to them in many ways, but at the same time, she was already partly in another place and period. A soft light fell in from the window, dousing the room in a flattering glow and intensifying the sensation that everything around her was diaphanous, and that she herself was half here and half not.

"You know, there's lots of illiteracy in *this* country," Devi said after a moment.

"That's why I've been volunteering after work," Fi said. "But there, it's different. They've never been exposed to libraries. Some have never held a book in their hands."

"Not to mention that it's more dangerous, which somehow makes it appealing to Fi," Chris said to Devi, shaking his head. "Nai-robbery."

Though he spoke lightly, his words echoed those of Fi's brother and two sisters—especially her brother. She was ready with a retort. "I'll mainly be in Garissa, not Nairobi," she said. "It's no more dangerous there than New York City. Anyway, I want to take some risks—different risks. Break out of my rut. Do something meaningful." Then she made her tone playful. "The idealistic Irish. What can you do?"

"Sometimes idealism imposes," Chris said. "What if all they want is food and medicine?"

"You know what I think. Books are their future. A link to the modern world." Fi grinned. "Besides, we want *Huckle-berry Finn* to arrive before *Sex in the City* reruns, don't we?"

Devi reached out to squeeze Fi's shoulder. "Just be home by March."

Home. Fi glanced around, trying to consciously take in her surroundings. She'd considered subletting, which would have been the most economical decision, but she'd gotten busy and let it slide. Now she noticed that Chris had stacked her magazines neatly and stored away the candles so they wouldn't collect dust. After she left for Kenya, Chris had told her, he'd come back to wash any glasses or plates she'd left out, make sure the post office was holding her mail, and take her plants back to his apartment. He'd thought of that, not her. A nice gesture, she kept reminding herself. Still. She gave Chris a wicked grin as she reached out to mess up the magazines on the coffee table. It felt satisfying, even though she knew he would just restack them later.

Chris was deep into what his colleagues called "ground-breaking" research on the human brain—specifically the hippocampus—at NYU Medical Center. He wanted a shared home and, eventually, kids. Her siblings thought they were a well-suited couple, but that was hardly persuasive. Fi's brother's wife's cousin was married to one of Fi's sisters, and they all still lived within eight blocks of their child-hood homes. They considered Fi a wanderer for moving from the Bronx all the way to Brooklyn. They wanted to see her "settled," and she doubted that it mattered much to them who she settled with—or for.

But even Devi, who had arrived in Brooklyn via Iran,

agreed about Chris. "He's a scientist who studies the part of the brain that processes memories, and you work for an institution that does the same, if you think about it," Devi said once. "How perfect is that?"

Remembering it, Fi took a gulp of wine. The assumptions people made about one another were invariably wrong, she'd found. Yes, she was a librarian; yes, he was a researcher. But Chris was disciplined and logical where she was—well, she liked to think of herself as whimsical. Eventually, she suspected, her spontaneity would start to drive him batty, and his take-charge confidence would curb her style. Sometimes Fi thought Chris had become a researcher to immerse himself in a world he could analyze and define. That's not what she sought from her work. Books allowed her vicarious tastes of infinite variety, but they didn't supplant the need to venture out into the big and the messy. In fact, just the opposite. Books convinced her that something more existed—something intuitive, beyond reason—and they whetted her appetite to find it.

Occasionally, though, she felt a shock of fear that made her legs ache. She was thirty-six, after all, not a kid, and what she sought—this "something more"—seemed amorphous, even to her. She couldn't say what she was looking for, precisely; she only hoped she'd know when she found it.

What if, through inertia and social pressure, she ended up with Chris, and children, and backyard barbecues, and everything except the loose housedresses, and then what if she woke up to find herself somewhere on the gentle slope past middle age, gazing over her shoulder at a life respectable and well organized but too narrowly lived? A life that didn't fit her. Couldn't that happen? Didn't it happen to people all the time?

"Well, here's to the Camel Bookmobile." Devi raised her glass. "Bringing literacy to the African bush."

"Hear, hear," Fi agreed. "It's going to open up whole new worlds for those people." *For me, too*, she thought, though she didn't say it. She felt light-headed with anticipation.

"My little library evangelist," said Chris in an ironic tone, shaking his head.

"Come on. Toast the project," Devi urged him.

"OK, OK," Chris said. "To Kenya. To the camels." From the end table, he picked up a book on camel husbandry—a joke gift from Fi's colleagues—and lifted it with one hand, raising his wineglass with the other.

The Girl

THE SUN HAD NOT YET SPIT ITS FIRST SPRAY OF DUSTY GOLD into their home when Kanika woke to a vicious buzz. *Mbu.* Not just one—a whole swarm, thronging within her belly. She'd never heard of mosquitoes invading an abdomen before, but there was no other way to account for the vibrating drone coming from within. How in the name of her blessed ancestors had the mosquitoes gotten inside? She pictured the bloodsuckers breeding in her veins, dumping eggs along her rib cage, their heads drooping as they guzzled down her precious moisture at its source.

"*Nyanya,*" she called, frightened, pressing a hand to her center, the curve of her flesh, to try to determine the numbers within. This was not the work of ten or twelve. There were a hundred twenty at least, plenty enough to rob her of life.

Her grandmother Neema, asleep next to her, opened her eyes a little, then wide, then sat up. She reached out for Kanika.

And in that moment, Kanika remembered. The hum came not from insects, but from an obscure emotion—one rare enough to frighten her. Anticipation. She rubbed her eyes and laughed at her own foolishness. "Lie back down," she said.

Neema shook her head as though to clear it. "You wake me to tell me to sleep?"

"A tickle inside scared me. But it's only the books."

"The books." The answer satisfied Neema enough to allow her to lower her head, but she kept her eyes open, watching Kanika.

This was Library Day. The day the books would arrive, borne in wooden boxes on either side of a camel's hump. Soon Kanika would be fondling covers and running her fingers over random words before settling on the two volumes she was permitted to borrow. Then she would grasp them possessively, carry them home, put them in the center of the room, and delay opening them as long as possible to stretch out the delicious pleasure. Finally—sometime before nightfall, she knew—she wouldn't be able to wait longer, so she would give up and dive in. Endless words in English or Swahili spilling one atop another, metamorphosing into sentences and paragraphs, leaping to life as Kanika deciphered them, revealing secrets that left her light-headed.

Kanika could read as fast as locusts devour, thanks to lessons from her grandmother, who had also grasped the gift as a girl. For years, though, Kanika's sole book had been a tattered copy of the Bible in English that a British missionary once gave Neema's mother—the first of Kanika's family who had been taught to read. For Kanika, the book had nothing to do with religion; she believed, as did her neighbors, in the Hundred-Legged One and in the spirits that lived in everything. Nevertheless, by the age of nine,

Kanika had reread the stories of Adam and Abraham and
David more than fifty times. That was the year she realized she couldn't stand to read them again—or the ones
about Samson, or Joseph, or Cain and Abel, or any of the
others. She'd had enough of abandoned sheep and feuding
brothers and mythically flawed men. She thought she was
finished with reading forever.

Now, five years and five months later, what unexpected
wealth! *True Stories of Grizzly Bear Attacks.* A biography of
Nelson Mandela. A history of Nigeria. And most recently,
Mosquitoes, Malaria, and Man: A History. Still on her back,
she flexed her feet and reached to touch the tome featur-
ing on its cover a magnified mosquito, head hanging, body
ballooned with blood. The cause, obviously, of her waking
imagery. All right then. No more insect books. She could
see the wisdom of that, as long as there were other words
to read. The camels had been lumbering into Mididima
not quite four months, and already their cache had become
essential to her.

Of course, they'd delivered more than books to Kanika,
more even than knowledge of the outside world. They'd
elevated her status. As a child, she'd spent so much time
with Neema's Bible that her neighbors had dismissed her
as a useless oddity. Words on a page were acceptable, barely,
as an occasional idle distraction. But to be obsessed with
them? If she wanted to read, the elders had told her many
times, far better to learn to read animal scents on the breeze,
or the coming weather in the clouds.

The library's arrival had made a leopard's leap of a difference, marking the start of a real school. Matani had always

called himself a teacher and tried to gather together the children to write letters in the sand. But how long could sticks and dirt hold their interest? Now, though, all the children were given books to explore, and being taught to chant the alphabet in Swahili and English and to translate squiggles on paper, and Kanika had become Matani's helper. "The assistant teacher," he called her. "With all these books, I cannot educate everyone at once, Kanika. Not even with help of the cane."

Kanika had never before been given a title, let alone thought to be someone who had valuable knowledge. Before, she'd been considered nearly as out of place, in her own way, as Scar Boy. Now, though, tiny bodies with sour-scented skin pressed close to her over open pages. Mothers watched with a mixture of envy and resentment as she shared some mysterious secret with their offspring. They didn't respect her any more than ever. But they were afraid of her, she knew—afraid of the skill she possessed that they didn't have.

She yawned and stretched and thought, then, of Miss Sweeney, the American who would, by the ancestors' blessings, arrive with the camels as she always did. Kanika extended a hand to pick up a flat, round object she kept next to her grass mat. Miss Sweeney's gift. A miracle smaller than a clenched fist. A dry water puddle that could be carried around and gazed in whenever one wished. A mirror, Miss Sweeney called it. None of the girls of Mididima had ever seen one before. She shifted it so that she could examine, in the dim light, her eyes, her cheeks, her effusive mouth.

"The sight of yourself pleases you," her grandmother said with a generous chuckle.

Kanika shook her head in protest. "What pleases is that I can see myself at any time. I won't be left wondering who that is when I catch glimpse of myself in a splash of rainwater."

Neema nodded, serious now. "There's magic beyond our world, it's true."

Moved by something in her grandmother's voice, Kanika turned, tempted to reveal her plan. But she stopped herself. Better to act before talking. And act she would, as soon as the camels arrived today.

She would hurry to Miss Sweeney's side and use the hem of her own *kitenge* to clean off each book. No matter that she personally found no offense in the sunset-colored dust that wasted little time in laying claim to everything that entered the bush. Unimportant if she, like her neighbors, believed it irresponsible to use up hours struggling against grains of earth. The powder bothered Miss Sweeney when it settled on the books, and that was enough. Kanika had watched Miss Sweeney stroke the books clean with her soft, pale palms. This time, Kanika would do that for her—quietly, yes, but ostentatiously enough to be noticed. The act of cleaning would be something more than an effort to ingratiate herself; it would be like a book's prologue—not the story yet, but a suggestion of the story to come.

Then afterward, she would approach Miss Sweeney, lead her apart from the others, take her hand, perhaps. Little by little—an elephant must be eaten a bite at a time—she would speak of her desires: no, her needs. A way to the Distant City. Or perhaps to even more distant Distant Cities. To leave the bush. To be an assistant teacher somewhere where shelves of books and walls of mirrors and other wonders were as commonplace as sand. If she could teach the children of Mididima to read, couldn't she teach other children, in places of greater potential?

Kanika knew her plan would sound, to most of her tribe, like a desert nomad's dream of snow. That's why she'd told only Scar Boy. He would repeat it to no one, of course; who talked to Scar Boy? And telling him had been enough. That had satisfied her need to press the words into another's ears, to make her vision real. He'd listened with his whole being. Though he'd said nothing, she was sure he supported her plan. After all, forsaken as he was by his neighbors, with his slow limp and his poor distorted face, he understood about dreams.

Miss Sweeney—clearly a daring woman herself, clearly someone who'd seen snow, perhaps even walked through it—would listen too, and understand, and help. Miss Sweeney, after all, had squeezed Kanika's shoulders. She'd leaned close enough for her hair to brush Kanika's cheek, and for her odor—that complicated, ornate scent that some here found disgusting—to fill Kanika's nostrils. She'd given Kanika the mirror.

Kanika vowed to find the courage to act today, before her great-uncle Elim or others began grumbling again, muttering that she was behind schedule to find a husband, that she must be married before the arrival of summer's dry winds. Before they trapped her.

A spiraling cord of nerves in her stomach, as well as a

morning pressure that needed to be relieved behind a bush, at last propelled Kanika to her feet. She glanced through the open door, surprised to see the day still hovering. She was rising earlier and earlier now that she was an assistant teacher, now that she had books to read. It seemed to have satisfied Elim, who'd lately been complaining less. He used to protest that she remained wedded to the earth far too long each day, depending on the sun to pry open her eyes.

"She's as lazy as a dying man," Elim told Neema once in a voice that boomed through Mididima, loud as a thunderstorm. It had not been laziness—even now, Kanika flushed at the public accusation. Sometimes, yes, there was a morning's heaviness after a late night spent talking to Scar Boy while Mididima slept—talks no one else knew about, because all would disapprove. But primarily, her lack of enthusiasm for daylight had been born of days carrying too few possibilities. Since the library had arrived, all could surely see that she was far from lazy.

She brushed her uncle's old complaint aside by flinging her right hand through the air. Today, she would not be disturbed by thoughts of uncles whose minds resembled mud pools, or lurking husbands or pointless chores. She would begin the morning with the speed and joy of a well-aimed spear, and that would make the moments fly faster until the Camel Bookmobile and Miss Sweeney arrived.

The American

IN A VACANT LOT NEXT TO GARISSA'S PROVINCIAL LIBRARY some three hours south of Mididima, two herdsmen struggled to strap wooden boxes filled with books to a camel's side. They'd been trying for fifteen minutes, and by now an audience of a dozen passersby had collected. Fi stood with Mr. Abasi. She saw the camel blink its long eyelashes against an arrow of early-morning light and then shift abruptly with uncanny timing. The boxes fell off. Again. Books thudded onto the ground, the sound reverberating. It was the fifth try and still no success. The camel's lips turned up in what looked remarkably like a smirk.

One herdsman spewed curses—Fi understood that much even without knowing the words. He picked up a book, *Practical Primary English,* and flung it down in frustration. She flinched as the book skidded on the ground. Still muttering, the herdsman grabbed a second book, *How the Pig Got His Snout.* Mr. Abasi stood immobile next to Fi. He was, Fi guessed, about forty-two or forty-three, but in his blue striped pants and pale pink button-down shirt with soccerball cufflinks, he looked like a boy playing dress-up. He stared dispassionately as the herdsman hurled one more book.

These were the moments when Fi, if she allowed herself, could regress to what she thought of as her early period: the days a dozen years ago when she'd been a new librarian and worked at the information desk in the children's and teens' section at the Bedford library branch. "Children! People are reading. Please, no roughhousing here. A library is not a playground—well, it *is*, actually, but not as you might think of it . . . " Trailing off, giving up, recognizing that she was particularly unsuited to make such reprimands because for them to be effective, one must be able to stick to black and white, while she always found herself slipping into intricate grays of "maybe" and "sometimes."

Here, she'd approached the matter freshly. She'd learned to admonish the herdsmen in Swahili to be careful with the books: "*Vitunze vitabu!*" She'd tried longer lectures, too, with Mr. Abasi as translator. She'd mentioned the vulnerability of a book's spine, the limited numbers of volumes, the trust of the benefactors. But then she found herself veering off, mentioning the first library of clay tablets collected in Mesopotamia; or the first horse-drawn bookmobile in 1905 in Hagerstown, Maryland; or even philosophical statements about books transcending time and space—and Mr. Abasi's translations would fade away and the herdsmen would stand silent.

Talk wasn't working. There had to—had to—be another way to infuse them with her own commitment to the bookmobile.

With both hands in front of him, Mr. Abasi held a brown bag that, she knew after these many trips, contained his lunch. He wasn't married; she imagined him packing the lunch for himself each evening, setting it next to the door. She reached over, smoothly took the bag from him, then raised her arm and threw it on the ground.

He opened his mouth as if gulping water. "What are you doing?" he asked.

"I'm a visitor to your country, Mr. A.," she said. "I want to fit in."

"I—" He was actually sputtering. "I have grapes in there. Do you know how expensive grapes are here?"

She gestured toward the camels. "And books," she said, "are expensive, too."

"That," Mr. Abasi said, waving a hand. "He's frustrated."

"Me too. The Camel Bookmobile was started so people living away from towns could learn to read. It can change lives. But if the books are ruined, the program fails."

Their gazes locked for a full minute. Then Mr. Abasi rotated his long neck and spoke curtly to the herdsman, who, with exaggerated gestures, lifted the thrown books one by one and dusted them off, placing them carefully with the others.

"Thank you," Fi said, bending to pick up the bag. "Your efforts will help our library survive."

"Along with my lunch," he muttered. But as he turned away, she thought she saw a glimmer of amusement in his eyes.

Light was seeping into the mushroom gray sky; the suspended wine-colored dust particles were becoming increasingly visible. Fi opened her mouth to take a bite of the grainy air, scented with animal dung, dust, and wood smoke. Nairobi had perpetually smelled of charcoal fires and diesel fumes, but in Garissa, scents never seemed to linger—they vanished in the aridity. In her apartment in Brooklyn, above Fleishmann's Coffee Shop, smells tended to seep up the stairs and plop in her living room like ornery houseguests refusing to leave: bitter coffee wrestling with steamed milk and burned sugar-dough.

Suddenly, unexpectedly, Fi missed the scents of home. She calculated: in Brooklyn, it was late evening of the previous day. "Going to make a quick call," she told Mr. Abasi, gesturing with her head toward the library building.

Inside, she used her calling card. The one luxury she permitted herself was weekly calls, usually to her brother or one of her sisters, sometimes to Chris or Devi, always made from the library because there was no phone in the nearby home where Fi had a room provided for by the Kenya National Library Service.

Sometimes, though, she lost track of the weekly schedule. Time felt elusive here, where the crocodile-laden Tana River eternally passed on its way to the Indian Ocean and flocks of ugly marabou storks perched atop acacia trees and men hauled carts along dirt roads as they had for generations. The battery on Fi's wristwatch had run down two weeks after she arrived, and she'd taken that as a sign, stuffing the watch away instead of getting it fixed. Devi, hearing that, said Fi had better keep calling, because she clearly needed a link to the twenty-first century—what Devi called the "real world," by which she meant Pilates, lattes, organic grocery stores, and, everywhere, clocks.

Fi dialed the number. "Hey," she said when Devi answered. "You still awake?"

"Fi!" Devi said. "How are you? No malaria yet?"

Fi laughed and reached inside her bag for her water bottle. "I'm so done with worrying about that," she said, because she was, mostly. "What's happening there?"

"The sun is up and crime's down," Devi said. "Though some baseball star was suspended the other day for using a cork-filled bat. And Lulu the transvestite has the hottest off-Broadway show. Now tell me about you."

"Mididima," Fi said.

"'Scuse me?"

"Where we go today. My favorite stop."

"You have a favorite now?"

Fi leaned her neck back into her free hand and rubbed. "The place rises up out of nothing," she said. "The people are stunning, with their burnished skin. And they're not as poor as the others. I mean, they're poor—my God, everyone's poor—but they created this irrigation system that I haven't seen anywhere else, and they never beg, and when the Camel Bookmobile shows up, they're eager. We're going to bring them into the modern world, Devi. These are the people I'm here for."

"They're eager? That means not everyone you meet is so thrilled to see a white lady and her books?" Devi's tone poked gentle fun.

"OK, not everyone," Fi said. "I mean, the others aren't unhappy to see us, just puzzled. In most places, they keep their distance, or stare with blank faces. I must seem so strange. And sometimes I do feel them thinking—with everything we need here, what craziness possessed this lady to come with a pile of books?"

"But I already know your answer," Devi said. "Books, books everywhere. So tell me about Mi—whatever."

"Mididima. In their tribal language, it means Those Rooted in Dust. I feel more connected to them than any of the others. Maybe because so many of them speak English—" Fi laughed at herself, "Well, three, anyway." She thought of the girl Kanika, her straight-backed grandmother Neema, and the teacher Matani, whose sudden smiles startled and charmed her. "But all the children are learning, and they practice on me. And there's one they call Scar Boy, who doesn't speak at all but cradles books like they could save him. How can I resist that?" Fi reached into a plastic bag to pinch off a piece of peppery-sweet fried bread. It was powdered with soil, and dry enough to require infusions from the water bottle before crawling down her throat. "Mr. A., of course, hates Mididima," she said.

"Mr. A. Isn't he the one who thinks you're a colonist, trying to homogenize the world? The one who hates everything about your project?"

"Especially Mididima, though. Mr. A. says it's too primitive and too far away. It's an isolated little pocket. Takes hours to get there."

Fi had been surprised that Mr. Abasi had any doubts at all about the bookmobile project, and even more surprised to find that he had enough reservations to fill a small set of encyclopedias. She hadn't anticipated objections from Garissa's chief librarian when she'd applied for the consultant position. She'd thought everyone in Kenya, and especially the librarians, would be thrilled with the idea of camels ferrying books to the isolated northeast region.

But, just for starters, Mr. Abasi didn't even seem to fully trust the seminomads. He had been educated briefly in London, and he sprinkled his speech with Briticisms like *bloke* and *lorry* and acted as if he preferred Europeans to either Africans or Americans. He'd spearheaded the imposition of a series of rules that seemed too rigid to Fi, but that he insisted were necessary. "We've got to follow a strict policy if we're going to be balmy enough to take books this far into the bush," he liked to say. She'd given way in exchange for a measure of his blessings.

"What are you doing in your spare time?" Devi asked now.

"Meeting with teachers, mostly," Fi said. "I talked with a local government official a couple of days ago to discuss future funding."

"But what about for fun?"

"Garissa is way off the tourist path," Fi said. "I see giraffes all the time, though, and hippos at the Tana River the other day. I was invited to hear some drummers a few nights ago." She heard a shout from outside. "I've got to go, Devi."

"You going to call Chris?"

"No time now," Fi said. "Just give him my best."

"Your best? You want me to tell him that?"

"You know what I mean."

"All right." Devi drew the words out. "Be careful, Fi, OK?"

As she stepped outside, Fi saw one of the herdsmen talking with large gestures and in an agitated voice as his fellow camel-driver nodded. The cantankerous camel was on its knees but baring its teeth and complaining in a loud moan. "Still no books loaded?" Fi called.

Mr. Abasi shrugged. "The driver calls the beast a fool-brained lump of dung, but I think the camel and I actually agree. It would be wiser to stick our heads in the mouths of lions than to make this trip."

Fi laughed. "Lighten up, Mr. A.," she said. "We're going to the village of Mididima, not hell."

"It's not a village, Miss Sweeney; it's a collection of wanderers best left alone, and it's too far into *shifta* territory. More than once, I've tried to point that out."

So convenient, this mention of the *shifta*, Fi thought. Downplayed most of the time, the desert thieves were brought up only when there was a chance that they might dissuade a foreigner from doing something a local found tiresome.

"*Shifta* steal cattle, not books," she said. She reached down to the pile of books stacked on the ground, picked one up—a biography of Napoleon—and placed it in Mr. Abasi's right hand. "Just think, Mr. A.," she said, attempting to sound like Mary Poppins, "books, books, everywhere."

Mr. Abasi stared at her skeptically. Then he set down the book, put his lunch bag on top, scratched his neck, and looked off searchingly into the saffron light, as though trying to discern, on the flat horizon, the makeshift, mirage-like gathering of souls—the settlement of Those Rooted in Dust—which was, to his obvious and immense regret, their day's destination.

The Grandmother

NEEMA WATCHED HER GRANDDAUGHTER RISE AND SASHAY through the shadows of their hut, her body a long blade of grass that swayed in time to a private breeze. Kanika settled her necklace and earrings. "I'll get your *chai*, *Nyanya*," she murmured. "And take out the goats before I go to Matani. You can move a bit slower this morning."

Neema reached to smooth her granddaughter's hair. "Up this early, with the air this dry, you'll be a wilted leaf by evening."

"This evening? I'll be like a fresh-fed calf," Kanika said as she stepped outside, dismayingly cheerful.

Neema shook her head. She still couldn't quite fathom how Kanika's demeanor had changed so radically over these last few months. Neema loved Kanika like a bowl of water at the end of a thirsty month, no matter what her disposition; after all, the girl had saved her life. But she couldn't deny that she missed the days when Kanika had been as moody as a pregnant bush pig. There'd been power in the moodiness. It was for that girl of tough volatility that Neema had hopes. It was for that girl that she'd screamed at her dead husband's brother Elim—may the wind eat him—when he, dreaming of the bride price, had pressed for Kanika to be married at age thirteen. "A hibiscus on a vine, a clam in a shell, and my granddaughter—all have nothing to do with you!" she'd said.

And though she'd sounded brave, that had been a risk. Neema knew she held a unique position in Mididima. As a widow who had successfully managed her dead husband's herds, she was often permitted to participate in discussions over grazing and resettlement decisions. Still, if Elim had chosen to fight her about Kanika's future, tradition and the neighbors would have supported him.

Neema spit on her palms and flattened the hair at her forehead, sighing. She'd told herself many times that she shouldn't be anything but pleased to find Kanika adjusting to life's expectations. At age fifty-six, she knew what it cost to spend years chafing against restraints others didn't even seem to notice. The journey was always easier, after all, for the beast that wore blinders. That had been her own mother's argument, though Neema had never been able to live by it.

Kanika returned, bringing Neema a cup of *chai*. She was humming. Humming! This was too much. Her granddaughter of spicy temperament, who had resisted the idea of being tamed before ever being untamed: where in the name of a camel's ass had that feisty spirit gone? Neema could feel something painful welling up within her. She didn't want to raise another one who compromised too easily. She took the cup her granddaughter offered and motioned for her to sit. It was time for something radical.

"I've never told you," she said, "about my *kutairi*."

Kanika cringed and grinned at once. "*Nyanya*, circumcision doesn't seem the topic for this morning—"

"I kept it from you," Neema spoke over Kanika, "but now you should know. It was my twelfth year. I'd heard of the custom before, of course. But I'd never thought of it in connection with myself. They came to me. Told me my time was two days away."

Neema felt hot just thinking of it. She dipped her fingers in a tin pot holding about two inches of water, and dampened her cheeks.

"Maybe later we could—"

"I want you to hear now," Neema said firmly. "I remember looking to my mother, hoping for help. But do you know what it is to have lost the ability to imagine life differently? That was my mother. So I fled. What else could I do? On the other hand, I was still a child. I only went to my aunt's home. From there, they dragged me back, though not before a cousin whispered of a certain rock that would change me into a boy if I sat atop it overnight."

"A rock?" Kanika's eyes went merry.

"There is magic in the earth, don't doubt it." Neema shook a finger.

"But, *Nyanya*, it didn't work," Kanika said, her voice still teasing.

Neema took a sip of warm *chai*, remembering how she'd found the boulder, perched on it, and begged to the moon as it rose. "In fact," she said, "I became half man that night. Only it was the wrong half. Outwardly, I still looked a girl." She scooted closer to Kanika, touching her knee. "The next day, they held me down and hewed away at my private flesh with a broad-bladed knife before covering the mangled mass with a leaf."

Kanika looked into her cup, shuddering slightly.

"I had to be propped up to make it home," Neema said. "My relatives began feasting on a slaughtered goat—such a celebration!—while I lay bleeding, half-delirious. Three days later, my wound filled with pus."

Kanika put a hand to her stomach. "*Nyanya*—"

"My mother was a good woman," Neema went on. "But she couldn't see that we didn't have to be cut like this. Or perhaps she lacked the courage to say no. Your mother—forgive me for saying it, but take it as a warning—lacked courage too."

Kanika stood and went to the door.

"Kanika, I say it for your own good," Neema said, rising too. "Dahira was my daughter, don't forget. And you know I almost didn't survive when she was killed. She was much sweeter than me; I've told you that too. But she married too soon, and became docile too soon. And what is hardest, she died without knowing more than"—Neema gestured out the door—"this."

"I know more. Already, I know more."

Neema touched the rim of her cup to her lower lip, sipped. They stood silently looking out the door. Soon, Neema knew, the strangers—or not quite strangers anymore, but at least not neighbors—would appear like distant dots, and slowly swell until they became three camels, three dark men of Africa, and one pale foreign woman. Heat rising from the cracked earth would blur their forms until they reached Mididima, where, finally in focus, they would spread grass mats onto a tiny spill of tree shade and unload their treasure. Then nearly everyone would toss aside the daily chores to gather. Perhaps even Abayomi's son, poor, feared Scar Boy, would again venture out of his home long enough to wrap his arms around a book, although with him it was difficult to know.

Neema's brother-in-law Elim walked by, brushing his teeth with a stick from the *miswak* tree, his oversize head floating above scrawny shoulders. "Women," he said. "Why do you linger at your door?"

"Thinking," Kanika answered boldly. "Of the books that come today."

"Books." Elim spit out the side of his mouth. "Matani should have stayed away, instead of trying to drag the Distant City here. We don't belong with that world. It will treat us like dung if we let it. It would wipe us out if it could. We don't want it."

"I do," Neema said.

Elim glared harder at Neema. "Then you are unspeakably misguided," he said. "If my brother were alive, he'd die to see you wasting good daylight peering at paper. You're better off spending your time teaching your granddaughter how to build houses, or telling her our stories."

"I'm bored by the old stories, Elim," Neema said. "They stick in my throat; so go ahead and put me to death. And please, do it this week, if I must squander the rest of my days on nothing more than helping girls learn to patch together twigs and camel dung."

She gave him, then, what she knew the neighbors called her "corpse gaze," mouth flat as the horizon, eyes distant and unfocused. This well-worn trick of hers, perfected at an early age, infuriated Elim, just as it had infuriated her husband, and her mother before him. Elim's last comment came as spit from over his shoulder.

"Lines and curves carved onto paper are meaningless to us," he said. "Worse than meaningless. The hours you waste staring at pages—that, Neema, is a rotten sin."

"Yes, good morning, Uncle Elim," Kanika muttered under her breath as he left. She reached for Neema's empty cup, but Neema refused to release it.

"You remember learning to read?" Neema asked.

"Of course."

"The first sentence I taught you?"

Kanika grinned at her grandmother as if she knew what was coming. Very well, then, let her hear it again. And again and again, until Neema could be sure it stuck.

"A chicken's prayer doesn't touch the hawk," Kanika recited.

"And that means—"

"I'm to be a hawk, I guess, instead of that feebleminded chicken," Kanika said, grinning.

Neema rested her palm briefly on Kanika's cheek and then let her leave. How lucky that her early reading lessons with Kanika had centered on wise sayings and the Bible. Of course it was only because she hadn't known of anything more, in those days.

She felt ashamed to admit that until the Camel Library came, she'd thought the Bible was the only book of stories in existence. Never in a lifetime of moons would she have imagined there were so many books, with firm outer skins of bright colors, and flexible innards so full of flavor that she liked to touch her lips to the pages as if to drink. Mr. Abasi, the librarian from the Distant City, told her in his tone of a man with a bug in his nose that of course there was a word to describe these objects. She surely had heard it before, he said. *Vitabu.*

And she had. *Vitabu.* But she thought it stood only for the long, pretentious statements tribal leaders issued against one another, statements less important than the sand beneath her toes. Or perhaps the dull, studious tracts that she imagined Matani and his father read in the Distant City. She never knew *vitabu* could hold so much variety, so much beauty, so many made-up tales more real than her own life. And so many women. Women who revealed and confirmed and challenged and comforted at once. Women who were like her in some essential way, some even as old, though their outward circumstances were unimaginably different.

In another moment, she knew, she had to go cultivate. She sat anyway, and opened the book she would have to return today in exchange for another. A story about a widow living near an ocean in America who is told she has only a few months left to her.

No living soul knew it, but in the months before the book-bearing camels first materialized, jutting up from the desert floor like thirst-inspired hallucinations, Neema herself had begun to feel Old Woman Earth waiting to claim her. Her bones seemed to grow heavy beyond her years. Her memory became a frayed and dangling thread, often distorted. Moments from childhood seemed fresher than those from a week ago.

One night she dreamed of floating above Mididima. It was a moving day, with the tribe packing up to resettle in another place. Animals were grumbling, tin pots clanging, beaded necklaces swinging; and she was above, her arms pointing down to the neighbors with whom she'd lived all her adult life. A group of women, some dead, others still living, walked one behind the other, chanting from a place deep in their throats. She'd watched a moment, and then glided on to the seaside where she'd been born and spent her childhood, where her mother had been buried. She sank to the circle of seashells she'd made to mark her mother's grave and found them remarkably, impossibly, still in place.

A woman approached, and though she looked paler and heavier, Neema knew it was her mother. First, the woman carried the same Bible her mother had given Neema shortly before she died. And second, when the woman got closer, she smiled, opened her mouth, and burped. It was scentless, virginal, resonating—exactly the sort of belch Neema's mother always had been able to produce at will. When Neema was tiny, her mother had used this skill to amuse her. Later she'd told Neema her burps served a larger purpose. They were meant to demonstrate that grasping a thing too tightly, even something she loved, would crush the life from it.

Later, after Dahira was killed, Neema remembered her mother's words, and worried that, though with good intention, she'd tried to grasp her own daughter too tightly. As a child, though, and unburdened by such concerns, Neema, who always giggled when her mother belched, giggled even more at this attempt to justify and exalt that act. Even in the dream, Neema had chuckled, and her own laughter awakened her.

But the laughter quickly faded. She understood the meaning of her dream right away, and felt something dry up inside like a root ripped from the ground. *Not yet.* Those two words swelled up from somewhere below her heart. She was too young. She wasn't ready to join her mother and daughter. She had more to do, though she wasn't sure what. And she couldn't yet leave Kanika.

A plea was pointless, though. The day a monkey is destined to die, Neema knew, all trees turn slippery.

And then the camels came. Kanika saved her life first, but the books saved it the second time—that was certain. The library returned her to a last breath of youth, days ripe with hope and possibility. When she sank into a page and heard the others' voices, music began within again, the tripping rhythm and beat that carried all life forward. No matter if her neighbors stirred and grunted and complained. The stories were her lifeblood—the stories and Kanika.

As she closed the book and rubbed the callused feet she would be standing on all day, she made a private vow. She would tend the crops, yes, and gather and carry and cook and build. But then, with whatever time she had left, until life was taken from her, Neema would touch more pages; she would encounter there more of those far-flung sisters; she would listen to them whisper the unuttered words of her heart.

The Teacher

Birds darted overhead with a surplus of energy as though fueled by the undercurrent of excitement running through Mididima. Or perhaps tension was more accurate. Inside Matani's house, his wife—her musical voice strained—was complaining again: the same old topic, the one that troubled the tribe's elders as well. The Camel Bookmobile.

Even in the midst of her irritation, though, it could not be denied that she was a stunning woman, with breasts that smiled up at her face and legs of a panther and eyes as welcoming as water in the Kaisut Desert. Despite, or maybe because of, this beauty, Matani sometimes thought, though briefly, that she had not been the right choice for a teacher's wife.

If only he could have wanted someone plainer who would not have felt so free to find fault. Or maybe someone with education who would have understood. Although what woman from Nairobi would have come back here with him? He did not deceive himself into believing that he was, after all, as good-looking or charming as that. He was lucky to have won Jwahir's heart. She was twenty-seven years old, nine years younger than he. She had delayed marriage much longer than other girls of Mididima, but not because there hadn't been offers. Many of his peers would have gladly wed her. He'd been the one to win her, and he still found that remarkable.

"These books of yours," Jwahir was saying, "are too foolish, even for the children." Matani managed—just—to stop himself from interrupting to clarify that the books were not actually his. "Kanika translated one for me." Jwahir pronounced the next words in slow, stilted English. "A cat. On. A hat." She shook her head, then switched back to her own language. "If such a book held facts for how to hunt a leopard, then perhaps—although even then, it's better for the knowledge to pass from father to son. But a book about a creature who, what? Sits on a head covering?"

"*In* a hat," Matani said absently, distracted by Jwahir's mention of father and son, wondering if it was off-handed, or intentional, perhaps a subtle female way to show that her deepest desire matched his own. Too late, he realized that he had corrected his wife, so he leaned closer, reached for her shoulder, hesitated, and stroked the air above it. "It's only because I am a teacher," he said apologetically.

His beautiful Jwahir glared. An apology had never been enough to soothe her temper. And on this topic of the Camel Bookmobile, she routinely displayed more thorns than the acacia.

"*On* or *in* doesn't matter. Either way, it's a story from the space between one's teeth," Jwahir said. "But the true ones are yet worse. I saw a book with pictures of what they called food. Food? How can they call that food? It is *we,* Matani, who should be teaching them what is important—not the other way around. Even the colors were unimaginable. And the lists of ways to prepare them—pshhh!" She pursed her full lips, almost as though she were readying for a kiss, though her irritated wide-open eyes made it clear that love, unfortunately, was not on her mind.

"Recipes," Matani said, using the English, since his tribe had no word for them.

Jwahir ignored him. "How many separate foods are wasted to make one?" she asked, and waited a moment to see if he would be foolish enough to try to answer. "Ten, sometimes fifteen. How much time is spent on such a project? A full morning? More?" She opened her palms to the ceiling, her shapely fingers extended. "What use is such a book, when maize mixed with camel blood and baked over an open fire is a treat for us?"

Wistfulness had slightly softened her indignant tone, and Matani slipped into that opening. "Perhaps the books' gifts are in what they let us imagine," he said.

He considered, then, telling her everything he believed about the sole topic besides her that made him passionate. How the Camel Bookmobile offered the only chance of survival for this collection of half-nomads with only one toehold in the future. How the children had to make friends of written words if they were ever to have prosperous grandchildren. How until the books came, he hadn't really felt himself to be a teacher—his only supplies, after all, had been a few pencils, which quickly disappeared, and not even any paper. But now he knew he could do it; he could help create a generation in which, instead of one man going off to study in Nairobi—as his father had done first, and he second—there would be ten, or twenty, who would then return to help their people. He didn't hope to be remembered as a father of his tribe, nothing so grandiose as that. He wanted to be thought of simply as one who helped shape the future and encouraged his people's dreams, like a father who would teach his own sons. And for that, the traveling library was crucial.

But Jwahir was speaking again, and wouldn't want to be interrupted. Besides, she would deem his explanations as lofty as the clouds, and end up only angrier. He patted her hand instead. She shrugged him off.

"They come here thinking that because we can't read these silly books, we are *mabardhuli*," she said.

"No, they don't think we're stupid," Matani said, though he felt a twinge in his chest as it occurred to him that Jwahir might be right.

"Not *you*. You can read. That's all they care about," Jwahir said, and then she launched into a discussion of another book she'd inspected. It seemed that, even in her disdain, she had looked at most of the volumes in Mididima. And she, like all the tribe, believed the library's arrival in their midst was Matani's doing. He himself was not sure how Mididima had been chosen; and he had never asked, considering the question immodest. But he suspected in fact that library officials in Garissa discovered somehow there was a man who lived in this tiny spill of houses and spoke English and had been educated as a teacher—courtesy of his father's connections, and in keeping with his father's wishes. This indeed made Matani responsible for the bookmobile's visits, or more accurately in Jwahir's view, blameworthy.

He tried to pay attention as she continued speaking, but found himself idly studying the nape of her neck, the shine of her hair, her eyes so alive with passion. He had married late, by Mididima's standards, and it was his dearest hope that Jwahir would become pregnant soon, and with a son. His deepest fear was that somehow it would not be possible.

There'd been an omen. A bird tumbled from the sky while he strolled in the hum of early evening two weeks ago. A black-fronted mosquito-eater. It spun through the air before crashing, splayed, two large steps in front of him. Though it bore no sign of violence, it was undeniably dead, its wings extended as if in objection, the purple ring around its neck bent back in final protest. A sign, clearly, though of what? He feared it had to do with the images that had been dancing through his mind the moment before the bird plummeted: him striding through the bush on a future evening, his own devoted son beside him, Jwahir waiting back in Mididima with their meal prepared. He hadn't mentioned the mosquito-eater to his wife. He was ashamed of his own superstitions, so unsuitable for an educated man.

Now he shook the bird's image from his head. Jwahir's voice still spiked the air. He lowered his chin, slipping into what he hoped she might mistake for a listening pose, and took a moment, as he did each library day, to form a silent prayer: *Let them all bring their books today; let all the books be whole.* Mr. Abasi was clearly an unforgiving man. Each visit, just before he departed, Mr. Abasi clapped his hands and announced in a voice full of capital letters, "Please be advised that under library rules, any settlement which loses or ruins a book will no longer be visited by the Camel Bookmobile." Unfortunately, Mr. Abasi's tone was reminiscent of rancid meat, so Matani feared that no one except him listened to the librarian's warning. Then again, Matani knew the warning was really meant for him anyway.

Matani wanted—in fact, he always intended—to remind Mr. Abasi that in the bush, there were many threats to a man's possessions, even to a man's life. Neglect, wild animals, fierce weather—one would be enough to account for a book's ruin, but all three made it an eventual certainty. This was too big, this responsibility. That's what Matani wanted to say, what he'd wanted to say for months.

Each time as he opened his mouth to make this short speech to Mr. Abasi, he noticed the foreign woman, Miss Sweeney, smiling at him with the innocent confidence of the doe who has not yet seen the spear. Somehow, that smile defused his energy to object. He let Mr. Abasi conclude, and then he vaguely nodded his head in reply. He wondered about that nod, about what sort of contract it implied between him and Mr. Abasi. So the joy that hung over him every library day was coupled with trepidation, fueled further this morning by the memory of the poor dead mosquito-eater, and by his wife's disappointment in his fondness for objects as vaporous and imprecise as words.

Babies, birds, books. All three were becoming braided together in his mind. He rubbed his forehead as though to put his mind in order. *Only let them all return what they've borrowed*, he silently intoned to the dirt floor, his head still lowered. *For now, only that.*

The Teacher's Wife

WHAT A PARADOX LAY SNARLED WITHIN HER CLEAN, CLEAR argument. Jwahir felt it even as she made her case, even as her husband, Matani, listened attentively with head bowed. Jwahir had no doubt that the white woman and the librarian from Garissa were dangerous invaders. The books they brought, full of false values and deluding seductions, threatened the stability and harmony of Mididima's cluster of families. If the young swallowed a foreign idea of what it meant to be alive, what would become of Jwahir's people? She knew the answer: they would be wiped out—history and tradition severed from the soul of every child as surely as if Matani had welcomed in killers. She was the wife of this misguided madman. It was her duty to speak.

But what would she do if Matani were to bend to her wishes? If he were to lift his head and agree to defend Mididima, to send the outsiders away?

What would she do if there were to be no more visits from the camels?

Looking at him now weighing her claims so carefully, Jwahir saw that his eventual agreement to her request was not only possible, but inevitable. He believed in his books, no doubt. But he would be swayed by her—was already being swayed—and would eventually meet her wishes. Out of love, that's how he would explain it, with a disturbing look of defenseless devotion in his eyes. And what then? What of her eagerness for this day that came twice a month? What of the welcome tightening of her chest, the tingling between her thighs?

This was the day she would see Abayomi, the drum maker. See him alone. She saw him every day, of course. And they wouldn't be exactly alone. Still, that's how it felt: the two of them together, the rest of Mididima in the distance, distracted by the books.

And there, in that narrowing space between her and Abayomi, lodged the inconsistency between heartfelt convictions and the heart itself.

Imagine no bookmobile. Would she and Abayomi have simply passed by one another, then, for the rest of their lives? And if the bookmobile halted its visits, how could they continue their conversation, begun by accident, sustained by design? She couldn't give up this bond, so unlike any she'd ever known, that dipped and soared and carried her through the bare bones of her other days, the days with no bookmobile. She needed it as a mosquito needs blood.

They'd met—really met, as she thought of it—the day of the bookmobile's first visit. Moments before, she'd stumbled away from watching Matani preside over a kingdom of paper, a kingdom so clearly false it made her stomach roil. Books, long irrelevant to their lives or the lives of their ancestors, had been placed on a mat as if they were honored guests instead of snakes waiting to strike. Her neighbors, most as illiterate as she, crowded around on hands and knees like animals.

As for Matani, he glowed. Glowed like a hunter who'd made a kill—only he was not a hunter at all; he had none of that instinct, none of that steel within. She'd been so disillusioned by the man she called husband—his exaggerated mildness, his fascination with the inconsequential—that she sprinted away from the camels and the books and Matani, her head down, sightless in her preoccupation, unaware of where her feet fell. Not expecting to meet anyone. Everyone else, after all, was with Matani and the camels and the books.

And there, between their huts, she'd run into Abayomi. Literally run into him. A form that cushioned her descent and led her gently back to earth.

She kept her head lowered, embarrassed. Discomfited by his solidity, his raw scent, her own flightiness. She stepped away, waiting for him to pass, but he didn't. The hands that took her by the shoulders, the same hands that pulled and stretched to fashion the drums that made the music she loved, were warm and firm. At first, she couldn't look up. He waited until she finally raised her eyes to his. The tenderness she saw there nearly drowned her. She felt as though she were floating. She wanted to touch his face to steady herself. She almost did.

"Are you all right, Jwahir?"

She caught her breath, got ready to say yes, pull away, move on. But when she opened her mouth, other words came instead.

"The books . . . " she said. "Matani . . . "

She stumbled at first, but he listened more intensely than anyone ever had, easing the flow of her words and soon making them come faster. While the rest of Mididima gathered near the camels and busied themselves with impermanent pieces of paper, she spoke about how she feared new ideas would destroy ancient wisdom. She grew passionate. If they weren't careful, she said, what was vital would be replaced by what was not. Finally, she turned the topic from Mididima to herself. The stories from her husband's books, she told him, seemed irrelevant, while the music that emerged from Abayomi's drums—and here her voice grew quiet—felt sacred.

He smiled. He did not answer. No answer was needed.

Then they spoke of other things. He told Jwahir of sitting next to his wife as she died, and of his sorrow over his son Taban, the one they called Scar Boy—a nickname Jwahir would never again say aloud, now that she understood. She told him of the longing she felt as she sat outside the *kilinge*, the sacred enclosure, listening to the drums joined with the nightly chanting.

The nakedness of the words she spoke surprised even her.

This didn't all come during that first meeting, of course. But it was one conversation, stretched over eight meetings, twice a month, while the bookmobile visited. Their looping exchange took on its own life, and Jwahir watched with awe and gratefulness. They teased and praised in the same breath. Banter and seriousness overlapped. They sank into one another's eyes; then their gazes darted away. Their secret conversation was alive and tangible, like a child whom they'd brought forth together and in whose care they shared.

A child, however, who withered and nearly died each time the camels drew away. Jwahir and Abayomi could not speak with such intimacy where others could listen. And without the bookmobile, they were never alone.

She would watch him, though. She watched—slyly, while warming camel milk over a fire or sweeping a patch of dirt—as he sat outside his hut building drums. He worked for days on each drum, and each was different, as one man is from another. The muscles in his arms shifted like a melody beneath the surface of his skin while he soaked wood and bent the pieces to build the frames, then cleaned the hides with long, broad strokes. She watched as he brought the drums to life, stretching the hides over the frames, giving them both bodies and heartbeats.

Life-giver. That's what he was, like the rain itself. And waiting for the Camel Library's next visit felt to Jwahir like holding her breath beyond the point of bursting lungs.

It was possible only because of the tiny talismans they gave each other as soon as they were alone again, words that hinted at how often one had thought of the other in the intervening days, and at what they felt now in each other's presence. Careful words, restrained, but she would repeat them a hundred times in her mind until new ones came to take their place.

"One evening last week I wished so much that I could tell you about . . ." she would begin. The event itself was inconsequential; the mention of the wish was meant to convey all her longings.

"That very evening, I went to sleep uneasy and woke in the middle of night. I must have felt you wanted to tell me something," he would reply, and she would feel the cord between them surge and strengthen.

They'd recently begun to speak of her marriage, but in coded terms, since this was the most precarious territory of all. She'd hinted at her frustration; he'd nodded in understanding. Their words had trailed off. They didn't touch, but she could still feel, from the first time, the pressure of his fingers on her shoulders.

How long had she known this man Abayomi? Her entire life. Longer even than she'd known Matani, who went away to the Distant City for many years. Abayomi had already been a man by the time Jwahir was born, and they'd seen one another nearly every day of her life. Seen without seeing.

It seemed to her now, though, that there'd always been a feeling between them, something large and substantial that she simply hadn't noticed until the wandering library made its way through the unmarked bush to arrive beneath the great acacia tree of Mididima. The books? They were for the foolish or misguided of Mididima. But the library did bring a gift, one known to her and Abayomi alone.

Here she was, then, caught in a contradiction of her own making. Fingering the beads that hung between her breasts, Jwahir fell silent in mid-argument, rose, and walked away from her quietly puzzled husband. She felt suddenly wearied by the balancing act required to sharply condemn the bookmobile aloud while, with equal fervor, blessing it within.

The Librarian

SITI, THE LEADER AND LOAD CAMEL, SEEMED TO GRASP FROM the beginning that she held the balance of power. First she forced a late start to the journey with her capricious shifts of weight that stunted the men's effort to pack her with books. Mr. Abasi, grumbling about the wasted time as they set off, thought he spotted victory in her eyes, though he quickly told himself he had imagined it. Then, ninety minutes into the trip, Siti glanced back at him, blinked her long eyelashes, sighed loudly, and plopped to the lunarlike desert floor. She tossed her head jauntily, exhibiting the yellowed teeth that jutted from her lower jaw.

At that moment, Mr. Abasi knew for sure what no one else could: Siti was possessed by the spirit of his own departed mother. When he looked closely, he even saw his mother's particular mulish expression reflected in the camel's stubborn gaze. A woman of aggressively colorful dress, his mother had been renowned for her strident refusal to be chained to household chores, as well as for her loud complaints that her husband, responsible for the happiness of three wives, failed to visit her as often as contractually required. She'd been, of course, three times the size of that husband. Her hugs had, more than once, nearly suffocated her slight only son. "I am a woman who must be embraced in full," she used to proclaim to anyone who would listen. "My expanses must be traversed like the land itself."

A full embarrassment, that's what she was. But frighteningly powerful. He'd never been able to completely accept that a mosquito caused her death. She'd seemed too substantial to be threatened by a *mbu*, even one carrying *onyong-nyong* fever—so it wasn't a total surprise to find her reincarnated now.

It was disturbing, though, to think that he could never be done with his mother, never leave her behind.

Then Mr. Abasi realized he had a chance to finally hold the upper hand with her, so he knelt and muttered into the camel's ear. "Listen to me, Mama. You continue to make this trip difficult and I will unload you, dump you with that primitive, nowhere tribe. I swear I will. They will slice your throat to drain your blood for their meal, and then close it up with a bit of your own dung mixed with hair. A month later, they will cut again to drain more blood. They are that hungry." He paused a moment to let his words sink in before concluding. "So. Get up now, or die a second time in Mididima, Mama. Make your decision. Be quick-quick."

It was his words, Mr. Abasi knew, and not the driver's lashing, that prompted Siti to rise at last and resume the lead, trailed by a second camel carrying Mr. Abasi, a third carrying Miss Sweeney, and a fourth carrying supplies. But the delay had been too long. With such a lackadaisical pace and so many distractions, they were lucky they hadn't encountered any *shifta*. The bandits, with rows of shiny gold bullets slung around their hips, would surely have killed this willful white American woman. What, then, would be the fate of Mr. Abasi?

Of course, what sort of fate was this, anyway? Since Mr. Abasi's boyhood, his dream of an ideal job was one he could do in the shade that required as little physical exertion as possible and even less human interaction. What joy when the foreign librarian, Miss Fetegrin, had visited from London looking for a worthwhile scholarship recipient, and he had been chosen, and thus discovered there actually existed work that would meet his requirements. Some shelving was necessary, of course. But the library's unambiguous rules against talking more than compensated for that light lifting.

Now, though, they'd changed his job requirements. They'd forced him to travel beneath the unforgiving sun four times a week on these exhausting excursions across a terrain naked except for the occasional thornbush or acacia. And why? Because foreigners with fervor in their hearts decided all children must be educated. *Educated.* The misconception buried in the word set his teeth to grinding. These foreigners couldn't understand that literacy was not the only path to education. In tribal settlements, the tradition was an oral one, bolstered by the evolutionary development of powerful memories, supported by a web of ritual and respect that books would not reinforce—could, in fact, destroy.

Besides, these simple people were at peace with themselves. Wasn't that a kind of wisdom? A little rain, a bowl

of maize, and they were happy. They didn't desire objects
outside their reach. This bookmobile project, overseen by
the Kenya National Library Service with Miss Sweeney
as "visiting consultant," bred envy of an unobtainable life.
Some suitable books were to be found among the donations,
of course. But what were a dusty desert people to make of
a movie star's biography? A do-it-yourself book for land-
scapers? A children's picture book about medieval castles?
Their inclusion highlighted Western idealists' underbelly
of ignorance, and even arrogance.

There were other issues. The tricky concept of borrow-
ing something that must be returned two weeks later in the
same condition, for one. No one could convince him that
this policy had been sufficiently explained to these tribal
warriors or their wives and children. And the requirement
that the library-on-a-camel be available only to permanent,
non-nomadic settlements. What did that concept mean,
here in the bush? Permanent until the seasonal well ran dry.
Permanent until the bandits threatened. Permanent until
permanence felt like a chore rather than a choice, until the
freedom of a new place proved irresistible to the men of
the clan.

These lines of reasoning he had outlined many times at
many meetings with American and British do-gooders as
they barreled ahead, devising a way to transport a library
across rugged land devoid of modern infrastructure, lining
up foreign funding, collecting books. He'd considered it his
responsibility to raise these issues, and had expressed himself in a manner that impressed him, at least, as admirably
articulate, though he'd tried to keep his pride from being

too apparent. Then came the afternoon his boss from Nairobi, Mr. Munyes, bent to whisper in his ear.

"No one wants to hear from the mouth of a librarian an argument against reading," Mr. Munyes said. Though
his tone was suitably restrained, Mr. Abasi understood that
convincing these people to abandon this foolish project,
to use the money for something more practical within the
library system, would be as likely as teaching an elephant to
sing. To continue the efforts might even cost him his job.

He was not ignorant of the problem of perception that
his boss mentioned. On the surface, he knew, his demeanor
could seem snappish, his comments peevish. Counter that
with Miss Sweeney, who appeared goodhearted and laughed
a lot. Mr. Munyes had described her as "charmingly casual."
Mr. Abasi understood this as a reference to the fact that she
attended meetings carrying a purple bag and rarely seemed
to brush her frizzy hair. She wasn't like the librarians he'd
known in London. She was so much more outspoken and
opinionated, and such a strange mix of casual and fervent.

She'd told Mr. Abasi that she dreamed of "putting something together here that will be bigger than you or me, and
that will keep on growing long after I'm gone." By *gone*,
she meant not dead, of course, but distant from the foul-
tasting local food, the uncomfortable sleeping quarters, the
lack of privacy. Back to her swimming pools and low-cut
gowns and confusing rounds of love affairs—he'd seen the
American television shows. Well, he supposed her motiva-
tion in leaving all that temporarily behind was admirable,
although some days it simply seemed meddlesome.

But he wouldn't worry over this further, he decided

as they drew into Mididima after a trip that had stretched to more than three hours. He'd insisted on implementing certain rules, and to that at least, they'd agreed. And he'd gone on record with his position regarding the entire scheme. Surely they wouldn't hold him responsible when the "non-motorized mobile library"—or the Camel Bookmobile, as they dubbed it, the very words making them smile in appreciation of their own cleverness—began inevitably wilting under the midday sun.

The American

IT WAS NEARLY NOON WHEN THE CAMEL BRIGADE PULLED UP
under Mididima's acacia, the tallest tree within a mile,
beautiful but severe like an elegant woman who'd become
too thin. Each time they traveled this lonely route—and
this was their ninth visit—Fi was struck by the moment
of impact, when the stillness of the journey collided with
the commotion of Mididima. Since Mr. Abasi routinely rebuffed her efforts to initiate conversation during these trips,
the only sounds she'd heard for hours had been a wet drone
of camels breathing and an occasional bird complaining
limply of heat or half celebrating a sliver of shade. She'd
imagined herself an ancient, isolated nomad, tossed back in
time, traveling in a bubble of dust.

Compare that with the motion and music that ran like
a swell through the air as soon as they first caught sight of
the acacia looming in the distance, and then a moment
later, the settlement itself. Conical huts with thatched roofs
sprouted like a cluster of mushrooms atop a table of green
and a natural shallow water reservoir, a gift to the eyes after
the desert hues of dried blood and wheat. Lemon-colored
plastic containers that she knew held extra water stood

lined up beneath a ramada. The people of Those Rooted in Dust were already gathering, pulled toward the acacia as if by an unseen puppeteer, followed by their animals—dozens of animals, more goats and camels, it seemed, than people. And cattle too, though most of the cows were raised in the higher lands.

Once at Mididima, Fi could not even dismount for the first few minutes. The ripple of excitement gave way to a flood that surrounded them and spiraled them into its center. This, she imagined, was what an athlete must feel on the shoulders of his teammates after the winning goal. The exhilaration, the thrill, the certainty that one would be young and strong forever.

"*Jambo,*" she said in greeting to one after another as the men set up the three-walled tent, spread grass mats, and laid out the books. "How are you, how are you?" the four- and five-year-olds called in singsong voices, running up to take her hand. Their local dialect was an obscure language she'd never heard of before, but they practiced their English and she practiced her Swahili, which most of them knew.

So thin, they were all so thin, and she noticed it still, but it didn't scare her as it did at first. She used to think their hold on life must be as threadlike as their bodies, but she'd lost that sense, perhaps because they seemed so alive and because, here in Mididima at least, they never gave a sign of thirst or hunger, and they laughed more often than not.

Kanika, the girl, was among the first to push close. Her smile claimed much of her narrow face. She braided her hair against her scalp and three necklaces corded her neck.

Not far behind stood the girl's grandmother, Neema, wearing a brilliant orange scarf, a sky-blue dress, and beaded earrings the size of a boxer's fist. Fi didn't immediately see the scarred young man who spoke with his eyes and long fingers. Of course, he was never among the first press of people.

Mr. Abasi unloaded the lead camel, who seemed to glare at him from under her fringed lashes. The teacher, Matani, helped.

"Matani! *Jambo*," Fi said, and brushed the tips of his fingers with her own. It had become their form of greeting since they'd first met, when she'd reached to shake his hand and missed, touching his fingertips instead as he stretched to lift a box of books. He must have thought the gesture intentional, a strange custom particular to her region of America, because the next time he'd brushed her fingers first. The flare of his nostrils and the thickness of his lips gave Matani a firm and authoritative face. His eyes, in contrast, reminded her of warm cocoa. When he got close, she smelled something pleasantly spicy, something akin to pepper mixed with cinnamon. Now, he wore dark pants, a light shirt, and a metal bracelet around his left wrist.

"How are you?" she asked.

"We've made good use of the books, Miss Sweeney," Matani said.

"Call me Fi," she said, as she always did. "I've brought another stack of magazines, and a few more pens and pencils. Plus six books for you. How are they learning, your students?"

Matani reached out to grab a boy by the arm and spoke

to him rapidly before turning to Fi. "Let Nadif show you," he said.

Nadif, who looked eight but was probably twelve, held out a hand on which he'd written some numbers in ink. He spoke and Matani translated. "Eight cows," he said. "Two die from drought. Then four calves come in spring. Next year, half of the remaining cows become mothers, so then you begin all over with fifteen cows."

"And, hopefully, lots of milk," Fi added.

"That is thanks to the mathematical primer," Matani said.

"Yes, thank you too much," Nadif said.

"Very much," Matani corrected. "Too much is in excess, Nadif." Then he growled playfully at the boy, drawing laughter from both Fi and Nadif.

"And how is his reading?" Fi asked.

"His English is coming along. Last time, he got a book about the Ivory Coast," Matani said, gesturing to the boy's arms, where he held the book.

"Can you read it?" Fi asked, leaning toward the boy. After a pause, Matani translated.

"Many large words," Nadif answered in slow English.

"But we enjoyed the pictures," Matani said quickly. "And we're learning the words."

Fi shook her head. Most of the books had been donated, and they were not always appropriate. "We need simpler books, don't we, Matani? And more in Swahili instead of English."

Matani grinned. "The boys, you know, won't take the easy ones anyway," he said. "And I want them to learn English."

"Miss Sweeney," Mr. Abasi called. "We're nearly ready." The grass mat had been spread beneath the acacia, and the books lay in neat rows. Standing stiffly, Mr. Abasi held out the clipboard for her to record the titles that were returned and those to be checked out. A child brought a large pail turned upside down, and Fi sat, clipboard on her lap. Then Mr. Abasi nodded to Matani. As though invisible doors had swung open, the children pressed forward, adults close behind.

Mr. Abasi was speaking authoritatively—telling everyone, Fi imagined, to line up in an orderly fashion. No one listened. Excited voices rose and fused. Matani slipped among the children, translating titles, reading opening paragraphs, helping them make their choices.

Fi patiently marked off each returned book, checking its condition briefly under Mr. Abasi's eye. He seemed to consider this chore beneath him. That amused Fi. She wasn't the perfect candidate for this kind of task either—in many ways, she often thought, she had become a librarian against the odds, being neither as organized nor as detail-oriented as many of her colleagues. Nevertheless, she enjoyed this particular job in the tiny, scattered tribal communities. She liked knowing which books were being checked out most often, and which were being ignored. And she loved it when these new, unlikely library patrons held out their choices and she looked into their faces and then both her hand and theirs held the books for a breath while she recorded the titles and their names. Even if she was guilty of romanticizing it, the connection she felt to these people at that moment was a key part of what motivated her.

That, and a childhood memory of her mother and the starving Biafrans.

When Fi was in grammar school, her quick-tempered widowed mother possessed patience enough to endure only ten minutes of whining from any of her four children before issuing the sharp rebuke: "Saint Brigid of Faughart! What of the starving Biafrans, hey?" If the offending child continued to cry—sometimes, depending on her mother's mood, if a bottom lip even dared tremble—a brusque pop on the backside could be expected. Fi's mother always spoke the warning phrase in a slurred rush, with a touch of accent from her native Ireland. Fi knew about Brigid, her mother's favorite saint—the beautiful daughter of a slave who, legend had it, could cure lepers and turn water to ale. But *starvenbeeoffrans* were mysterious to her. If she could only discover the meaning of that word, she might at last be able to understand her complicated, baffling mother—a woman who turned up her nose at Irish Catholic charity and worked instead as a "personal secretary" for a scholar in Manhattan about whom she spoke so seldom that he could have been entirely fictional for all Fi ever knew.

Fi could not find the inexplicable phrase in any dictionary, though—not the one in the classroom, or the one in the school library, nor in the home of her best friend, Lizzie McElroy, who lived down the street in their neighborhood in the Bronx. The only time she dared ask, "And, Mom, what are *starvenbeeoffrans*?" she received the pop that really should have gone to her little sister—the whiner on that occasion.

By the time she was in middle school, Fi had developed

a whimsical style at home, performing gymnastic tricks or telling corny jokes to try to make her straight-backed, overburdened mother smile. It sometimes worked. Her attempts at closeness, on the other hand, were routinely rebuffed: her mother refused to answer the few questions that her children dared to ask—about her childhood, for instance; or her work; or even their own father, who had died after being struck by a car while walking home late one night when Fi was a toddler. "May you never forget what is worth remembering," her mother would say, "and never remember what is best forgotten."

So Fi continued to wonder, intermittently, about *starvenbeeoffrans.*

It took a high school social studies class to teach her who Biafrans were, and then she began hunting down their history at the big mid-Manhattan library branch. For weeks, she was a daily fixture on the fifth floor, round-shouldered at the library's substantial wooden tables, concentrated as if the Biafrans were a secret she had to uncover to learn at last how to connect with her emotionally distant mother. She read about the Biafrans' failed rebellion against Nigeria, the political indecision that led to four cities' being named the capital, the 2 million dead, children roasted alive, young girls ripped in two by shrapnel, and of course the starving—everywhere the starving that her mother must have seen in the newspapers, that prompted her urgings to her own children to buck up.

Fi's friends implored her to stop the daily research, but she couldn't. Eventually, in fact, her interest took her far beyond her mother's reprimands, driving her teenage cynicism underground for a while and spawning a wild idea: that she should help these Biafrans. She didn't know how, though. And she recognized, finally, that helping them wouldn't get her any closer to her mother, who by then had fallen ill, and who in fact died during Fi's second year of college. Her death marked the last time Fi had ever cried—tears of frustration as well as sorrow, she recognized even then.

As it turned out, Fi ventured only as far as Europe, in a trip taken one summer after college, and she became a librarian instead of an aid worker. It was the library, after all, that brought her the answer to at least one of the riddles of her childhood, her mother's mysterious admonition. Besides, she felt embraced by those tall, narrow stacks; she felt nurtured in the library and supplied with information, as she might have felt in her childhood home if things had been different. If her mother hadn't needed to work so hard, which made her taciturn. If her father had lived instead of being crushed beneath an oncoming car.

Nevertheless, she dreamed of traveling to Africa. When a posting appeared on a librarian website from a group of American companies seeking someone to work temporarily as a consultant and help start a camel-borne library in Kenya, she almost couldn't believe it at first. Some god who knew her secret desire seemed to have created a job tailored for her. She applied immediately and would have gone even if her employer hadn't agreed to give her a leave of absence.

Kanika was dusting off the books, an endless chore, and reading the back covers as she worked. Sometimes she opened the inside to see if whoever donated the book had written a message—"Greetings from North Carolina" or "Hello from Mark Twain Elementary." Once or twice, Fi had seen Kanika touch her finger to those written words, though Kanika surely didn't know where North Carolina was and couldn't imagine Mark Twain Elementary.

Kanika always checked out nonfiction and considered her selection carefully, unlike some who chose as though they were on a live game show and had only seconds to pick door number one, two, or three. They often didn't pause over the title, or even flip through a book looking for pictures. Instead, they judged by color, size, or sometimes scent. Fi had watched them lift books to their noses, sniff loudly, open the pages, inhale again with their mouths open, and then either tuck the book beneath their arms with pleased smiles or return it to the straw mat with crinkled noses.

"Wilt thou take some *chai*?" It was Kanika's grandmother. Neema spoke an odd stilted English influenced by the language of the Bible—*thee* and *thou* and verbs ending with *est* and *eth*. She extended a cup, which Fi took. In her other hand, she held a paperback novel called *Projects for Winter*. Fi had read the back cover earlier that week. She knew it was about a woman whose affair goes sour, whose husband divorces her and wins custody of the children. A modern version of *Anna Karenina*, apparently. Fi wondered how that story could possibly interest a woman like Neema, even given her fondness for fiction. Fi considered suggesting something else—but no. The ferocity with which the grandmother always made her selections forbade meddling.

Besides, Fi was convinced that instinct could determine a body's literary needs, just as physical cravings pointed to dietary shortfalls. She'd experienced it herself more than once among the library's dense shelves; not knowing what she should read next, she'd wandered, sniffing slightly, palms open. When intuition hit, she felt a sensation she couldn't describe exactly: her hands seemed to know where to go. And when she reached, invariably she found exactly the book she needed at that moment—sometimes fiction, sometimes biography, sometimes a slim volume of obscure poetry.

Two young women stood to one side of the grass mat, trying hard to mask their interest in the bustle beneath the acacia. One was lean but well formed with strong arms, her neck and shoulders adorned with yellow and blue beads. The other was rounder, with the heavy, drooping breasts of a nursing mother. Both had a reddish dusty blush painted between their eyes, down their noses, and onto their cheeks, as well as tattoos on their chins—three dark straight lines— that indicated they were married.

The crowd around Fi was thinning a little, so she turned toward the two women. "Please," she said, urging them closer to the books.

The women, aloof, gazed off toward the horizon.

Fi picked up a book called *Baby's First Five Years*. "Help me," she said to Mr. Abasi. "Tell them this is loaded with simple games for a child's early development."

"Miss Sweeney, these women have no-no interest in games."

"Humor me, Mr. A."

Mr. Abasi pursed his lips a long minute before he translated—at least, Fi hoped he did—as she pressed the book into the hands of the young mother.

The woman took the book, but didn't glance at it.

"There are more," Fi said. She reached for another book that showed photographs of homes built by craftsmen in America and Europe, and handed it to the second woman. She knew wives and daughters here built the houses, so she wasn't surprised to see the woman look at the pictures with some interest.

She turned back to the mother, who was still holding the book on child-rearing. "What's your name?" Fi asked in her rudimentary Swahili.

The woman looked shyly to the ground and then glanced up again, smiling slightly. "Leta."

"Give this a try," Fi urged, tapping the baby book. "Matani can help you." Fi wasn't sure the woman understood. She looked around and saw Kanika, holding two books. "Tell her, will you, Kanika?" Fi asked.

Kanika said something to Leta while Fi smiled encouragingly. The young mother stared into Fi's eyes, as though the two of them were making a pact, before nodding and moving away with the book.

"What do you think of this one?" Kanika asked, offering a book for inspection as Fi jotted down the title taken by the young mother. Fi glanced over. *Snow Sense: Staying Alive in an Avalanche.* She bit her lower lip. Some of these titles they were carting around by camel were beyond absurd.

"Interesting topic," she managed, making her tone neutral. "You know that word, *avalanche?*"

Kanika shook her head.

"You remember snow?" Fi asked. "Well, an avalanche means a large rush of snow and ice and rocks sliding down a mountain." Fi used both arms to demonstrate the movement of a landslide.

Kanika tipped her head, considering, and then held out the other book, a biography of Gertrude Bell. "And this?"

"She was a woman from England who became powerful in the Middle East," Fi said. "She helped settle arguments between men."

Kanika set down the book on avalanches but kept the other.

"By the way, Kanika," Fi said, "I've got something for you." From her bag next to the overturned pail, she extracted a copy of a glossy American magazine for girls. "Some of it will seem silly," she said. "But I thought, maybe . . . "

Kanika smiled broadly, showing all her teeth. "*Asante*," she said. Then she leaned forward and lowered her voice. "Miss Sweeney. Can we speak together?"

Fi bent toward Kanika. The girl wanted to confide something, perhaps? Or sought some advice? Fi felt pleased out of all proportion.

Before Kanika could speak, though, Mr. Abasi's voice came between them. "Miss Sweeney," he said, gesturing her back to her clipboard. "A dawdling sun would never rise, and then what?"

Fi never understood how he managed to speak like that, entirely through his nose. "I'm headed your way, Mr. A.," she answered, tossing a smile at him over her shoulder. She touched Kanika's arm lightly. "We'll talk soon," she said.

The Teacher

MATANI FELT A LOW RUMBLE OF APPREHENSION AS HE saw Scar Boy's older brother Badru approaching. Badru's expression was that of one carrying news of death or drought. But then, Matani reminded himself, Badru often looked foreboding. He had a way of holding his head—chin thrust forward, forehead back—that hooded his intense eyes and left his cheekbones bold above the fierce line of his mouth. At the same time, there was something commanding about him, a bold quality that attracted attention.

"You are here to chose a book?" Matani shaped his tone so it would not betray his doubt.

"Taban sent me," Badru said, using his brother's given name. "He is not well today."

Scar Boy unwell was not news. There had to be more. "And what else?" Matani asked.

Badru didn't reply at first. He seemed to absorb the scene beneath the tan tent, where his neighbors knelt before volumes spread on a piece of burlap. "I do not find his books," he said laconically after a moment. "The ones that came from the backs of these camels."

Matani moved closer. "So ask him where they are."

"He was not able to tell me, Teacher." Badru added the title with heavy politeness.

Matani opened his mouth, but nothing emerged. He didn't know whether to yell or strike the young man or turn his back. He couldn't tell whether Badru was simply obtuse or outright defiant. Badru so feared being pitied as the older brother of Scar Boy that he always seemed guarded, as impenetrable as parched earth.

Matani felt the weight of Mr. Abasi moving close. "What's this? We're missing books?"

Matani massaged a fresh throbbing at his temple. "One young man is unwell today," he said. His voice sounded faint, even to him. The missing books seemed an omen that stretched far beyond Scar Boy's irresponsibility. He wished, suddenly, that he had mentioned the mosquito-eater to Jwahir. She would have comforted him, surely. She would have told him the incident was unimportant.

Mr. Abasi shrugged. "So let the sick recover. We do not need a roll call. We need only the books."

Badru must have seen the look in Matani's eyes that recommended—even pleaded for—silence, but he ignored it. "We do not know," the brother said, "where the books are."

"And you are?" Mr. Abasi demanded.

Now Badru did not reply. Now he chose to stay quiet.

"The brother of the ill one," Matani said after a long moment.

Mr. Abasi shifted from foot to foot, gazed over at the camels, then out to the horizon. "So the books are lost, then," he said.

"No, Mister Visitor," Badru said.

Oh, the arrogance in the boy's tone. It was clear now, and not only Matani could hear it. Mr. Abasi glared. "You don't know where they are. Isn't that the definition of lost?"

Matani cleared his throat, then spoke. "The boy means that his brother knows where they are—he must, of course he does—but he is not well today."

"Not well enough to speak?" Mr. Abasi asked. "Unusual. But if so, then what about yesterday? It is a surprise that we have come to you today, the very same day twice a month that we make this jarring, endless trip?"

The chatter under the acacia tree, Matani noticed, had evaporated. The others all paused, their attention drawn to the knot of Badru, the librarian from Garissa, the teacher—and now the foreign woman, who was approaching with her clipboard.

"Matani?" Miss Sweeney said. "Is something wrong?"

"A young man has failed to return two books," Mr. Abasi said.

Among the people of Mididima, whispers moved like wind swirling through the bush. Matani made out two words, and he was sure Badru heard them also: "Scar Boy."

Mr. Abasi's voice floated above all their heads. "We will pack up our load now," he said. "No one will be allowed to keep any books. If you find the missing volumes, send word. In that case, we will come back to you again—unless, of course, your day is already filled by another tribe wishing to be visited by this library."

The murmuring undertone was replaced by the subtle sound of grips tightening around book covers, and then a sharp-edged belligerent silence. One young boy bent down and snatched up a volume at his feet. Matani felt the eyes of his neighbors turn toward him.

A long-necked bustard, half-tamed by some of the children, landed near the acacia tree. Matani stared at the bird a moment, feeling tightness in his chest.

"Perhaps, before we . . . " he began.

They were waiting, his neighbors, his students, exchanging glances with each other: some squatting on books as if these were eggs to be laid; others slipping books beneath thin shirts so their stomachs looked rectangular; still others holding books between their legs, spine out, as if that made the books invisible.

"I feel certain that . . . "

Matani fought to find the words. It was he, after all, who cajoled and scolded them into learning, who caned the younger ones when necessary. It was he who, in his neighbors' eyes, made the library appear on the horizon. He was the go-between linking the villagers to the outsiders. Now that he and they faced this snake of an unfamiliar species, he had to be the one to defeat it.

"Once the young man is well . . . " he said.

But then his voice trailed off again, and he knew it would not return. The man who carries no weapon when he meets the snake must run, and fast.

It was not two missing books that defeated him. They would be recovered. It was a fear—unreasonable, surely—that Scar Boy's irresponsibility foretold a larger loss, a more extensive unraveling.

"Hold it a minute here," Miss Sweeney said. Kanika

stood by her side, and she'd been translating. "Who's misplaced his books? Can I talk with him?"

Someone had spoken. Someone on his side had assumed a tone of authority. Matani surged with a gratefulness that he hoped Miss Sweeney could feel. "It is Scar Boy," he said quickly. "He is unwell today. That is his brother."

"This is the policy, Miss Sweeney," Mr. Abasi said in a warning tone. "You agreed to it and it exists for good reason. If every settlement loses books, soon we will not have enough to continue this project of yours."

"Scar Boy," Miss Sweeney said slowly. "He's . . . "

She let the words drop, but Matani met her eyes. "Yes," he said.

She looked down at her clipboard, tapped her pen on it three times. "If he is unwell, of course he's not brought the books," she said. "Can't someone else bring them?"

"The family," Mr. Abasi said, "doesn't know where they are."

"Can't someone run and ask him directly?" Miss Sweeney asked.

Matani spread his hands. "He goes mute from time to time. A reaction, perhaps, to his . . . " He felt censored by Badru's gaze, even though Badru did not understand English. "To his circumstances," he finished.

Miss Sweeney nodded as though she understood, but how could she? How could she know that the people of Mididima still couldn't stand to look Scar Boy full in the face, even after all these years? It was not only his disfigurement. It was his attitude: the way he stood, the way he held himself apart as if morally superior, and his very silence, which seemed to remind them of their own moments of shameful inattention like the one that had led to his maiming. That is what made him an outsider.

Miss Sweeney looked directly at Badru, studying him a moment. "Tell me, has your brother lost the books?" After a pause during which no one spoke, Matani translated.

"They are not lost," Badru said without elaboration, and Matani translated his reply.

"If you don't know where something is, it's lost," Mr. Abasi muttered.

"The books the boy checked out," Miss Sweeney said, looking down at her clipboard, "were a child's illustrated copy of *The Iliad and the Odyssey* and"—she hesitated—"a collection of Zen meditations?" She named the last one as a question and pursed her lips as though holding back some strong emotion—laughter? tears?—but when she spoke a moment later, her voice was calm. "Aren't they somewhere in the home?"

"Or in the bush," Mr. Abasi said, "or swallowed up by a leopard or burned in a fire or eaten in a meal." He shook his head and muttered again. "Zen meditations. Dear God."

"Let's think a minute. What can we do?" Miss Sweeney addressed her question to Matani, who had no reply. Into the space left by his silence, Mr. Abasi spoke.

"This program of yours is well intentioned but flawed, an ill-fitted idea for tribes such as this," Mr. Abasi said. "I've said this many times."

"Not now, Mr. A.," Miss Sweeney said.

But Mr. Abasi was unstoppable. "If we must transport library books across the desert, we must have rules," he said, voice rising. "Books are expensive to replace. Our standing library in Garissa could use a more extensive collection, but we are funding this instead. And these places have not a shilling to pay a fine. So we have to be absolute regarding the rules. Give each settlement an equal chance. Remain committed only to those who show full dependability."

"And no room for the slightest error, Mr. A.?"

He shook his head adamantly. "No room," he said. "You agreed to this when the program was established. Not all people are going to be able to learn your Western responsibility, Miss Sweeney. Not all people want to."

The lead camel stirred next to the acacia, kicking up dust with a rear hoof.

"Matani, couldn't you collect the books before we come next time? Then we'll get them back, just a little late," Miss Sweeney said. "There should be a grace period, after all." She faced Mr. Abasi. "Every library I've ever heard of has a grace period."

"Grace period? We don't have that in my province," Mr. Abasi said. "Besides, how can he guarantee?"

Matani had to restrain himself mightily not to nod at the reasonableness of the senior librarian's words. Nothing could be guaranteed—not offspring, not rain, not recovery of a missing possession. Miss Sweeney was reminding Matani of his own sweet, outspoken Jwahir, and he wanted to help this foreign woman—he did—but he felt powerless to dissuade Mr. Abasi, who was gathering steam. He rubbed his temples again.

"Your policy, as I understand, is meant to prevent the willful destruction of books," Miss Sweeney said. "Or their misuse—like someone throwing them on the ground, Mr. A." She tucked her clipboard under her arm. "People have already selected their books," she said. "I've already written it all down."

"Perhaps in the next place we will make sure each book is returned before any are allowed to be taken."

"I suggested that," Miss Sweeney said. "Weeks ago. You said it would take more time." Matani detected a sharpness in her tone, faint but clear, that he couldn't help but admire.

His neighbors were packed in close now, touching each other, breathing one another's air, listening intently to words most couldn't understand, tasting the intent of Miss Sweeney and of Mr. Abasi. Their arms, Matani noticed suddenly, were empty. Nor could anything be seen beneath their shirts. Undetectably, all the books had all been secreted away. Mr. Abasi would not be able to reclaim them today anyway.

Mr. Abasi must have observed this too. After a moment, he grunted. "We'll give it two more weeks, then."

"I think you've got a good idea, Mr. A.," said Miss Sweeney.

"In the meantime, you'll file a report explaining it."

"Of course, Mr. A. If an explanation is needed, which I doubt. Matani will recover the missing books," said Miss Sweeney. She grinned at the teacher.

Matani returned the smile, though he knew himself as trapped as an ignorant elephant in deep mud. What trapped him he could only sense, not yet name.

Kanika, whose expression showed she understood most

of what had occurred, was whispering to her grandmother and two others.

"Enough," Mr. Abasi said. "We're finished for today."

Miss Sweeney glanced at Matani. She hesitated, and for a moment she seemed so unwilling to leave that Matani thought she was going to say good-bye to Mr. Abasi instead of to them. She looked over her shoulder toward Mididima's homes, and then back to Mr. Abasi. "Fine," she said. The youngest children ran forward to be patted by her one last time.

"If he's not well, I'll let him recover, but tomorrow I will see Scar Boy," Matani told Badru. "Let him know." His manner had stiffened now into what, for the first time today, might be considered teacherlike. His tone was, he knew, a worthless effort to mask the fear of failure that rose like bile in his stomach. He felt Mr. Abasi at his side and turned to him. In the librarian's eyes, in his silence, Matani saw reflected Mr. Abasi's utter conviction that the next library visit would be the last to Mididima. That meant there would be no education for his son, the one he intended to have.

Mr. Abasi turned away. "Load up," he told the driver.

The lead camel stopped scratching her side against the acacia and gave a loud, dissatisfied snort from deep in her long throat. Matani, without words, watched as the drivers began repacking the boxes on the ground and the villagers, ducking as they would in a sandstorm, moved quickly toward their homes.

Part Two

Humans in love whisper "forever" and "always" and convince themselves that they mean it, every time. Mosquitoes, on the other hand, take romance to the opposite extreme. The female mosquito need make love only once in her life. The sperm, stored in her body, is then hers to use at will.

—*Mosquito Habits,* Dr. Sarah Jenkins
German-language edition, 1987

The Teacher

MATANI WAS SITTING BEHIND HIS HUT READING BY THE last stingy pinch of sunlight when he was distracted by the sound of men working in concert to secure the thorn fence that would discourage wild animals from entering Mididima and attacking the livestock overnight. He stopped to listen to their voices—smooth chords sliding beneath the scratchy melody of bushes being dragged across the dry ground. He closed his book and tapped his fingernails on its cover, keeping time with the fluid rhythm of the men's conversation. Why, he wondered, had Miss Sweeney given him this book about a poor baby boy poisoned by a scorpion, and a father with nothing more than eight graceless pearls to offer a greedy doctor? *The Pearl*. She called it a classic. Was it, instead, another omen? Combined with the overdue books and the dead mosquito-eater, it signaled something, he thought. Or maybe a lack of something. No water? No food? Or a son who would remain unborn?

No. He was rushing to conclude the worst when he'd read only the first dozen pages. It was because he'd had no time to calm down in the few hours since Mr. Abasi and the bookmobile had left. It offended him that Mr. Abasi considered Mididima's people unreliable and unworthy of the library books, and that he did not expect Matani to recover the two that Scar Boy had checked out.

He was wrong, Matani decided. The matter with Scar Boy would be resolved, and easily, in the morning. The infant in the story would recover. Matani himself would have a son, many sons. He would shed his superstitious side, so unbefitting a teacher.

"Husband?" called Jwahir from inside the house, more formal than usual but in a tone rich with unexpected tenderness. He'd thought she was still angry about the bookmobile, but in her voice he heard only love. How much he still had to learn about this creature, his wife.

"My dear?" he answered eagerly.

"My father of mine is here to see you," Jwahir said.

My husband of mine. That's what she used to call Matani, letting her voice slip into the charcoal range. It had always been a prelude to intimacy. But it had been many weeks since she'd used that lusty phrase with him.

Matani cleared his throat, rose, and extended a hand as Jwahir and her father approached. Her father's beard was dyed orange in honor of his age and position in Mididima. He'd only recently begun coloring it, and the sight of it still startled Matani. "Welcome," he said. The two men shook hands for a full minute, the expression on Jwahir's father's face enduringly solemn.

"News of the night?" asked Jwahir's father

They moved together into the hut. Jwahir left them alone there. "All is well," said Matani. "And your news of many nights?"

"My family is well, thank you," said Jwahir's father. "Although can you tell me of my daughter?"

Of course, Jwahir spoke to her father every day, and perhaps, Matani realized uneasily, more frankly than she spoke to her husband, with whom she was so elusive. Nevertheless, custom required him to answer his father-in-law's routine questions before the conversation could move forward. And forward it must go—Jwahir's father never visited Matani simply to chat.

"Jwahir is my home's adornment," Matani said. "I thank you for her."

Jwahir's father nodded stern acknowledgment. "No dust storms have troubled you?" he asked.

"Not one."

"And you are eating as needed?"

How wearying, this old-fashioned, time-consuming practice of asking and answering to display a certain stiff decorum. During the six years Matani had spent in Nairobi, he had not once missed it. He managed—just—to keep his smile as he nodded at Jwahir's father. "Thanks be for your concern," he said, attempting a tone of polite finality.

His father-in-law replied with another question, signaling that he was prepared to go on for some time yet. "How are the children learning?"

Only a substantial bride-price had persuaded Jwahir's father to agree to Matani's marriage to his sole daughter. Jwahir's father was a wealthy man by Mididima's standards, but with two wives and eight children, he always needed more. He would be less formal, Matani knew, with a son-in-law he liked, one with whom he could identify. He viewed

Matani as a man disappointingly trapped by his own brain and unable to contribute meaningfully to his people.

Still, how much of this distantly polite conversation was necessary in order to make that point?

"Please," Matani said, gesturing decisively to the rug.

"May you have many children of your own," his father-in-law said—a bit pointedly, Matani thought. Then he sat at last, allowing Matani to do the same. "Forgive my rudeness if I come quickly to my topic," he said.

Matani couldn't keep his eyebrows from rising.

Jwahir's father cleared his throat. "There once lived a family in our tribe," he began, "who'd long been known as the best of hunters. They knew how to run in the night. They were respected, and brought much food." He nodded solemnly and placed his hands on his lap, palms up. "This was long before you were born, or I, or even my grandfather, who told it to me, having heard it from his own grandfather. This is one of *our* stories, Matani," he said, as though Matani might miss the point.

"I probably know it, then," Matani replied.

"It would do you to hear it again," Jwahir's father said. He cleared his throat. "One spring day, into the family came a cross-eyed baby. A boy, as fate decreed, though a girl in such a condition would have been easier to embrace. The family, of course, feared the son would spoil their reputation, though no one spoke of it."

He looked expectantly at Matani, who shifted his weight from one side to the other rhythmically to try to demonstrate interest in the story being told so slowly by the father of his dear Jwahir.

"At the same time, we fell upon a harsh year. A Little Hunger, not a large one. We could have survived it. This family still wanted to be known as exceptional hunters, but they came home each night without a kill. Finally, two of the family's young men stole from another tribe and claimed the bounty was their own. The tribe gave the family thanks and ate the food without knowing it was tainted. We didn't know until the other tribe's elders came. We had to give three cows in compensation, although they were three we could hardly spare."

Jwahir's father sighed. "You've already imagined the outcome," he said, and Matani sank a little in relief to think an outcome was approaching. "It took only this for every-thing to change. In the next year, eight of our tribe died, including the cockeyed boy. When one is shamed, disaster follows. Always." He pressed forward from the waist, his face close enough to Matani's for them to drink from the same cup if they'd had one between them. "You understand my meaning?"

There it was, the question Matani had hoped to avoid. He looked up to the ceiling and down at the floor, waiting.

Jwahir's father betrayed impatience in his tone. "The books," he said, "must be returned," he said.

Matani sat straighter, now keenly interested. He had not expected Jwahir's father to touch upon this topic of Scar Boy and the missing books. "You mean you want the library to keep coming?" he asked. This would be a change, and an important one.

His father-in-law's eyebrows knitted in impatience. "The threat to end the camels' visits has nothing to do with

my topic. This is a question of honor and survival. For all of
Mididima. For you personally."

Matani rubbed his temples and took a deep breath. "So
you mean to compare stolen meat to missing books?"

"I am speaking of disgrace. And the fact that you are the
husband of my daughter. She is not to be dishonored."

Matani studied his father-in-law for a breath—not too
long, or it would be disrespectful. They were getting to the
heart of the matter, he thought, but he had no wish to discuss it. "This is a simple misunderstanding," he said, "that I
will resolve with Scar Boy by midday tomorrow."

Jwahir's father dismissed Matani's words with a wave of
his hand. "Scar Boy. He talks to evil spirits and, beyond that,
opens his mouth only for eating."

"Evil spirits?" Matani could not completely stifle his
scoffing tone.

"In becoming civilized, you've lost touch with the basic
forces of the world," Jwahir's father said. "The fact is, your
father should never have helped save the mangled child."

"My father . . . " Matani felt blood beating beneath his
eyes. "My father—"

Jwahir's father interrupted him. "Please, Matani. We've
grown more heated than I wished. Your father was, in essence, a good man, and I don't wish to dishonor him or
discuss history now. It is the future that concerns me."

"My father—" Matani began again.

"You can better understand it this way, perhaps," Jwahir's father said. "The luck of our tribe is like a stockpile of
grain, a guard against future drought. In his unlikely survival, Scar Boy used up our store of good luck. That's all.

But we can't let Scar Boy waste it again. It is better for you to speak to the boy's father."

"Abayomi?" This was an unwelcome prospect, though Matani would have trouble explaining why, even to himself. Abayomi, seven years Matani's senior, was quiet and deliberate, both in making the tribe's drums and in living his life. The exchanges between him and Matani had always been polite. Yet in Abayomi's presence, Matani always had the sense that he was being evaluated, and coming up short.

"It is really a matter to settle between the two of you," his father-in-law continued. "After all, Abayomi is responsible for Scar Boy. And you are responsible for your library."

"I can see this through with Scar Boy himself," Matani said. "Also, it is not my library. To hold me accountable for every book in every hand—it's unreasonable."

Jwahir's father frowned. "Recover the books," he said. "Then, let *us* choose to send the library on its way." He waved his hand as though to stop Matani from speaking. "Let us tell them that when an elder dies in Mididima, a dozen libraries are lost, each more valuable than the one that comes on camels' backs."

"No one thinks to replace one with the other."

"Intended or not, it will happen. The young will begin to think the words of the books are more important than the words of elders. And then we will slide into a world that you would say holds greater learning, but that I would say holds less."

"Before the library, our young had already started—"

"And we are fighting to discourage that, not embrace it."

"If we are to survive as a tribe, we must gauge the wind's direction," Matani said.

"Or shield ourselves from it." Jwahir's father cleared his throat. "This slim disease that sucks the body dry—it is worse than drought. Even in places where they can read, they cannot find a cure. We have been spared. Why? Because we remain apart. And what of these children you are teaching? Do you want them to live among the girls you described to my daughter—what are they called?—the Coca-Cola girls? Do you want them to become that?"

Matani felt himself flush. He regretted sharply ever telling Jwahir about the girls, as young as nine years old, in the dusty, destitute towns on the way to Nairobi. Men bought them a cool drink that no one but he had tasted in Mididima—Coca-Cola—and got sex in return.

"Books have nothing to do with that," he said.

"They are all of the same distorted world." Jwahir's father waved both hands in clear frustration, his voice raised. "And they think to teach *us*?" He took a deep breath. "But let's not discuss this further now. Get the books back quickly from Scar Boy, so we don't have to act against the boy ourselves. Reestablish Mididima's honor. On the importance of this, we can agree?"

Matani hesitated before answering. "As far as that bird flies, yes."

Jwahir's father rose. "May the sun shine warm on your left shoulder, cool on your right, until we meet again," he said, moving quickly toward the door now as though he couldn't wait to get away. "And may my daughter be well."

Matani sank down, conscious of a throbbing behind the

bone on the outside corner of his left eye. He felt a flash of anger at Scar Boy. He'd hoped to postpone a debate about the future of the bookmobile until after the camels and their load had become a force of nature, more difficult to stop than to accept. Now, Scar Boy's stubbornness had caused the issue to be raised too soon. Even after Matani had recovered the books, he feared he couldn't defer this argument further.

He was roused from his thoughts by the pressure of Jwahir's stare. She stood at the door. Her eyes held something intangible. He wondered if she wanted to lie with him this night, create a child. He reached for her.

"You will talk to Abayomi tomorrow?" she asked as she turned, deftly slipping away from his grasp.

Though she eluded him, her gaze seemed seductive and her tone undeniably held an undercurrent of risk, excitement, and anticipation. This sort of foreplay was unfamiliar to him. But, praise the ancestors, he would jump at it.

"Well?" she asked.

"If that's what your father suggests, then I'll do it," he said, making up his mind then, a private bargain of sorts, the father's will in exchange for the daughter's intimacy. "Now, come to me, my Jwahir."

But she shook her head. "Read your book," she said. "I will go to Leta. Come there for dinner when your stomach protests."

And before he could think of a reply, he was left staring at the empty place where she'd stood.

His Jwahir wanted to visit Leta. That was not bad, he reminded himself. That should be comforting, in fact. He could imagine the two friends together. Jwahir would bounce one of Leta's little ones on her lap, and they would discuss motherly emotions, mother love. Leta would fan that nurturing fire within his Jwahir.

So this chill that ran down his body was insignificant, caused by the vanishing of the sun—or, more likely, by the book Miss Sweeney had given him. It was not superstition—who, after all, would not be made anxious by the desperation of a baby puffed and feverish from an insect's sting? That was not a story for evening. He found the novel and hid it in a corner beneath a spare blanket. Then he went out to pace alone around the inner circle of Mididima, just inside the thorn fence.

Scar Boy

A MAN'S VOICE SLICED THROUGH THE SEEPING DARKNESS, beckoning like a bent finger. "The daa-aay," he sang, "the day is turning its corner."

Half a dozen others answered him. "Its corner turns."

Taban stopped drawing to listen to the sound swell.

"Gather," the chanter sang, "against its turning."

"Its corner turns," the men answered again, their numbers already growing, a dozen now, maybe two, more on the way, assembling to meet the moment of day's collapse. This was the time when camels and cows that normally disdained human company fervently sought it. It was when the earth was turned over to creatures not only stronger of eyesight and hearing, but bolder and more cunning than their daytime brethren. This was when *tame* was revealed to mean *weak*.

Taban savored the shift in the quality of light that came with this boundary, and he welcomed the cover of night. But the men, like the domesticated animals, feared it. For the next hours, those in the *kilinge* would keep the tribe safe with their drumming and stories and recollections, their praises to the ancestors. Already, the drums—a barrier against nothingness—thumped faster than a frightened heart.

Taban knew things about the men in the *kilinge*, even though he'd never been among them there. He knew that the flames burnished their cheeks, making them glow as if from within. And that the fire distorted the shadows so that outside the circle, everything was exposed as alien and undesirable. And that beyond those shadows, absolute darkness gathered like a force and everything that fell within this darkness was deemed irrevocably apart, the other.

His father, Abayomi, was at the fire now; and so was his brother, Badru. He could be there too, raising his voice with that of the other men, perhaps even playing the drums that spoke so many stories.

But he could imagine what would happen if he appeared there. They would turn to him, expressions hooded. They would step back to allow him his own space instead of stepping forward to meet him. They would lower their eyes to avoid his gaze, as though it could infect them. And later they would whisper, words like *horror* and *evil* and *cursed*.

They liked men who resembled them, men with unblemished skin and wide-bridged noses and eyes of polished *shona* stone. Men who shunned shade, not hovering indoors. They were suspicious of those who were even a little different—and maybe, after all, that trait didn't belong only to those of Mididima; maybe that's how all men were, even men of the Distant City or beyond. What did a boy like him know? To them, he was Scar Boy, the distorted. To them, he belonged in the dark, beyond the outskirts of the *kilinge*. So there he would stay and from there (he repeated now an old vow), he would never ask for anything. He would do without, when he could. And what he needed, he would take.

He lowered his head, then, and focused, eyes narrowed, shutting out the drumbeat. Soon, all he heard was the sound of his pencil dipping and curving and circling across the page.

The Girl

KANIKA CURLED HER TOES INTO THE DIRT, WAITING FOR her eyes to grow strong enough to thin the darkness. She inhaled the odors of the night: nearly dead fires spitting tendrils of smoke and the musty, sour scent of sleep. When her eyes found their way by the light from the moon and the spill of stars, she went to Scar Boy's hut and stood outside the wall against which he slept. She felt the ground for a stick and then poked it through a gap between the twigs and dung, low in the wall. On very cold nights, Scar Boy plugged up the breach, but always in such a way that she could push the stick through and reach him. Tonight it was open to the air. She extended the stick until it touched something solid. His side, she knew, at his waist. She probed once, gently, and paused. She didn't have to poke again. She felt the stick turn—his signal that he was awake.

She went to wait outside his door. When he came out, they began walking immediately, though slowly, to accommodate his limp. The quiet of the night felt large, and they didn't break it until they'd eased past the thorn fence and put the huts at a distance. Then he stopped, turned, and faced her. Even in the dark, she could see the drag to his left eye and the twisted, concave deformity of his left cheek, though the mottled purplish skin of his face was not visible. He wore a scarf over his face sometimes when he came outside, but never when he was alone with her.

"Where are they?" she asked.

"You don't say 'How are you?'"

"How are you?"

"You don't take my hand?"

She took his hand. "Where are they?"

He smiled the only way he could, the right side of his mouth lifting. It made him look as if he were sneering, but Kanika knew he wasn't. "They can't be returned," he said.

"Oh!" she said, dismayed. "You lost them? But how?"

He cocked his head to one side, looking at her. "I have them. Look at the moon," he said.

Tension drained from the soles of her feet. "Good," she said. "Good, good. Now give them back."

"Feel the air," he said. "The night air is so new, every night."

"Do it tomorrow," she said.

"They wouldn't want them."

"Of course they want them." Sometimes he was totally clear, clearer and cleaner than rain. And then he could turn into a mysterious creature, speaking an exotic language filled with riddles. Those were the times she dreaded. "Listen to me. It's more than the bookmobile I'm worried about. I didn't have time to ask Miss Sweeney about leaving because your brother came and Mr. Abasi got angry and—Badru must have told you. And now, if you don't give back the books, they're going to come and gather up everything and it will all be in a rush and I'll be like the middle cow, I'll be stuck. I won't get to ask her and I won't ever get out of here."

He sank to a crouch and stared up at the moon. His feet were buried under shadows, but a fragile light softened his shoulders. They'd grown broad over the last year, Kanika saw. "That would be so bad?" he asked.

"If I have to stay my whole life here, without ever experiencing *there*, I'll evaporate," she said.

"Evaporate?"

She couldn't help smiling a little at his gentle mocking. "So then don't think of me; think of yourself," she said. "Everyone's angry with you. They say you've shamed the tribe. They say by shaming us, you've opened the door to evil spirits, and something bad will happen to us now."

He looked over his shoulder as if to catch someone eavesdropping. But he did it in an exaggerated way, to tease her. No one was there, of course. All those in Mididima were safe within their homes or the *kilinge*. Most were nearly as terrified of the dark—and of the spirits that ran in the night and could bring drought and famine—as they were of Scar Boy.

Scar Boy should have been afraid, too, considering that the hyena's attack came at the edge of night. He didn't fear the blackness, though. He seemed, in fact, most comfortable with the sun out of sight. Kanika thought that was because the darkness masked his scars, made him almost whole. Kanika could talk to him anytime, noon or midnight, and sometimes she felt her voice going on and on, like water pouring down a dry throat, longer than she even intended, because he listened so well. But for his part, he waited for the dark to talk.

She squatted next to him. "Please tell me," she said. "Why do you want to keep the books?"

He lifted his shoulders and she thought he would answer, but he only kept staring at the moon.

She closed her eyes. She considered what it meant to hold a book in her arms and run an index finger along the pages, letting her mind tumble with the words. How it took her away from Mididima, and how, when she closed the book and came back, she felt bigger and smarter. Scar Boy knew how to read too, though not as well as Kanika. Matani's father had taught him. Reading, in fact, had been the first thing Kanika and Scar Boy had talked about when they first spoke, years ago now.

"The books are like the night for you, aren't they?" she said. "You can hide in the stories, and grow there, and come out different." She turned toward him. "I'll send you books from the Distant City. As many as I can afford. Only give these back, so I can leave."

He didn't even glance at her. She felt her cheeks grow warm, blood pulse in her throat and temples. She was the only one in the whole tribe, besides his brother and his father, who spent time with him. The only one who cared. She was his closest friend.

"Are you going to howl at the moon," she asked, jumping to her feet, raising her voice, "or be human? Are you going to answer me?"

The fury in her tone made him look at her, then, full in

the face. He seemed to hold his breath for a moment. "Say my name," he commanded. His voice trembled.

She looked at him, surprised. She opened her mouth and shut it again. "Taban," she said. "Taban."

He exhaled audibly and motioned for her to sit. He put his arm stiffly around her shoulder. He'd never done that before. He looked at her sidelong. His wide-eyed expression, the rigidity of his arm, quenched her anger, almost making her want to giggle.

How to understand this quiet, mysterious friend of hers? His gesture must mean that he would give back the books. After all, he wanted what was best for her. He wanted that more than anyone else she knew. This arm on her shoulders was, for Scar Boy, as good as making the promise aloud.

"I want what's right for you too. You know that, don't you?" she said.

"Yes," he said, and his tone held no doubt at all.

"Good." She was glad that they could be here together looking at the moon, and that he understood, and that he would give back the books so she could talk to Miss Sweeney and leave. She slumped against him then, resting her head against his left cheek. She felt him tremble for a moment. "Relax," she said softly, though she knew that he couldn't. "Relax."

The Grandmother

THE TRIBE HAD SPENT YEARS ROAMING TOGETHER, UPROOT-
ing and settling and moving again. In the process,
they'd become as intimate with one another's moods as
they were with the shifting wind, the drifting dust. And
they felt each other's habits as distinctly as they felt the
weight of the midday sun or the pressure of a belly too long
unfed. Even a break in routine they sensed in advance.

Thus Neema knew, without deliberation, that if she
wished to speak to Matani that morning, she must be outside his home extra early. She slept weakly and was waiting
when he emerged. Although they'd had no plan to meet
and Neema had never before greeted him at such an hour,
he nodded without surprise. "This morning, Neema, has
as many sharp teeth as a hyena's jaw," he said. "Perhaps we
could talk at evening?"

"The other teeth will have to wait," she answered, taking
him by the arm. "We will walk together. At this age, the
tongue is more productive when the legs are going, too."

She was too old, she knew, for anyone to raise eyebrows
at her and Matani. Nevertheless, she waved and called loudly
to the three men who stood talking near the camels so they

could see she had nothing to hide. "Let's walk to the cassava shrubs," she said. They passed the rows of maize, beans, and an experimental crop called sweet potato, all watered by the bucket irrigation kits Matani's father brought to the clan years ago. Neema walked as far as the crops and the water pan every day, but she rarely walked farther. Beyond the crops stood a hut and a fire hole where the young sometimes danced, and at the same place, a second water pan the tribe had dug years ago. Sometimes the children took the animals there for the day. It was smaller, but had, so far, held water consistently.

The grass in the area still grew tall, but already she could see the barren patches that were a precursor of the Big Hunger. They lived, her husband's tribe, with an ache deep in the abdomen that they called the Small Hunger—that is, when they spoke of it at all, which was seldom. They accepted the Small Hunger as proof of life. It was the Big Hunger that pricked like a thousand thorns, and then split apart and at the end felt like nothing at all. It was the Big Hunger that worried them.

She wondered what the men would decide if the Millet Rains did not come again this year, if the buckets lost their usefulness and a sea of brown engulfed the land around their settlement. Already they were pleading with the Hundred-Legged One in their nighttime songs, begging for water. But He, seeing things they did not, would respond in His own impenetrable way. Last time, after the land grew dry and the rituals failed, the elders decided not to risk another Great Disaster, and they had taken the tribe to a feeding center. She knew it was a humiliation they would not repeat. She wondered about the changes a long drought would bring this time.

"Is it Kanika?" Matani asked, intruding on her thoughts. "Some problem I don't know of?"

Neema, already a few steps ahead, shortened her stride. She stood only as tall as Matani's shoulders, but her gait had always been intentionally broad so that—though she would never acknowledge this aloud—all those in the tribe would feel they had to walk quickly to keep up with her. Now she reminded herself to slow her pace to the teacher's. He must be able to hear her words.

"You were in the Distant City when Kanika's mother was killed." She stopped walking for a moment. Saying the words aloud hurt, even after all this time, and she hadn't expected that.

"It's an old sorrow," Matani said softly, "but it belongs to us all."

Neema inhaled silently, steadying herself. "Because you were gone, what you may not know is that before my daughter's death, I was very ill," she said. "I had a cough that would not vanish, that sometimes took over my body. Because of that, I was in my hut when they came to tell me what happened to Dahira, and to leave Kanika with me. She was only four then and needed attention, of course, but I—weakened by the cough and further by the news— couldn't move. They didn't think to help me—they didn't even notice. Their minds were on revenge." Her voice lost its trembling. "And that is fine; that is as it should be," she said.

She stopped walking and turned to Matani, who halted too. "Here's what happened next," she said. "My granddaughter and I stared at each other without speaking for a full day and a night. In the morning, she began to whimper." Neema placed her hand gently on her own stomach. "Hungry, of course. Her crying brought me to life—a little. I managed to get up and ask one of the women to fetch camel milk. I gave it to Kanika, but she gestured that I must drink first. I had no desire, but she insisted, so I took the smallest of sips. Then she took a sip, and returned the glass to me. She wouldn't drink more until I did. In this way, we had our first food since her mother's death."

Matani put his hand on Neema's shoulder. "Neema," he began. She cut him off.

"For a month, camel's milk was all I consumed. As I drank it, my cough of many months disappeared, the edges of my sorrow softened, and I no longer wanted to die. I didn't want the milk at first, not at all. Just as many here don't want the library." She tilted her head. "But thanks to Kanika, I drank. Our children's children can pull behind them a joy as big as the moon, Matani. You will find that out yourself."

Matani rubbed his forehead with the palm of one hand. "If you have something crucial to say, Neema, we must start."

Neema had a single point of vanity—her strong, flexible back. It was, she knew, unusually supple, even for a much younger woman. She lengthened it now and let her eyes run over the horizon as she walked. She pressed her fingers against her cheekbones. "I am reading another book from your library," she said after a minute.

"Not *my* library," said Matani.

"The white woman's, then."

Matani opened his mouth as if to object again.

"We need not quarrel over this, Matani. It's because of you that the librarian from Garissa even thinks of us, living as we do like the windblown bloom of the acacia tree. But what I want to speak of is this particular book."

"And I do want to hear," Matani said. "Though this morning, I say with all honor, may not be——"

"It's the story of a woman who feels without space or movement. She has the heart of a nomad, but nowhere to wander, and her husband does not wish to move. He listens without hearing, looks without seeing. So she——forgive me, but I am old now; you will not misinterpret my words——she becomes enmeshed with a man who is not her husband."

Matani smiled. "Please don't mention this story to Jwahir's father, or he will pay me another visit this evening to further discuss the seeds of corruption *my* library is sowing."

"She's a good woman," Neema said. "But the choice she makes is wrong. Those who break rules must be punished."

Matani sighed and sank to his heels. "I relent, Neema," he said. "I will stay. I will listen. Only give me the gift of coming quickly to the point."

She was not doing a good job with this. She had not planned what to say——she'd counted on its coming to her. She favored speaking in a way that suggested rather than dictated meaning, but Matani preferred directness, words that were clear and quick. He'd picked up a taste for that in the Distant City. She took three broad steps, circling him, then stopped.

"I was thinking last night of your resolute side, Matani," she said. "I've known you since boyhood, after all. When you were about twelve, I saw you kill an aging cow that had been your pet. You did not once recoil. Because of this—your unflinching—you were chosen to put to death one of the favored camels that had broken its leg when you were, what, Matani? Only sixteen?"

Matani squirmed and smiled at once. "You mean by this that you remember me as ruthless?"

"I would put it differently," Neema said. "There is no room for tenderness in our men, little enough in our women. But some fight against indiscriminate compassion. You, Matani, you know what must be sacrificed. And that is important now. We don't send a boy to fetch honey. We send a man."

He leaned back on his heels, staring at her.

"Survival and change are linked," she said. "Who better than we knows that? We've always adjusted to stay alive, moving to follow drops of water, to avoid enemies, to find grass for the animals. Now a different kind of altering is needed."

"Ah," said Matani. "We arrive near to your subject."

"Some among our elders see the bookmobile as a raiding enemy tribe," Neema said. "They say that the books are touched by evil spirits, that they will destroy our culture. That our young will be lured to the cities, where the boys will work as street-sweepers and our girls as street-sleepers, and their hearts will be forever empty because they must live in one place instead of wander free."

"I've heard this muttering, too," Matani said softly.

"But we know, you and I, that even if books are pieces of other worlds, they are not inhabited by evil spirits. And that learning to read will bring necessary change."

"So you disagree with the elders?"

Neema bent from the waist, lifted a handful of dirt, and let it fall. "We'll survive what is to come only if we make it to the modern world," she said. "Those who stand in the way must be ignored if possible, displaced otherwise."

"It's not in my power to displace—"

"What we will lose from having the books," Neema said, "we were going to lose anyway. What we gain cannot be measured. When you see Scar Boy, you must tell him that. Tell him, too, that his place among us has always been tenuous, that he shouldn't risk the wrath of his people, and that he will not in any case be able to keep what isn't his."

Matani shook his head. "In the end, I fear Scar Boy will have little enough to do with the future of the bookmobile here."

"I am an old person," Neema said. "I can be spared. But I'm not the only one who depends on the life these camels bring. You. The children. Even your Jwahir. And my Kanika, she needs it too—tell Scar Boy that."

"I think these words will do little good directed at Scar Boy, Neema. I do not think the books are gone. He is just irresponsible, or defiant."

"Just tell him," Neema said. "Mention Kanika."

"After all, where does he ever go, that he could lose the books? He must have them. And if he has them, this will be a simple matter, so why—" Matani's tone had become almost musing, as if he spoke to himself.

Neema shook her head, cutting him off. "What's in the heart and head of Scar Boy," she said, "is yours to determine. You are connected to him by history and by fate. Only, please, as you meet him, remember our survival."

"Survival." Matani lowered his head, his smile slight. "You give me a large task."

"We women are allowed to do so little," she said. "We do know, though, to stretch the hide while it's still green, even if we think the winter will be warm."

Matani laughed, and she smiled too.

"What I have left to say to you is briefer than breath, and then I will release you," she said. "Whoever hurts my granddaughter's future"—she gripped his wrist for a minute and then let go—"I will kill them."

"What words!" he said.

"It's my job," she said. "And whatever would hurt Mididima's children, you must put to death."

"What words," he said again, more softly this time.

"Do not underestimate the importance of what you say and do with Scar Boy," Neema said. "Take with you your unflinching."

The American

FI HESITATED BEFORE THE DOOR, STRUCK BY AN UNEXPECTED
wave of shyness. Mr. Abasi might not welcome her spon-
taneous visit. But then she chided herself for her hesitation:
he wasn't dangerous, after all, and she'd already considered
and dismissed real risks on this trip. Some guidebooks, in
fact, advised travelers not to venture at all to the remote
northeast region near the Somalia border. In addition to
the references to malaria and *shifta*, the books warned of
deadly clashes between tribal groups, and of *kumi-kumi*,
bootleg liquor that could be laced with enough methanol
to kill. One handbook, referring to the high rate of violent
crime, even quoted a billboard that urged drivers: "If you
are carjacked, try to establish rapport with the hijackers.
Remember: they are human also."

What, then, should be so alarming about the prospect of
knocking on Mr. Abasi's door?

Still, she hesitated, watching three scrawny chickens
claw and peck the ground a bit desperately in front of Mr.
Abasi's clay-brick home. Next door, the house was patched
with rags and scrap metal, and an emaciated donkey stood
in the yard.

She'd found Nairobi memorable mainly for its slums collapsing into valleys; its street kids called *chokora*, or "those who eat garbage"; and the *matutu*, the minibuses that careened through the city bearing names like Thriller Ride, No Honx, and New Orleans Shuttle. Nairobi was a tough, seething town, full of corruption and racial suspicions, both blessed with modern conveniences and burdened by modern woes. It reminded Fi of the line from Dambudzo Marechera's *The House of Hunger:* "Life stretched out like a series of hunger-scoured hovels."

The five-hour drive northeast had been a shift in time even more than space. The region began to feel more exotic just twenty minutes outside of Nairobi as Fi and her driver reached the tin houses near Thika, and increasingly exotic after she bought short, fat bananas along the road in Yata and then hit the hot, barren desert. They passed solitary herdsmen with goats or cows, and the occasional family walking camels to water. Fi felt an excitement and urgency about her mission that grew as she traveled toward Garissa's entrance, marked by a sign that said *Karibu*, Swahili for "welcome." As far as she knew, she was the only white staying in Garissa, and at first she was viewed with enormous curiosity. Children gawked openly; grown-ups, attempting more subtlety, stared from beneath lowered eyelids. But after a couple of weeks, she woke up one morning to find that everyone seemed to have forgotten her skin color, or at least had become willing to overlook it. She forgot it herself, though perhaps that was partly willful, stemming from a need to fit in here, to have a place and purpose, not to be an oddity.

She felt glad that Garissa differed so from the modern, hurried, distracted world she'd left behind. She reveled in the difference. But sometimes, she had to admit, she missed surfing the Internet, knowing the latest news instantly, following the blogs of fellow librarians. And she even missed the crazy patrons, like the Asian woman with dyed lipstick-red hair who spent hours reading everything on gambling, including the novels, so she could learn how to beat the slot machines in Atlantic City. Or the would-be poet who always carried a notebook stuffed with his precious papers—some frayed or food-stained—and repeatedly insisted on showing her where his book should be shelved, if it were ever published—or ever written, though he never added that. Or the retired tailor who came in to read the newspaper every day. He vanished for a couple of weeks, and when he returned, he told her in a hushed voice that he'd been on a trip with extraterrestrials. That was the day she'd seen the ad for the consulting position in Kenya. That was the day she told herself she had to do something with her life beyond listening to patrons whisper about their adventures with men from outer space. Now, she wondered how the tailor was doing.

Abruptly, Mr. Abasi's door swung open, as though he'd been expecting her, except that he looked astonished. He didn't speak at first.

She smiled. "Mr. A."

"Miss Sweeney?" He made several small hiccuping noises. "What are you doing here?"

"Can I ask you something?"

"Now?" he managed.

"It's a bookmobile matter," she said. "I'm sorry about the intrusion. It's important, though, and I was afraid we wouldn't have enough time later on."

He looked right and left and then made rapid scooping motions three times with his right hand. "Come in, of course."

She dipped her head slightly to step into his dimly lit home. "Shoo!" he said over her shoulder, and she turned and saw two little boys hiding behind a worn wooden cart that was parked in front of the house next door. She was used to being followed by children here. She waved at them.

Mr. Abasi's two-room home was sparsely furnished with a mat rolled up on the floor and a small pantry made of blond wood. Three hardcover books were stacked in a corner, and he'd put up a map of the United Kingdom. But her attention was captured by a stylized painting in shades of brown and red that hung on one wall. It showed a large woman with her back to the artist, both arms raised to her neck and shoulders as if she were massaging them. She wore a full skirt but seemed naked from the waist up. The painting's hedonism conflicted with Fi's image of Mr. Abasi. She moved in for a closer look and saw, stuck in the corner of the frame, a snapshot of one of the camels loaded with books. So he did care about this program. That boosted her confidence.

When she turned back to him, he was still standing a bit stiffly, staring with an expression that seemed almost a parody of surprise. His chest rose as he took a deep breath, and then he finally appeared to recover. "Sit," he said, gesturing to a maroon mat, stuffed with stiff straw, on the floor. His tone held a certain note of command.

She sat cross-legged.

"Would you like some *chai*?"

She felt so impatient; she felt so American all of a sudden. She didn't want *chai*. She wanted to leap directly to the point. But she'd come, unannounced, into his home. She had to do it his way.

"*Chai* would be fine, thank you," she said.

She watched him move to a corner, where he lit what looked like a slightly larger version of a single-burner camping stove. On it stood a sky blue kettle, already steaming. He opened up a small pantry and pulled out a coffee mug decorated with a drawing of a leopard—it looked, she thought, like a souvenir from Africa that one might buy from an airport shop. He shook tea leaves into the cup from a small plastic Baggie and then poured in the hot mixture of milk and water. He didn't look at her as he worked, and she sensed that she shouldn't speak. After a few minutes, he brought her the cup and sat across from her.

"Thank you," she said, and then she made herself take a sip. The *chai* was unsweetened, a little spicy, unexpectedly good. After that sip, though, she couldn't restrain herself any longer. "Mr. A." she said, "why did you become a librarian?"

He gave her a look that was at once amused and impatient. "Miss Sweeney. How is this about the bookmobile?"

"Bear with me, Mr. A. Is it that you love books? Or maybe reading?"

He was silent for a moment. "I like some books quite a

lot. I like Shakespeare, for instance," he said at last, and then he lowered his voice and intoned, "Eye of newt and toe of frog."

She laughed, and he smiled, seeming pleased for the first time since she'd arrived.

"But if you really want to know," he said, "I'm a librarian because of Miss Fetegrin."

"Who?"

"Fetegrin. The first librarian I ever met. A no-nonsense Londoner with short hair. She wore these tight two-piece suits and had a tiny waist; but it was her eyes—they held such passion, and especially when she talked about the library on Saint James Street." His tone had become fervent, and then he cut off, as if realizing he was getting carried away. He cleared his throat. "Anyway, she came from London and found me at my school—I guess my teachers recommended me. She interviewed me for a scholarship to study library science in England. I got it."

"Once there, did you consider staying abroad instead of coming home?"

He shook his head. "I like it here, Miss Sweeney," he said, and looked as though he was surprised by his own words. Then he fell silent, and she could tell he was done revealing himself.

"Me, I was slow to learn to read," Fi said after a moment. "Some undiagnosed learning disability, I guess, but I was nearly nine before I could read a book on my own. I loved it. I realized right away that books could take us out of ourselves, and make us larger. Even provide us with human connections we wouldn't otherwise have." She paused.

Mr. Abasi watched her without expression. "Back home, I help with the adult literacy program. Do you know how many people go to the library—even people who can't read—to find answers and solutions?"

"Well," Mr. Abasi said. "And what is this about, Miss Sweeney?"

She smiled at his tone, suddenly abrupt and impatient. "Mididima."

He nodded, a satisfied expression overtaking his face. "I thought so."

"Mr. A., you must think literacy is important. How can you be a librarian and think otherwise?"

"I didn't say—"

"Do you know," she said, "—but of course you do—that literacy increases one's income?"

Mr. Abasi's eyebrows climbed. "In the bush?"

"And there are less tangible benefits, too. For instance, a boost in one's sense of self-worth."

"You Americans," he said, his tone at once exasperated and indulgent. "With your unflagging belief in your ability—and your right—to change the course of another's history."

Fi stretched her legs and flexed her toes. "You know, Mr. A., I've always hated the word *administration*. It's a clipped, deadly word, don't you think? After they told me I was in library *administration*, I start seeing images of myself being executed by a firing squad."

"Yes, Miss Sweeney?" Mr. Abasi prompted after a minute.

"But those people in Mididima, they make me value my

job again, Mr. A. They are smart. They deserve a chance. And I can help them. Without an education and exposure to the modern world, they have no future."

"Of course they have a future." He looked away for a second, his face creased in apparent frustration, and then spoke with exaggerated patience. "The people of Mididima have existed, in one shifting form or another, for thousands of years, Miss Sweeney. Longer than your country. You see them so abstractly."

Fi stared into her cup of *chai* and then took a sip. She decided to try a different tack. "I've been thinking," she said, "about a special trick of mine. I can always find books. No, seriously, Mr. A. It's an amazing gift to have as a librarian. Whenever a volume is misshelved, I'm called to locate it. I don't know how I do it exactly; I just put out my arms and walk through the stacks, as if I'm a book-dowser. It astonishes even me."

"Do you know," Mr. Abasi said, "how many people live in Mididima, Miss Sweeney? Maybe one hundred seventy-five. Think of that."

"You are saying that's too few people to worry about?"

"I am saying there are many other places for your bookmobile to visit, now that the people of Mididima have broken the rules."

"That seems unnecessarily hard-hearted."

"Hard-hearted? No. It's practical." He stood up and poured himself more *chai*. "There is something else, Miss Sweeney," he said as he added more to her cup as well. "Something I learned when I lived in London. Sometimes countries like your own can begin to believe theirs is the only way."

"I'm not disagreeing, but I think I'm missing your point. I'm talking about books, not a military invasion."

"You love the idea of what you think you are accomplishing in Mididima. But they have their own approach to their lives, Miss Sweeney. Don't assume it needs to change."

"What kind of life? Not enough food. Not enough water."

"Let me tell you a story," Mr. Abasi said, sitting again, "about another settlement not too far from Mididima. The people there fetched water from a well that was a four-hour walk away. A few years ago, a Christian mission raised money and started to build a well that would be only fifteen minutes away. Before they could finish, it was destroyed. They began to build again, and again it was destroyed. Finally, they asked the people of the settlement if enemy tribes were wrecking the well. No, the people said. They were destroying it themselves. The women had always walked those four hours, once a week, and it didn't seem too long to them. It allowed them a break from daily chores and a chance to visit their neighbors. Also, it had become a rite of passage from girlhood to womanhood, a part of their culture. They didn't want a well fifteen minutes away." He rubbed the back of his neck. "These people have connections to the land and their traditions that outsiders might not understand."

"But what, Mr. A., can be wrong with learning to read?"

"The books we bring are in Swahili or English, not their local tongues. They are not books about *their* lives," he said. "These are books that might even make them feel ashamed of their lives."

"We need other books, I agree," she said.

"I'm not sure, Miss Sweeney, that there exist the kind of books they need." He sighed. "But your mind is settled, I see." Then he gestured for her to take another sip of *chai*, and waited until she did. "Have you heard," he said, "that many of our people believe if you know five colloquial expressions in their tribal language, they must always provide you with nourishment and shelter? But—" He paused as though to make sure she was paying attention. "But if you know fewer than five, they owe you not even a sip of water."

She nodded, understanding his point, but he pressed it.

"Learn those five phrases, Miss Sweeney," he said.

"Maybe even ten, Mr. A.," she replied.

The Teacher

H E WOULD HAVE EMERGED A DIFFERENT MAN IF HE'D BEEN born someone else's son. A hunter. A warrior, perhaps. It wasn't predestined, his current life as Mididima's teacher. As a boy, he'd moved with the silence of held breath, which the tribesmen mentioned regularly and with meaningful gazes. As a young teen, he'd sometimes imagined chasing and slaying, returning to his people bearing sustenance.

But Matani, who loved his father to the point of worship, always knew he would finally succumb to his father's wishes. He learned to spear words instead of animals. He compensated by telling himself that he was, in the end, a warrior of sorts, strong and passionate, fighting for the future of his wife, for his children who were soon to be, and for his neighbors. It wasn't the same, he knew.

"Hello, Teacher," Nadif called to him. "Time to start?"

Matani touched the boy's shoulder. "Go drink some milk and gather your energy. I'll be ready soon." Nadif did not ask where Matani was going: everyone knew he was headed to see Scar Boy. Matani felt the pressure of eyes and thoughts on him; his neighbors were waiting to see if he was truly worthy of the new respect he'd lately been given.

"Okay, Teacher," Nadif said.

Only since the arrival of the bookmobile had the children begun addressing him in this way, as if the library had conferred the title on him. He knew that their respect might not last. A furtive step, a muscular arm, a closed mouth: these were the most esteemed of male virtues. And he, after all, was only a man who could read, and who could speak unknowable words in irrelevant languages, and who spent hours among children. His sole act of bravery was to support a contentious camel-borne library. If he'd been a more traditional sort of warrior, maybe Jwahir would have found it easier to understand him.

To keep loving him; that's what he meant.

That, after all, was the real source of his self-doubt. Jwahir had become distant, as if she'd moved on to a different watering hole and left Matani behind on spent land. Even during the previous night, as he tossed wakefully, she'd spurned him. He could tell by her breathing that she was awake too, so he'd reached for her; thinking they could talk; that they could share this worry about the bookmobile; and that then, he might finally rest freely. But she feigned sleep—a sort of lie—and rolled heavily away. He preferred her passionate anger to this withdrawal.

As he quietly reached the door to Scar Boy's hut, a vision came to mind: he was returning from hunting, his shoulders well built, his skin shiny with sweat; Jwahir was staring with admiring eyes, taking his hands, putting her thumb in the middle of his palm, stroking there, moving closer.

So preoccupied was he with this image that he was startled when Badru swept aside the cloth door of his hut.

Badru's unsurprised expression made it clear that he'd heard Matani's approach, that Matani no longer possessed even the quiet step of his youth.

"Hello, Teacher," Badru said.

Coming from Badru, the greeting sounded dismissive.

Matani stepped closer, gathering himself, not expecting this task to be difficult but still focusing on the responsibility that had been impressed on him by so many—not only Neema and Jwahir's father, but children, young women, even Jwahir's best friend Leta. "I'm here, as promised," he said. "To see your father."

"And he's not within."

Badru spoke smugly. But Matani had expected Abayomi's absence. He'd been counting on it, in fact. "Your brother, then," he said.

Badru hesitated before beckoning him forward.

In a corner of the room, Scar Boy sat cross-legged. He did not glance up as Matani entered. He held a stone, triangular with one sharp point, brown in the center, gray around the edges. It looked like the meat-filled dumplings Matani had eaten on the streets in Nairobi. Scar Boy had been using it to draw in the dirt in front of him, Matani saw. A spiral shape. And an animal—a camel, perhaps?

Even after all these years of watching the boy's scar stretch and soften, Matani still could not help cringing inwardly for the first moment or two each time he was in Scar Boy's presence. He didn't admire this in himself, but he had to forgive it: his reaction was involuntary. The scarred skin of the boy's left cheek was dark and vivid at once, an almost luminous cobalt, the sort of color Matani suspected might be found on large leaves in the dense, tropical regions his father used to talk about. The boy's nose had been torn from his face, and in its place stood a wartlike lump with two holes. Half his lip was wrenched downward, as if the left side had abandoned its fight with gravity.

But this was not what frightened the villagers most. It was Scar Boy's eyes. The right eye, untouched by the hyena, was higher and wider than the other. Too much of the white showed. The left eye had slipped almost onto the cheek. The boy looked permanently unbalanced, feral.

"Hello," Matani said.

Scar Boy shifted his rock from palm to palm and grimaced in greeting.

Something in Scar Boy's harsh expression produced a spiky pain in Matani's stomach and, at the same time, triggered a sharp memory of the afternoon when Abayomi had carried a chewed, bloody mass into Matani's home.

Matani had been a young man, only a few years older than Scar Boy was now. He'd been preparing to go to Nairobi to study. His father had been giving him an English lesson. Matani could still remember clearly how his father sat cross-legged, hands cupped on his lap, his voice dipping and soaring in a gentle rhythm—and how the lesson ended when a force punched into their hut with the thrust and velocity of a sand blizzard. A rush of air, a sour smell, a sound of panting, and wild-eyed Abayomi with the writhing toddler in his arms. Matani had never, not before or since, seen anything as brutal, as reeking, as glaring. The child seemed to be wrestling with death itself.

Matani had stuffed his fingers into his mouth and bitten

down on them to keep from crying out as he ran witlessly from his home. He was afraid to run far with night coming on, afraid of whatever nameless horror had attacked a child, so once he got out of sight of the settlement, he turned and crept back, cowering like a child, and hid in the shadows of the *kilinge*. He stayed away from his hut for hours, precious hours when of course his father could have used his help in dealing with the injured boy and his stunned young father.

Now Matani straightened, gently massaged his stomach, and took a deep breath, refocusing on his purpose. "I've come," he said, "about the books." Matani was not one who liked long speeches about important matters, so he wanted that to be enough for him to pronounce the sentence, and for Scar Boy to pull forth the overdue volumes.

Scar Boy cradled the stone in one hand, then dropped it into the other.

"They have to be returned each time the camels come, as you know," Matani said. "The library gave us an extra two weeks in this case. But the tribe grows uneasy when it falls behind with its responsibilities."

Scar Boy did not answer even with his eyes.

"So I've come to collect them now," Matani said. "I'll keep them until the library comes again." He heaved a loud sigh to show that he was getting tired of stating the obvious.

Badru, in one corner of the room, stirred slightly. Otherwise, everything was still.

On that earlier day, although Matani could not imagine anything except fleeing, he had still been ashamed. He wished he'd stayed, not only to help, but to watch his father at work. His father always knew how to kindle a fire for himself, as the expression went; he was the most resourceful man Matani ever knew. An English anthropologist, David Barkin, had befriended him when he was a boy, seeing something unusual in his easy, enthusiastic manner. Barkin had paid to send Matani's father away for an education. Three times, Matani's father had gone to Nairobi to attend schools, and three times he had returned with new knowledge. But his neighbors grew wary when he told them he was learning how to prolong water and ration it to a thirsty earth. They believed the earth should be worshipped, not manipulated. They grew even more suspicious when he returned carrying pills that he said could ease a fever or cut pain. Tiny tablets stronger than the chilled heat that could overcome a body? It made no sense. But what, after all, could you expect from a man who thought he could control water?

On that day, however, Abayomi would not be numbered among the skeptics.

In fact, Matani's father didn't have much with which to treat the toddler; Matani understood that now. Antibiotic cream, a few large bandages, some sedatives, and other tablets intended more for aching muscles than torn ones. But somehow, with his meager supply, Matani's father had sterilized and wrapped Scar Boy's shredded wounds and softened the pain. He'd worked until the bleeding nearly stopped and the child's cries quieted. Then Abayomi had carried the boy on to the medicine man for the next stage of treatment. But he always credited Matani's father with saving the life of his son.

When Matani had returned home, his father hadn't criticized, or pointed out that he'd had to save the boy's life alone. He was brushing away the bloody dirt on the floor of their home, but he stopped to look full into his son's face. "The boy is alive," he said. "And I think perhaps he will stay so."

From that day until his death three years ago, Matani's father had taken a special interest in Scar Boy, teaching him things that once he'd only taught Matani. It was an interest that none among their neighbors shared, that even Matani did not fully understand, and that, frankly, Scar Boy had done nothing Matani could see to earn—unless one counted nearly dying.

Now Scar Boy sat before him, stubbornly silent. Matani tried to summon up the patience for which his own father had been famous. "Though it's not up to me," Matani said, "I'll do my best to make it possible for you to check out books in the future, if that's your worry." He hesitated, struck by the sense that the bond between them had grown so weak that Scar Boy could no longer even hear his words. "You understand, don't you? The library will stop coming if they don't get their books back. And you of all people know how we benefit from contact with the world beyond ours."

"Contact," said Scar Boy, and his voice sounded raw, as though he hadn't spoken for days. "The world beyond."

"Yes," Matani said pointedly. "For our survival. We must end our isolation. The bookmobile will help with that."

"I want only this hut, and what is within it, and what I allow in."

The words were many, for Scar Boy, and spoken in a rush, as though he feared he would be unable to be allowed to say them unless he said them fast.

"Don't leave your hut, then," Matani said, finally allowing a measure of disgust to creep into his tone. "Only give me the books."

Scar Boy looked at him scornfully, as if he'd missed the point. "Your father used to come to me," he said.

"I know."

"He never took anything back."

"This is different. This is a library. They've lent us the books. And now you've put it all at risk."

Scar Boy's face grew dark. "They look different," he said. "They eat different, talk and think different." Each time he said the word *different*, he pounded his stone into the ground, gouging the dirt, obliterating his drawing.

"If my father were here—"

"I'm not the same as them."

Matani inhaled deeply and tried to make his voice as gentle as his father's had been on that day long ago. "My father would tell you to give back the books," he said.

Scar Boy's grip tightened around his stone, and Matani noticed the long muscles of his arm. It surprised him to realize Scar Boy was a young man now. "No," Scar Boy said, his voice fierce.

"It's not a choice. These aren't our—"

"I'm done," Scar Boy said in a piercing voice.

"They belong—"

"Done."

"You'd better go," Badru said.

Matani didn't understand Scar Boy. But he didn't care about that. He needed the books. The longer it took, the more difficult the issue of the library's future would become.

And the harder it became to quiet his superstitions, notions that he should have outgrown, but that clung to him like his very flesh. It wasn't only the library. Books, birds, babies. What happened with one seemed to be a portent of what would happen with another.

Scar Boy was right, though, Matani thought as he rubbed the ache in his stomach. It was clear that Matani was done. At least for the moment, he could hope for nothing further from this life that sat before him, angrily digging in the dirt—this life that his father, for better or worse, had saved.

Part Three

You have to hand it to the little buggers. They nibbled at the ankles of the earliest cavemen. They even knocked back dinosaur blood. That elevates them above most other insects. Their lives really count for something. Right up until the moment they're crushed.

—Interview with the scientist Rich Hutchins
Entomologists' Quarterly, Summer 2000

The American

I HAD NEVER ACCEPTED MR. ABASI'S CLAIM THAT MIDIDIMA and settlements like it could disappear with a stiff breeze—that the next time the Camel Bookmobile came, there might be no sign that life had ever huddled there. She'd considered this assertion nothing more than another attempt to talk her out of making the trip he hated. It seemed to her, in fact, that the houses of Mididima were rooted directly in the earth's subsurface, and that during the coming generations the settlement could only spread.

But this time, as she approached Mididima, it looked transient as it never had before. Perhaps that was because no one expected her. No heap of people gathered beneath the tall acacia; no buzz of anticipation vibrated in the air. Mididima looked, in that moment, like a desert plant gone too long unwatered, preparing to shrivel.

Books, it occurred to her now, were enduring, even immortal. Some, like the two she was going to recover, had been part of the world's consciousness for so long that they were no longer singularly identifiable. The maxims of Zen masters and the stories of Homer had been tossed into the soup of human consciousness, blending and emerging at lunchtime as one's own thoughts, as if they were original. And they would become the thoughts of one's children, and eventually one's grandchildren. Mididima, on the other hand, seemed a flimsy fancy once briefly considered and then abandoned. The plants were frosted with sand, the rays of the sun themselves dusty with neglect.

Mr. Abasi had declined to accompany her, of course— "I'll come to fetch you instead," he'd said. That had seemed for the best at the time, but she wished for him now. With his loud, abrupt voice, he'd get someone's attention. She thought of calling "Anybody home?" or "Yoo-hoo." Neither seemed like proper etiquette for the circumstances. The two men who had traveled with her on a second camel scrutinized her curiously, waiting to see what she would do.

Two young boys came out of one of the huts and stared. "*Jambo*," she said, waving. They giggled and dashed away. She dismounted. One of the men sharing the other camel handed her the duffel bag, then climbed onto the camel she'd ridden. She took a few steps toward the nearest hut and turned back to see her traveling companions with their eyes fastened on her movements. She needed to say good-bye, to release them to make the return journey. Yet she felt uncertain and unable to send them away yet. She hovered clumsily at the edge of Mididima.

The two boys emerged again, this time with four other children and Matani in tow, Kanika right behind. "How are you? How are you?" the children began calling in English, laughing and running to her.

"How are *you*?" Fi answered, smiling. Then she caught sight of Matani's face. He looked surprised, maybe even a little horrified. "*Jambo*," she said to him, trying on a tone that held more confidence than she felt.

"You have just come? You've come for Scar Boy's books already?" he asked, glancing uneasily behind her. "Where is Mr. Abasi?"

"You've found them?" How stupid she'd been not to consider the possibility that the whole visit was no longer necessary. But his face quickly told her they'd not yet been recovered, and she was flooded with relief—the irony of which was not lost on her. "I've come . . . " And here she wavered, wondering how to express why she'd come. To help Africa toward literacy? Too grandiose. To help some spit of a place find a couple of books? Too insignificant.

Both her argument with Mr. Abasi and her decision to show up in Mididima with little more than six bottles of water, a toothbrush, and mosquito netting had been fueled by a confidence that had since fled.

She took a deep breath, waiting for the end of that dangling sentence to occur to her. She felt the stares of the children, who were inching closer to her. This time, she'd come with no payload of books. She rummaged in her bag and pulled out a pencil. "See?" she said in Swahili to the children, holding the pencil up between her thumb and her index finger. She reached out and took the hand of one of the little girls, and smoothed open the palm. "Now, watch." She tapped the pencil once, gently, onto the girl's palm, and then lifted it high and brought it down, tapping a second time. Improvising, she twirled around, holding the pencil above her head, waving it, winking at them, and calling "Woo!" She knew she looked a bit mad, but a sense of flair was critical. She blew on the pencil, demonstrating, urging the girl, without words, to do the same. The child did so, hesitatingly. Then Fi tapped the pencil for the third time on the girl's palm, raised both hands, and lowered them to show that the pencil had vanished. "Where's it gone?" she asked, sweeping her arms in front of her like a vaudeville player. Even without their understanding those words, the children's eyes widened appreciatively.

Fi gestured to the sky, then to the ground, and reached behind the ear of little Nadif, the boy who'd had numbers scrawled on his palm. "Voilà!" They had no idea what that word meant either, but the way she exclaimed it as she held out the pencil sounded impressive, she knew.

Magic Tricks 101, learned the summer before she started high school, seldom used after that. This act wouldn't hold the attention of most eight-year-olds in New York, but the audience in Mididima was easy. Little faces stared at her as the children soaked up every move. Behind them, by now, a few young women lingered, more skeptical but still curious.

Matani watched silently, hesitant, with a half-smile, probably wondering if she'd come all this way just to do the trick with the pencil, maybe thinking it was another strange custom from her country. "Whispers of the flames," he said.

"What?"

"It's the literal translation for what we call magic."

"Whispers of the flames," she repeated slowly, willing herself not to forget the phrase—the first of the five she had to learn. The children hovered nearby. One took her hand and squeezed. She leaned conspiratorially toward Matani. "That wasn't real magic," she said in a stage whisper. "But I *am* good at finding missing books. So I thought . . . Well, that's why I'm here."

He looked her full in the face as if to see whether she was joking. Then he broke into a grin that stretched so wide she felt a moment of pure gratitude, and he took her bag from her hand.

"It's all right?" she asked.

He glanced at the two men who had accompanied her. "When should they return for you?"

"They can't until Friday. Four days. Is it too long?"

Matani spread his arms. "It's a gift for our tribe, Miss Sweeney," he said.

Fi wanted to kiss him; he'd made so easy what could have been agonizingly awkward. "Thank you," she said, reaching forward to brush his fingers.

He spoke quickly to the two men on the camels, more authoritative than he usually was around Mr. Abasi. They smiled with visible relief, turned their beasts, and were gone.

By now a larger audience had gathered, still mainly children. "You will stay with Kanika and her grandmother," Matani said. "That's fine?"

Kanika gave that full smile of hers, the one that took over her face.

"Thank you," Fi said.

"They'll get you something to drink and you can rest," Matani said.

"But I'm not tired. I'll put my things down, and go see the young man."

Matani's grin shrank slightly. "You have four days," he said. "We'll talk first. And then, perhaps, go together? Now I'm teaching, and—"

"Of course," Fi said. "I don't mean to rush you. Maybe I can watch you teach?"

Matani gave a small shrug as he ran his fingers over one eyebrow, smoothing it. His shyness was appealing.

"The books," she said, sweeping her arm in an arc. "I'd like to watch how you use them."

"Of course, then," Matani said.

"Come, Miss Sweeney," Kanika said. "Let's put your bag away."

Kanika took her by the hand. Despite the exoticness of Mididima and the age difference between Kanika and Fi, the gesture made Fi think of her own elementary school in the 1970s, with its promise of untainted friendship: soothing secrets and notes passed in class and simple rhyming poems and all the pure earnestness of those years.

"Fi. Call me Fi," she said.

As if by real magic, Mididima had become inhabited again. Laughing children were fiddling with one another's ears as if they hoped to find other pencils there. Men's voices poured from one of the huts, three goats rambled by, women were bent over work in the nearby fields, and Fi felt a breeze that carried the scent of bread baking.

"I'm glad you've come," Kanika said.

"Me too." As she said it, Fi felt a rush of renewed confidence in her decision. It wasn't silly; it was right to be in Mididima. She'd find the books; she'd ensure that the bookmobile would keep calling on Mididima for years to come. And this visit—it was more than a hope; it was an intuition now, or maybe a vow—would be the pinnacle of her trip.

The Teacher's Wife

JWAHIR BENT AT THE WAIST, LEANING OVER THE HOSES
that ran from the buckets and lay on the ground in twelve
straight rows, the buckets Matani's father had brought them
years ago. It was her job to inspect each one for signs of
wear, discoloration in the rubber, hints of holes that might
leak even a single drop of water somewhere a plant was not.
An easy job, normally. Today concentration eluded her.

All around, cousins and aunts and neighbors were hoeing,
or kneeling to tend young plants, or uprooting unwelcome
weeds that sought to steal the moisture. But the presence
of the other women generally did not distract her—they
always worked together on the crops, and quickly, as a rule,
so they could move on to other chores.

Usually, though, the laboring women were silent. Even
she and Leta saved their conversation for later. Sometimes
a chant would emerge, of course—a song about a child, or a
marriage, or the work itself. It was brief and passing, like
a shared gulp of water to quench a sharp thirst.

Today there was no chanting, and still the voices of the
women worked far harder than their hands, with less pleas-
ant results. An unnatural commotion grew from them like

a desert plant obscene with bloom after an out-of-season shower.

"Why has she come, this colorless woman?" Chicha, one of the young mothers, asked Jwahir, her voice sharp.

These days, Jwahir didn't like Chicha, who seemed to feel superior ever since she'd given birth to twin boys. In any case, Jwahir shouldn't have to face this interrogation. The white woman had nothing to do with her. Only because she was married to Matani did Chicha and the others treat her as if she were somehow responsible for the visitor, as well as the bookmobile.

Leta, sensing Jwahir's mood, as she often did, answered for her friend. "She says she's come to help find Scar Boy's books."

"But of what help can she be? She doesn't know our language," said Chicha.

"And why should Scar Boy talk to her when he won't to us?" asked Chicha's older sister.

"She has a magic for finding books," Leta answered. "That's what I hear."

"Why waste her magic here? She doesn't care about us," Chicha said.

"The children like her," Leta said.

Chicha shook her head. "Something else brought her. Matani may be too trusting to know it, but I'm not."

"I believe what the white woman says," said Neema. They all stopped talking to listen to her—a sign of respect, which was a blessing because Jwahir's head was beginning to hurt and she wanted the chatter to stop. The stranger would be sleeping in Neema's hut; they waited to hear what

Neema would say. But Jwahir already knew that Neema's words would not subdue anyone's doubts for long. Neema's views were always unusual.

"She's as clear to me as God's voice was to Moses," Neema said, refering to the Bible, as she often did. "She wants to find the books so the library can keep coming. Perhaps you're right that she doesn't care about us—this I can't say. But the library . . . " Neema hesitated. "She loves it the way we love the food we've grown, the goats we raise."

"Why? Books—" Chicha made a spitting sound. "What are they? They won't give her milk."

"There are many ways to drink," Neema said, and then Jwahir stopped listening. She already knew what Neema would say, since Matani himself had made the same arguments many times. Besides, she didn't want to waste the few free moments that Neema's talk would give her, moments when the women's attention was focused on something besides her and her association with the white woman.

She stood and stretched her sore neck. At a distance, she could see men tending the animals. She easily identified Abayomi. He stood straight, among the tallest, and his arm rested on the back of a cow. As she watched him, her stomach tightened. She replayed, as she already had many times, the day of the bookmobile's last visit.

That was the day she'd finally found the courage to reach out her hands and touch him. Only, in truth, it hadn't been bravery so much as desperation; she didn't know what else to do with this lightning rush of emotions.

Without preamble—without a word, in fact—she'd

stretched to trace his cheekbones. And she could recall perfectly his expression—startled, then full of trembling and warmth. She'd let her hands drop to his shoulders and soon they'd fallen together, she and Abayomi, lips meeting, hands feeling flesh through clothing, not yet fully merging but still unable to separate until they heard the sound of the camels being reloaded with books.

She wanted to do that again, and more. To run her fingers along the base of his neck and then down into the muscles of his arms, to the hands themselves, and beyond. She wanted him to take her shoulders again; she wanted to smell his scent like fresh milk, and to feel the roughness of his cheek brushing against hers. No matter that she risked being stoned or left to starve for even the hint of adultery. She wanted the feel of Abayomi's flesh against her own so much it felt like a gaping cavity that began below her neck and stretched across her chest.

"Jwahir, stop sleeping! We've been waiting to hear from you."

She swallowed, collected herself. "What is it, Chicha?" she asked, her voice cool.

"What does Matani say?" I asked.

"And when would Matani and I have had time to speak since sunup?"

"Then, what *will* he say?"

Matani. How difficult it had become to speak to him. Their evenings overflowed with dense silences. She thought every day that she would find a way to tell him how she'd slipped with Abayomi into something unexpected and astounding, something encompassing and cha-

otic—it was love, she guessed, though she'd never felt it
before. But even if she managed to express her feelings in a
way that seemed at once honest, honorable, and—this was
important—chaste, what would she say next? There was no
word in their tribe for divorce initiated by a woman. It was
always a man. Even if a wife was consistently mistreated, the
woman's father or brother had to take the step of seeking to
break the bowl of marriage. Her father had no great affec-
tion for Matani; still, she doubted that he would encourage
her in what—she could almost hear him now—he would
call a shameful whim.

"This woman has nothing to do with Matani," Jwahir
said, "or with me. She came here on her own. And this interrogation makes me tired."

She turned her back on the others, walked a few steps
away, and squatted.

"Let her sit," she heard Leta say. And then she cut them
out. She closed her eyes and pretended—but it was more
than pretense, this skill she'd developed; she actually was far
away, apart from people and noise, someplace not completely
silent, but dominated by a muffled, musical beat; someplace
she could think.

In that space, here's what she remembered. When she
was still a girl, no taller than her mother's waist, there'd
been talk about a woman of her family's clan whose husband beat her harshly every night and idled through his
days. One morning, as Jwahir had heard, the wife awoke
and immediately sat down. She refused to get up, refused to
cook or fetch water, until the tribal elders heard her complaint and ordered her husband to reform.

After this, the man improved—he was kinder and more helpful—though only for a couple of weeks. Then the woman repeated her protest, sitting once again. The elders again negotiated, and this time, the man changed for two full moons. After he slipped inevitably into his former patterns, all expected his wife to complain again, and for a few days there'd been a sense of waiting, because watching the couple had become a pastime for their neighbors. But instead, the man fell suddenly ill. Within a week, he was dead.

A whisper moved in a wave through the tribe: the wife had cast a spell on her husband. No one knew for sure, but everyone regarded her with fear, distrust, and distaste. Everyone except Jwahir, who even as a young girl understood the usual outcome of conflicts between husband and wife. Of what real use had the elders been? What choice, after all, did the woman have?

Matani, of course, did not beat Jwahir. He treated her tenderly, and her complaints—that he was too passive, too weak, too misguided—would be dismissed by the elders if Jwahir were to seek help there. She'd made her choice, they would say. He was not a bad man. If she were simply to tell them she loved another, she would be punished. If they suspected adultery, the punishment would be death. And Jwahir's father would be forced to stand aside.

For divorcing, however, Matani might be the best of all husbands. He was a modern man. In other clans that lived far away, she'd heard that women could break the bowl on their own. Matani had surely heard of them too. And he loved her. What if she could find a way to ask for freedom, if she kept it private, between the two of them? Perhaps he would accede. And if the decision seemed to come from him, the tribe would accept it. And then, with time, they would accept her being chosen by another man—as long as none of it seemed to be her doing.

She wanted to discuss this with Abayomi, though she feared his response. Would he think she was rushing too quickly forward to catch this rainfall of emotion?

But he felt as she did, surely. This was only the period of self-doubt, the same phase she'd also suffered through at the beginning of her joining with Matani. In those days, her insecurity stemmed from the very air that swirled around this Mididima man who'd been away and now returned. Matani had seemed so exotic and educated. Jwahir couldn't read; she'd never been anywhere else; she wasn't someone who ate in giant rooms where people paid for food, or went into dark huts to watch pictures on a screen, or did any of those things he told her about. How could she hope to attract his attention away from all the women he must have met in the world beyond?

It turned out, of course, that *exotic* meant the one who could travel into her soul, and knowledge had nothing to do with all the books a camel library could bring. Abayomi had taught her that.

Besides, she'd soon understood that Matani admired her walk, her hair, the line of her legs, all of which were surely as pleasing as any woman's in the Distant City.

As for Abayomi, she stilled her qualms by reminding herself that he understood her, and she him. They were, in fact, so similar as to be nearly one. And she recognized, she was sure, his wanting in his eyes—and now in his touch.

She turned her head slightly. She knew she had to return to work, or the complaints would begin. Before she rejoined the women, however, she made a private vow. She would find Abayomi alone—today, if possible; otherwise, tomorrow—and whisper of her feelings, plain and clear. Her legs trembled slightly at the thought of that conversation, until she recalled Abayomi's expression at the bookmobile's last visit. He might be surprised at first, but he would quickly turn warm as an evening fire's coals. Together, they would find the words to speak to Matani.

Still, it was an act of bravery she planned, to seek him out before the camels returned, and she might as well get in practice. She would need a sky full of bravery for the path she was choosing.

The Teacher

"SHE LIKED THE WAY I MAKE THE CHILDREN CHANT," MATANI said. It pained him to realize how much he wanted Jwahir to congratulate him, to do a little dance of pleasure, but he couldn't stop himself. "She appreciated the rhythmic quality and asked if she could record the children as they echoed me. We did the alphabet in English. She said it would help them memorize." He sounded, he recognized, pathetic. "Of course, they were well behaved today," he added.

Jwahir didn't look up from the necklace she was stringing with paper beads made from pages of the magazines Miss Sweeney had brought. "You've told her we don't want the library anymore?" she asked.

"Let's give her back the books first," Matani said carefully. "Then the tribe will discuss what's best."

Jwahir dampened her fingers with her tongue and picked up another bead, sliding it onto a thread of fiber from a sisal leaf. "I don't understand her presence here," she said.

"And I know of no explanation other than the one I've already offered, which seems straightforward enough."

That wasn't strictly true, though. Matani also felt there was something more to Miss Sweeney's visit than the missing books. Or maybe it was simply that this tiny tribe, drifting without notice through the desert for centuries, was not accustomed to an outsider's interested gaze.

"To come among us and watch, judging, waiting for punishment to fall on our heads," Jwahir said. "It seems a strange way for a foreigner to pass the days."

"Judging?" Matani said. "And who says punishment is coming? Scar Boy will give back the books."

Jwahir turned her head slightly and fixed him with a stare that made him uneasy. "You like her here, this white woman?"

"Like?" Matani paced the room, then stopped before Jwahir. The acidity of her tone surprised him. But he didn't want to argue about Miss Sweeney. "She is a responsibility to me," he said.

In fact, responsibility had been his food lately. Miss Sweeney, the books, Scar Boy, Jwahir, her father, the library's future. Sometimes the faces of those to whom he felt accountable rolled around within his head like boulders; at other times they shot through like hurled stones. This morning when he'd risen and stretched, his shoulders made a disquieting cracking sound.

"What does she say about Taban?" Jwahir asked.

Matani was surprised to hear Jwahir refer to Scar Boy by his given name. "We haven't much touched on that topic," he said.

"No? Then I ask again. Why is she here?"

Matani knelt before Jwahir. "Don't worry, my beloved

wife," he said. "And tell your father not to worry either. When Scar Boy sees the trouble he has caused, Miss Sweeney coming all this way, he will be chastened and stop his nonsense and quickly turn over the books. Then we will be spared further shame, and our tribe will be unharmed."

Jwahir stared at him silently. Matani wanted so much to reach forward and touch her. But she'd placed her beads in a line in front of her like a thorn fence between them. He rose and shifted back and forth on his feet awkwardly.

It hadn't always been like this. It would reverse again, sooner or later; Jwahir's mood would surely soften. But when? This passing stage in a woman's life was simply beyond his meager understanding. A book that explained the tangled emotions of women—now that would be a welcome volume in the Camel Bookmobile.

"Let's not speak more of this library," Matani said. "Jwahir, my love. We are at an important moment, the two of us."

She looked up quickly, searching his face. For a breath of time, her expression was as it had been in the beginning—wide open, without protection. Full of love. It gave him courage.

"I know you want children—a son—as much as I do," he said.

Her eyes widened. Then her face turned to one side, as though she'd been slapped.

She did want a son, didn't she? All young, newly married women did. Even to ask it would insult her womanhood. "You do," he said. "You do?"

She looked down. "Hmm," she said, mumbling.

With the sharpness of a bee sting, Matani understood. She shared his fears. She felt inadequate, afraid she would be unable to have a child. How ridiculous that he'd imagined her so different from himself, that he'd looked for some woman-symptom, when all along she suffered from qualms that matched his own.

He knelt before her. "Jwahir, you'll be the best mother in all the desert. From Nairobi to Mogadishu. And I promise we will have a son. Many, in fact."

She kept her gaze averted.

"My dearest, I have only now understood your worries. But they are premature. There are steps we can take. You know better than I." He'd heard, vaguely, of ways to overcome infertility. A woman could bathe with the blood of a newborn camel. Or she could walk into the bush, return by a different route, and find the path to pregnancy unblocked. There were more methods, too; Jwahir must know them all.

"Matani?" she said.

He leaned closer, took her hand. "Yes?"

"Have you spoken to Abayomi yet?"

He brushed away a rush of irritation. "Jwahir, don't think more of the books, not now. When we have our son, you'll know why it's important to be educated." In the past, he'd even imagined Jwahir reading *The Cat in the Hat* to their son, though he didn't mention that now.

"Matani."

"When I look at you," he said, "I see so clearly what our son will be. He'll have your wide, beautiful eyes. And the calm spirit of my father. He'll—"

"You must speak to Abayomi."

"Of course, but why worry when . . . " He stopped, trying to interpret her. She used to be so transparent, before her face turned as bland and distant as a cloudless sky. As it now had become again.

"Jambo?" A woman's voice, in English.

Matani jumped to his feet and turned. "Miss Sweeney."

"Fi. Please, Fi. I hope I'm not bothering you?"

"No, of course no," Matani said. "This is my wife, Jwahir."

Miss Sweeney reached to take her hand. "A pleasure to meet you. You have a wonderful husband. He's done so much for Mididima."

Matani translated, but only the first sentence.

Jwahir nodded, face downcast.

"Would you like to see the area around Mididima?" he asked.

"And perhaps the boy? But I don't want to take you from anything."

"You aren't," Matani said. Then he told Jwahir, "I'll be back as soon as I can."

As he followed Miss Sweeney from his home, he glanced back at Jwahir. She sat unmoving, head lowered, studying her hands. Soon, she would be smiling again, he told himself. Things between them had been settled. They were clearer, and they would move forward in new ways from this moment.

But something small, a doubt he didn't have time to try to find a name for, niggled within, taunting.

Scar Boy

TABAN WAS SKETCHING WHEN HE HEARD THEM AT THE door—sketching so intently that he'd become the soft scratch of the pencil; he'd vanished into curves and shadows, the shapes he wanted to make pop off the page. The curve of a cheek, a set of eyes, those lips. Maybe this time, he thought. Maybe this time he would succeed; he would pull life from a scrap of paper. He couldn't give this obsession of his a name, even to himself; he didn't know the words. He knew only that when he drew, he felt part of something.

"Hello, Teacher," he heard his brother say in that way of his, respectful sarcasm.

"Hello, Badru."

The sound of shuffling. Then Matani spoke again. "Miss Sweeney and I are here to see your brother." *Of course* hung, unspoken, in the air. This was often how Matani spoke, Taban thought—as though he were surprised that he had to speak at all, that his intentions and commands weren't automatically understood, and followed.

Taban bent more deeply over his paper, exhaling, trying to recapture concentration.

"My father," said Badru, "says you are to save your talk for him."

"Fine," Matani said.

"So come back tomorrow."

"Tomorrow?" Matani said. "Why?"

Taban straightened, imagining Matani's expression. Everything showed on Matani's face, as though he were still a child. By the time boys grew up, they should have developed the skill of dropping a veil over their emotions. Why had this ability eluded the teacher? Every time Matani met Taban, for instance, his eyes still revealed his revulsion at Taban's deformities.

Taban heard no reply to Matani's question and knew his brother was shrugging. Even the thought of it made him smile. Badru's shrug was peerless—a drawn-out, dismissive gesture, usually accompanied by a single cocked eyebrow. Taban hated it when Badru used that shrug against him, but had to admire it when it was aimed at others.

"The men haven't gone anywhere. The cattle still have water; we have food," Matani said, as if running through a list in his mind.

"My father went alone," Badru said.

"By himself?" Matani's voice rose.

Matani's surprise was understandable; even Taban had been taken aback. They were not a people given to solitary acts; nor did he think of his father as a violator of tradition. Abayomi blamed himself for the hyena's attack on Taban and rarely left his sons alone at night; as the only parent, in fact, he carried so much responsibility that Taban expected him to eventually end up with a camel's humped back.

Neither Taban nor Badru could guess why their father had gone, though Badru wouldn't admit his ignorance to Matani.

"He said if you came," Badru said, "I was to tell you to return after one moon."

Taban heard another voice then, a woman's, speaking words in that language he didn't understand. The foreigner. It amazed him she'd come all this way. It was funny, and a little sad, that Matani thought he needed the white woman to get the books back. That he believed it would make a difference.

Taban dropped his pencil—a gift from Kanika, who'd taken it from Matani's school—and let his back slump, giving up any pretense of working. Perhaps he would try again later; perhaps he would have to use a fresh sheet of torn paper. With one finger, he traced the lines he had drawn—the arc of a cheek, the stroke of a nose—as he listened.

"Does your brother know Miss Sweeney has come to help recover the books?" Matani asked after a moment.

"We've heard," Badru said.

"So I needn't speak to Abayomi at all if Sc— if your brother is ready to hand them over. I can also collect them from you."

"Teacher," Badru said. "My father's instructions were so clear I could follow them in the darkest pitch of night."

Matani sighed. He spoke to the woman in her language. "Fine," he said to Badru after a moment. "We will come tomorrow morning. But we don't want to take up too much of Miss Sweeney's time with this nonsense."

"Good-bye, Teacher," Badru said.

Taban heard Matani and the woman move away from their stick-and-dung hut. As Badru came into the room. Taban picked up his pencil, rolled it between his palms, then looked up. The two brothers exchanged a glance. Taban couldn't say who started laughing first—it seemed to him their laugher came simultaneously. It widened and stretched and filled the room, expanding beyond its original cause. It became powerful and loosened a tightness that had constricted Taban's chest for days. He rarely laughed as unguardedly as this.

This degree of intimacy between the two brothers was rare. Usually Badru held himself aloof from his strange, deformed sibling. And Taban couldn't blame him. What if he'd been the normal one, and Badru had the torn face that almost no one could look at without recoiling, that deformed his soul and mangled all his friendships save one? Wouldn't Taban, too, have sought distance?

Badru stood over Taban's shoulder, close enough for Taban to feel his warmth. Slowly his chuckle softened and died, and Taban's died with it. "Kanika," Badru said, looking down. "You've got every detail. I've never even noticed her before. But you—you really see everything. How do you do it? Make it so alive?"

This, Taban wasn't ready to discuss. He didn't want Badru's reaction, even a positive one. He may have healed from the outward wounds inflicted by the hyena, but on this matter of his drawings, his protective scab was far too thin. He shielded his picture with one spread hand. Badru took a step away, acknowledging and quickly accepting the distance between the two. In the dart of a lizard's tongue, the moment was gone, and Taban found himself already nostalgic for it.

"Badru," he said. His brother met his eyes—a receptive version of his brother, not yet the one of shrugs. "You're driving him mad, our teacher," Taban said, gesturing with his head toward the door.

"Me?" Badru grinned. "In truth, you are. You've always been a brave one."

Badru's words, their unexpected accuracy, thickened Taban's throat. He didn't think anyone had noticed the courage required to simply go on as he was. A wave of warmth gushed from his toes to his cheeks and settled, as water, directly behind his eyes. He didn't reply, though. He couldn't. He looked down at his hand stretched over the purloined paper, and waited until Badru turned away.

The American

FROM THE SLIGHT RISE WHERE SHE STOOD, FI COULD SEE IN the thin, late-afternoon light the full panorama of Mididima, with its mushroomlike homes and its shallow reservoir, and the sight made her flush with a sense of awe. She felt herself a tiny speck, improbably carried by an Irish mother's scolding and a library pilot program to this fistful of concentrated life. Men, women, and children were scattered like a hundred colorful handkerchiefs dropped in the grass, their cows and goats with them, untethered, as though favored companions. Where did they find the brilliant reds and yellows in which they wrapped themselves? In New York, fashion favored colors associated with soggy soil and clammy foods—blacks and browns and grays renamed as nutmeg, platinum, eggplant, midnight. Here, the tints were as if from tubs of kindergarten finger paints, the garments like a rap poem, or a shout to their primary god, the Hundred-Legged One—a reference to the sun with its rays as legs.

Fi and Matani stood next to the irrigation system, simple with buckets and hoses, but extraordinarily successful in channeling each drop of water. Matani had apologized repeatedly for the need to wait a day to speak to the one they called Scar Boy. Fi dismissed it as understandable. She knew deep currents had passed between Matani and Scar Boy's brother, the meaning of which she could only guess. They would get the books back, she was certain. The father clearly wanted to make some particular point first, some issue that must be pressing to him but remained elusive to her.

Letting her eyes slide over the horizon, she spotted a zebra. Watching it, she noticed a movement and picked out a giraffe, and then two others. With their chestnut-colored patches, they were as effectively camouflaged as objects in a hidden-picture game. They were revealed only when they dipped their necks to munch from the top leaves of an acacia. The zebra circulated among them, then stood below like a sentry, front legs splayed, swaying slightly.

"He follows them everywhere," said Matani, watching her.

"Dreaming of being a giraffe?"

"I imagine he lost his family somehow and he's longing to find another one to fit into. The young girls, though, like to believe he's fallen in love with a particular giraffe. They've named him the Pining One."

Fi laughed, then gestured to the irrigation system. "Your father was foresighted. The people of Mididima must feel fortunate."

Matani gave a small smile. "We have a saying: a donkey always says thank you with a kick." He shrugged. "But by now, yes, they see that this lets us live better than most. More settled, with more food. Parents are willing to let their children learn during morning hours. In many other tribes, they need the children's help all day."

"Books instead of chores. The children must be grateful."

"Sometimes they are," Matani said. "Sometimes I use the cane."

Fi couldn't stop herself; she cringed. She'd seen the cane in Matani's home, a deceptively narrow stick that she suspected would make a shrill scream as it whipped through the air. She'd read the human rights reports about children whose bones had been broken for not being able to answer a question, or even for fidgeting in class. She wondered if that had happened to any of Matani's students.

Matani made a sweeping gesture with his arm. "Do you want to walk?"

The sun was on its way down, leaving dark creases in the land. The people of Mididima were being drawn into the settlement's core as Fi and Matani moved together in the opposite direction. Matani took gliding steps, his arms swaying so that to Fi, it seemed he was responding to music instead of simply walking.

"How often do you use it?" Fi asked after a moment, willing neutrality into her tone.

"Hmm?"

"The cane."

She felt Matani's gaze. "Our children are unaccustomed to the demands of formal education. Sometimes they need to be reshaped."

"Education liberates, but only after one puts on chains, is that it?" Fi asked. "Discipline civilizes, though its methods can be brutal." She tried to keep her voice light. They walked in silence for a few moments.

"Perhaps, when we think to teach another people about what is right—even if those people don't know how to read—we presume too much," Matani said, his voice controlled.

"I didn't mean—" Fi broke off. "Knowing how to read," she said, "has nothing to do with this."

"For us, for instance, it is remarkable that you travel alone."

"Touché," she said. "What a quick turn of the tables."

"What do they think of this—your husband, your parents, your brothers?"

Fi took a deep breath. "I'm not married," she said. "My parents are dead. I have two sisters and a brother, but they don't care—or, it's not exactly that," she corrected herself. "They do care. My brother, especially, hated it when I moved out of the Bronx, a subway ride away."

"Bronx?"

"But they don't get me, especially my brother—I've always seemed eccentric to him. Not settled enough. He feels sorry for me. And they do worry." Fi paused. She was talking too much. "What I mean is, yes, they wish I'd stay home. But they know that ultimately, these decisions are mine."

"Yours alone?" Matani looked at her closely.

"It's not the same there," Fi said, "in terms of family."

Matani paused next to some dwarf bushes. He pulled off two thumbnail-size grayish leaves, began to chew one, and handed the other to her. "This is a loss, don't you think?"

Instead of answering, Fi put the leaf into her mouth. It tasted surprisingly refreshing, and not unlike chewing gum. She wondered if Matani would swallow it, or spit it out.

"Why do people have this—what would be the word? To break something?" Matani shook his head. "Why don't they stay with their families?"

"Dreams and ambitions take some of us far from home."

"Like you coming here?"

"And you going away to study."

He looked away then. "My questions are rude," he said. "I'm sorry."

"No ruder than me asking you about the cane." In fact, she liked him better for his questions. People had been curious about her from the start, but their curiosity was of the sort one might have about an exotic animal, possibly dangerous and definitely unpredictable, best observed from a distance. No one but Matani had been brave enough to try to get to know her.

He spit out the chewed leaf and said suddenly, looking directly at her: "I wish for a son." The words seemed to emerge of their own volition, making his comment feel like the most personal thing anyone had ever told her. She could see that he had surprised himself by what he'd revealed.

"I can see you as a father," she said softly.

He looked at his feet, then back up at her. "You've been married before?"

She shook her head.

"But you have someone who is yours?"

Such an antiquated way to put it. "Women get married much later in America," she said. "Like your men do here. I'm thirty-six. It's not young, but still I think—"

"It's my age," he said, grinning, reaching to touch her arm and then slapping his own chest.

His gesture made her laugh. The fact that they'd been born at the same time somehow made Matani seem more familiar. Fi started walking again, long strides that kept her a few steps ahead of him. "How long have you been married?" she asked after a moment, slowing her pace.

"Four years. Almost."

"Your wife is a beautiful woman," Fi said. "I'm sure she's proud of you."

Matani looked away.

Something was going on between the two of them, probably something simple, a marital spat that she'd interrupted. Fi couldn't tell him to spill it out, get it off his chest; she hadn't reached a point in their friendship where she could put a hand on his forearm and say, "Don't worry, everything will be OK." In fact—what was she thinking?—she'd never be able to say that. This was a fleeting acquaintance, a few days shared between an American librarian and an African teacher. Why should that recognition leave her feeling, suddenly, so bereft?

There were limitations to language, even when it was shared. Sometimes words were not sturdy enough to hold all the needed meaning. She'd discovered that as a child, when she sought to find her mother in the harried and unreachable widow, and she felt it again now.

"Hey," she said. "Have you ever tried a cartwheel?" She felt odd asking; she knew it was an unexpected question. But cartwheels used to make her mother smile.

Matani looked at her quizzically. "I don't know the word."

She laughed and shook her head, mock-scolding. "A gap in your education."

Actually, she didn't even know if she could still do a cartwheel—it had been years. But she tried anyway, demonstrated twice, the bend in the wrist, one hand and then the other, the reach of the legs, the palms as dusty as bare feet, ending it with a yelp, and they weren't perfect cartwheels but they were fine, and she told him to try. He resisted at first, but she kept calling out encouragement—"Only the giraffes will see"—and finally he plunged forward, his legs bent and raised no higher than his waist.

"Up, up, up to the sky with your feet," she called.

"Watch me hurt myself," he answered.

She shook her head and urged him on. "Be more free with it." And so he did one more, his shirt slipping toward his head to reveal his coiled, muscular stomach—the sight of which caused her own stomach to make an unexpected flip. And then he rocked on his heels and looked at her, grinning sheepishly, but self-satisfied too, and it made her smile, amazed at the power of something so simple in Mididima. And she felt drawn to him at the same time, and she pulled her gaze away and turned her head toward the sky, which had gone dark while she wasn't paying attention, and finally he spoke. "You are hungry?"

And though she wasn't, she felt it would be best to nod,

and to follow him away from the edge of the settlement, away from their shared giggles and soaring legs, back to the safety, the embrace, the company of so many others.

That night, sitting outside Neema and Kanika's hut, Fi heard the music begin, the drumbeats scattered at first, then melding together into a trancelike throb that lunged through the darkness, then chanting added to the mix, creating a conversation so profound she couldn't imagine it would ever be repeated.

She didn't know the words, so she was left to make up a song, and she invented a summons to the insects of the bush: the fat yellow worms and the menacing long-legged mosquitoes and the flies that lingered on children's cheeks. And to the animals: the cantankerous camel, the zebra full of longing, the hyena that had attacked Scar Boy. It was a summons, too, to the ancestor-spirits of the men who were making the music; and to the women who were their mothers, wives, and daughters; and even to the ancestor-spirits who gave birth to her: white Irishwoman drawn to an African tribe, a zebra among giraffes.

She thought of the words of Isak Dinesen in *Out of Africa*: "Here I am, where I ought to be." She imagined herself for a moment, not an outsider as Dinesen was but living here with an African man; known perhaps as the Library Lady or, even better, the Cartwheel Queen; falling asleep every night with her body spooned in his; absorbed within Mididima's ancient, chaotic, potent heartbeat.

The Teacher's Wife

JWAHIRANDLETA, LETAANDJWAHIR. WHEN SHE WAS A LITTLE girl, Jwahir used to imagine that the night wind whispered their names, exactly like that, weaving them together, turning them into one. Jwahir and Leta had been friends for longer than either of them could remember, and by now they fit together, though they were vastly different physically and, certainly, temperamentally. Where Jwahir was slender, almost wispy, Leta was solid, her feet steady on the earth. When the mercurial Jwahir grew overly passionate, Leta would take her arm and wander with her across the bush until she calmed. When Leta, on the other hand, turned too serious or was drained of spontaneity, Jwahir—strong despite her slenderness—would wrestle her friend to the ground and tickle her. Their friendship was so intense that when they were younger and still unmarried, they had even talked in giggles about a shared future as co-wives, though secretly Jwahir knew that it could never be, because no one man could love them both equally—if he loved one, the other would not be right for him, since they seemed, to all but themselves, nearly opposites.

Few childhood intimacies, even ones as powerful as

theirs, survive the onset of adulthood. But Jwahir and Leta were close even now, with two female circumcisions and two husbands and two babies between them, though their friendship was altered by their female responsibilities. They had less time together. On the other hand, they knew each other so well that three words in conversation often took the place of twelve.

On this morning, Jwahir sat cross-legged next to the drab asabini bushes with her toes touching Leta's leg, their goats around them, wondering how she could tell her friend what she felt for Abayomi. But that would involve revealing what she didn't feel for Matani, and Leta liked Matani. Leta would defend him. Jwahir didn't want anyone talking her out of anything—not now, not when she was so vulnerable, her mind full of the uncertainty of the recently decided.

Yet not telling felt wrong, too, and there seemed no easy solution, so she was preoccupied as she sat with Leta, letting Leta's latest baby—a beauty, with its wide forehead and wise eyes—curl its fingers around one of hers.

"Jwahir!" Her father's voice cut through the air. This habit of his, yelling out a summons as he approached, always annoyed her. Now, though, his interruption was welcome, relieving her of the need to decide whether or not to tell.

"I'll go meet him," she said, getting to her feet. One of the goats, Juju, blond with a brown spot on his ear, followed her, as he always did. Leta liked to joke that Juju believed Jwahir was his mother.

"You call to me as though I were a favored cow, Father," Jwahir said curtly as he approached. She could get way with a bit of brusqueness because he adored her.

"You have some news for me?" he asked.

News. The word hung in the air. Jwahir's heart pushed into her neck. Had he somehow guessed about her and Abayomi? Had someone seen them together, deduced the truth, and told him? Might this be her only moment to save herself from the tribe's punishment? She wished then, and urgently, that she had practiced by telling Leta. To confirm it to her father first would be more difficult than erecting a home in a windstorm.

A moment of silence sat between them. He looked at her appraisingly, frankly curious. "The books," he finally said, impatiently. "The books. Has Matani recovered them?"

She giggled before she could stop herself. Why should she think what was in her heart was written on her face for all to see? She was relieved, of course, that he didn't know. But she also noticed a small pit of disappointment. Her secret, she sometimes felt, weighed more than twin elephants.

She stopped smiling then, and looked to the sky. "Father, why do you bother me with this?"

"You're his wife," he said, drawing the last word out, giving it special emphasis "Matani, like his father before him, is too fond of a remote and dangerous world. He might sway the young, who don't yet know that if we stand tall, it is because we stand on the backs of those who came before us. You must act to preserve our traditions. You have strength and ability, my daughter. That is one reason I arranged the union."

Jwahir dipped her chin to hide another smile. Her father still did not know that he had arranged nothing. Matani had been Jwahir's choice. Jwahir's maneuvering, along with

Matani's hefty bride-price, was responsible for the match. It served her, though, to have her father think he'd made the decision.

"I expect more from you," Jwahir's father said.

"What, exactly?"

Jwahir's father sighed in frustration. Jwahir knew that exhalation well; it was an exceptional sigh. It could fill an entire hut and last as long as a year. She reached down to scratch the ear of Juju the goat while waiting.

"The library is from another world," he said at last, pointing off toward the horizon. "A world that does not serve us. In the Distant City, they've lost their connection to what is real. Nothing is as it seems."

He took her arm and walked a few steps, his voice growing impassioned. "They inject their food with false flavors, Jwahir. They build monuments that do nothing more than spit water. They even capture wild birds, dip them in blue paint, and then set them free to make the sky appear more brilliant. This is the work of the educated?"

Please. Not the birds again. But Jwahir knew from experience that once he'd launched himself on this diatribe, it was best simply to let him finish. Juju the goat lifted his head to nibble at her hand, and she stroked his back.

Her father knelt down and picked up a handful of dirt. "The soil is turning pale," he said, drama in his voice.

Jwahir knew what that meant. "You think it will be serious this time?" she asked.

Her father let the sand fall through his fingers without speaking. Then he nodded. "Don't misunderstand," he said. "We've made a place for ourselves on this land for two millennia. We are survivors of the Great Disaster. Few are as self-reliant as we. But we will need all our energy and all our virtue to withstand what is coming."

"Some say the threat of drought and famine is reason enough to allow our young to learn to read, to find another way," Jwahir said.

Jwahir's father shook his head. "Those are words from your husband, not you. The issue is values. Ours are not theirs. *We* respect our ancestors' lessons. *I* know the name of my father's father's father's father. Do they in the city with their books know this?"

Here, Jwahir was tempted to interrupt, to ask whether he could recall the name of his mother's mother's mother's mother. She knew the answer, though. She'd heard this litany before, along with the recitation of the endless list of male preceded by male preceded by male. As if the women did not exist, except as containers shaped by others' visions, holders of the dreams of fathers, husbands, sons. She felt a surge of irritation coupled with resolve. Like her father, she was traditional. But her father's words fed her conviction that she had to break with tradition on some matters at least. It was right to risk everything do to what she believed, what she desired and needed—as a woman.

"What is it you want of me, Father?" she said coolly after a moment.

He shook his head. "Sometimes I wish I'd never chosen Matani for you," he said. "Otherwise, I needn't be so discreet in pressing for what is best." He linked her arm through his. "But because I must be judicious where my son-in-law is concerned, your role is crucial. Two things must happen.

Matani must recover the books, immediately. And then he must tell the woman we do not wish her further visits."

Jwahir knelt and put an arm around Juju. "And that is the end of your advice? After all, this is no small job you press on me."

Jwahir's father gently touched her cheek with the back of his hand. "There are none more beautiful than you, Jwahir."

She raised an eyebrow. "Yes, you often say so. But what, at this moment, is the purpose of such flattery?"

"Use your influence," he said meaningfully.

"Influence?"

"Yes," he said, raising his voice as though he thought her deaf. "Yes, your . . . "

And then she understood what he meant, the power that he was too delicate to spell out, the power of a wife to give herself to or withhold herself from her husband. He didn't know, of course, that she'd already been avoiding joining herself with Matani for weeks, that there was nothing further to withhold.

"He has turned gentle, your husband," Jwahir's father said, and the emphasis he put on the word *gentle* made it clear he did not consider this a compliment. "Persuade him to be less so in his efforts to reclaim the books from Scar Boy and Abayomi."

At the mention of Abayomi, Jwahir felt her cheeks go hot, and her mind grow distracted. Her father noticed but misinterpreted this. "I'm sorry," he said, "to be so blunt in regard to the use of your womanly gifts. I would not do it if another way occurred to me."

Jwahir shook her head to clear it. "Why do you needle

me so?" she asked. "If the library stopped coming, that would suit your needs. So let the books go unfound, and the problem will be solved without my involvement."

Jwahir's father took both his daughter's hands. "And that's why I mentioned the coming drought," he said. "Honor. It helped us survive the Great Disaster, when we needed not only our wits and our skills, but also the support of our brother tribes and the avoidance of ill-wishing spirits. We must keep our word, always, even to those who intrude without proper knowledge or respect for our people. We must return the books. And then, blameless, we can send them away."

Jwahir fingered one of her beaded earrings silently.

"I know you understand," her father said, turning to go. "Just as Matani is a product of his father, you are a product of me."

Jwahir walked back to Leta, who sat with her baby in her lap, her head lowered. "He's wrong, you know," Leta said after a moment.

"Yes, I know," Jwahir said with a smile. "But about what, precisely?"

"What the camels carry on their backs, we need. The contact with the outside world. The new ways."

Jwahir stared at her friend, and then raised her hands to the sky. "You want the books to keep coming? I thought you agreed with me about this." Her voice, she knew, was sharp. Jwahir was accustomed to differences between them, but this one irritated her severely.

Leta hesitated before meeting her friend's eyes. "I did. Before."

"And then, what? She gives you some book to explain the way other people take care of their babies, and suddenly —"

Leta interrupted her. "It's not that, Jwahir." She looked down at the baby she held in her lap, the little one reaching for her hair. "It's her," she said. "And her older sister. My girls need the bookmobile. They need the possibilities it brings."

"You sound like Matani," Jwahir said, more bitterly than she'd intended. "This is not a bad life, Leta."

"Once, the land gave us more, so we owed it our loyalty," Leta said. "Not now."

"A couple of bad years," Jwahir said, "and you act like it's forever."

"Everything changes, Jwahir," Leta said. "Your father and mine won't admit it, but they're old men."

Everything did change; Jwahir couldn't dispute that. Everything had changed, in fact. That was how she'd explain herself to Leta, someday. When the time felt ripe. But now, Leta was still pressing her point.

"I look at her," Leta said, pointing her chin toward her baby, "and I see it. I understand, and you will, later, too. Matani is right."

"But you and my father argue as though the matter belongs to me."

"Jwahir." Leta rubbed her nose against her baby daughter's cheek. "You know where you sit in Matani's heart. But think, before you use your influence to try to change his mind. Consider mine. Consider the ones *you* will have," Leta smiled, "someday soon."

Jwahir felt a shudder, thinking of all that Leta did not know.

The Grandmother

THIS WAS NEEMA'S SPACE. NOT THE ROOM ITSELF, FOR which she felt little attachment, but this mat woven of sisal fiber and covered with scraped cowhide on which she slept each night in the company of her granddaughter's warmth and breath and scent. Over time, this bed had become molded to embrace Neema's body. It smelled of cattle and earth, and was solid. And whenever she wanted, she could reach out to touch the daughter of her daughter. She'd heard of faraway people who slept in rooms alone, on cloth or feathers. What a sorrow; what a loss. Whosoever slept without others, and on such a bed, would not be blessed with the voyages she'd taken in her dreams, the places where the brushwood and cowhide led her. That person was destined to what she thought of as white sleep, blank and without insight.

As much as she loved her bed, though, she couldn't deny that tonight the hide felt implacable, tickling her right leg at the back of the knee. The twigs beneath her shoved against her left arm and jabbed at her back. So she tried tricks. She silently recited words from the Bible. She forbade herself to move. She imagined her mother sitting at her feet, rubbing them. She breathed in a pattern: three short gasps in, one long sigh out. That sounded like a cow in the rain with a cold; it did nothing to invite sleep.

The problem was not the bed, she knew. The space around it was the impediment. Normally, Neema lay between her granddaughter and the door. Sometimes she slipped close to her granddaughter, breathing with her, thinking of her own daughter—Dahira, Kanika's mother, the one who linked them.

Now someone alien lay between her and Kanika, beneath a mosquito net hung on sticks. Miss Sweeney, with her own peculiar noises and smells. Miss Sweeney, who kept flinging a hand onto her forehead and clearing her throat. The people of Mididima had never had a foreigner of any color sleep in their midst. Now this pale woman was right within Neema's hut.

It must be even stranger, Neema admitted, for Miss Sweeney. To talk and eat and drink among unknown people was one thing; to sleep next to them, another entirely.

Lying in the dark, eyes focused lightly on the ceiling above, Neema tried to imagine Miss Sweeney's New York. Even with Matani's descriptions of the Distant City, even with the descriptions she'd read in the library books, her visions of Miss Sweeney's home were vague and confusing. She pictured one building precariously balanced atop another, people glancing up nervously as they rushed past on foot or sped by in cars that Neema had heard could move with the speed of gazelles. She tried to imagine the unlikely, invisible waves that performed jobs like running machines that cleaned clothes while people slept. And the water that poured out during any season with a turn of a wrist. Food of every imaginable color. Books everywhere. These seemed impossible stories; they could prove only that the teller had somehow been driven mad.

She turned to her side. She couldn't see well through the net, but Miss Sweeney's fidgeting indicated that she too was awake. As was Kanika.

Kanika was whispering. "Are you uncomfortable?"

"No, no," Miss Sweeney answered. "I'm keeping you up. Sorry."

"Miss Sweeney?"

"Fi," said Miss Sweeney. "Call me Fi."

"There's something I want to talk to you about," Neema's granddaughter said.

Miss Sweeney rolled to her side and supported her head with her hand.

"I want to go to the Distant City," Kanika said.

What was this? Neema, too, leaned on an elbow, trying to catch her granddaughter's eye, but Kanika was concentrating too hard to notice.

"Wonderful," Miss Sweeney said, with subdued enthusiasm—or perhaps she was just restrained because she thought Neema was sleeping. "You'd like it," she said.

"Go there and teach," Kanika said, emphasizing the last word.

Neema involuntarily put a hand to her mouth. To teach? To the Distant City to stay? From where had this dream come? Neema had known Kanika so well when she'd been little, had known every crease on Kanika's skin and the texture of her sleeping breath and the sound of her cries right before they gave way to weary hiccups. How had Neema passed from that full knowledge to this ignorance?

"Teach," Miss Sweeney repeated.

"I can do it here. Can't I do it there?" Kanika's voice held a touch of uncertainty, but it was barely discernible. The thrust of her tone was brave and determined, and that triggered in Neema a rush of love and admiration.

She understood with a sudden clarity rarely granted to her anymore. What she'd interpreted as a calm acceptance of Kanika's female role had actually been an emerging plan to escape it. That both broke and warmed Neema's heart at once. "You never told me," she said to Kanika in their language.

"You're awake," Kanika said.

"Away from my eyes, you've been plotting."

Miss Sweeney, who could not understand their words, poked her head out of the netting. She looked at the mesh web as if she'd never seen it before, as if she weren't the one who had hung it before nightfall, searching for the sticks, pushing them into the ungiving ground, spreading it over the place she would lie. Now she flapped a dismissive hand at it, crawled out, and pulled it down.

"You kept this secret," Neema said. "For how long?"

"*Nyanya*, I have to go."

Miss Sweeney sat cross-legged on the edge of the hide, out of the line of sight between Kanika and Neema as though to permit conversation to flow between them unimpeded. But for a second, Neema didn't know what to say. Yes, she'd wanted Kanika to be strong and self-reliant. But why in a different place, why away from her grandmother?

"It's hard there, too," she said. "Harder than you think. When we ask for rain, we must expect mud as well."

"I don't want *this* to be my whole life."

The words sat baldly between them. Neema's insides contracted. Miss Sweeney reached into her bag and pulled out something dark and hard, which she broke into three pieces, offering one to Neema and another to Kanika. "Chocolate," she murmured. Kanika popped hers into her mouth immediately. Proof, Neema thought, that she was far too trusting for the Distant City.

"I lost my daughter all at once," Neema said. "I cannot lose you."

"If I stay, I'll grow angry," Kanika warned.

"Like me, you mean."

Kanika shook her head. "You're strong, not angry."

Neema wasn't so easily hoodwinked by a compliment. She waved away her granddaughter's words. As she made the gesture, though, she heard, unbidden, her mother's voice. "Hold, but do not grasp," it said.

When Neema was young, there'd been no Camel Bookmobile, with its whiffs of another, larger world. Her "dead look" had been her only outlet for frustration. What would she have done, if she'd had the chance?

She sniffed at Miss Sweeney's chocolate. She would suffer through Kanika's absence, then. At least there would be, thank the Hundred-Legged One, one thing to look forward to: throwing the news of Kanika's departure in the face of her annoying brother-in-law, whose voice would hit the clouds as his chances of claiming Kanika's bride-price slipped away.

Before she could reconsider or change her mind, Neema spoke in English. "It comes to pass that I give my permission for her to go, Miss Sweeney."

That, however, apparently was not what Miss Sweeney had been waiting for. She tucked the crumpled mosquito netting beneath her like a pillow. "Kanika," she said, "you would have to go to a special school for a teaching certificate."

"Yes."

"It would take some time—a couple of years."

"I'm willing."

Miss Sweeney was quiet for a moment. She tugged on the back of her hair. To try to hold it away from her face, she'd tied a bandanna around her head. But it still flew in many directions; Neema decided she would offer to braid it in the morning.

"OK. Let me see what I can find out," Miss Sweeney finally said, and Neema was relieved that she did not offer yet another objection. Three would seem too many. "First, I've got to get the books back," she went on. "If I don't, Mr. A. . . . " She hesitated, and then gave a half-laugh. "Mr. A. might kick us all out of the country."

Surely this was a joke. Surely Mr. Abasi did not have that authority, or if he did, he would not exercise it just because of Mididima's missing books. But Neema wasn't certain. She'd heard of the Mau Mau rebellion, when people were beaten and jailed and sent away for mistakes smaller than missing books. And she knew that men often wielded unconscionable power over women.

"I'm sure you'll get the books," Kanika said.

Miss Sweeney lay back on her mat. "Kanika," she said, "what's Scar Boy's real name?"

"Taban," Kanika said.

Taban. How long had it been since Neema had heard that pronounced aloud? But it was right, she realized, that they should begin to call him Taban. After all, he was not a boy anymore. He was seventeen years old, a young man, and one who wielded a surprising amount of influence. Taban, once mauled by a hyena, yes, but now with an identity forged by other events. Keeper of the secret of overdue library books. Decider of his tribe's fate.

"Taban," Miss Sweeney repeated slowly. "Can you tell me about him?"

Kanika rolled on her back. "He's . . . " She hesitated. "He listens. He doesn't like to talk, though. You have to pay close attention to understand him."

"Does he want something?" Miss Sweeney asked. "Is that why he keeps the books? So we'll listen to him?"

Kanika turned to stare at her. The girl seemed to be considering. Then she held both hands, palms up, toward the ceiling. "He will return them."

Miss Sweeney reached over and squeezed Kanika's hand. "Yes," she said. "Yes, of course he will. And even if they're misplaced, we'll find them. Of course. You're right." She nodded as if to herself, stretched, and yawned.

"He must return them," Kanika said again, quietly.

Miss Sweeney did not reply. Her breathing had at last become regular. Lulled by Kanika's apparent confidence, the foreigner was falling asleep. Now maybe they all could sleep.

Neema lay back, thinking how much she admired Kanika—for her clear desires and brave plans, for her way of appearing so self-assured before this foreign woman, and for her ability to hide misgivings. She'd sounded so confident about Scar Boy returning the books, in fact, that Neema was sure only she could detect the note of doubt in her granddaughter's voice.

Part Four

What they prefer most of all is stagnation. Lumpish, unaroused immobility. They adore the thick, grimy scent of inert water, of course, but anything that languishes too long—a half-eaten peach, a glass of wine, a human arm—sucks them in.

—Tape-recorded woman's voice
"The Mad, Marvelous World of Mosquitoes"
Children's Museum exhibit, London, 1999

The American

HER PEEVISH ABDOMEN WOKE HER. FI OPENED HER EYES
to find, on either side of her, the girl and the grandmother immobile, almost leaden, as though sunk in the
kind of heavy slumber that follows a night of insomnia. If
they hadn't been so deeply asleep, she thought her raucous
stomach might have awakened them. She slipped outside,
tenderly patting her middle as if to hush it.

It wasn't that she felt hungry, exactly. She was being fed
generous portions by the standards of the tribe. But how
many extra helpings of maize mixed with milk or camel
blood could one take? Last night before bed, Matani
offered her a local treat: "milk that has slept." Left to stand
overnight and then whisked with a twig, the milk was
considered more filling and flavorful than fresh milk. He'd
gone to some effort to get her a cupful, since usually only
the elder men were permitted to drink it, so she suppressed
the urge to sniff it before taking a large, polite gulp. It tasted
curdled and grassy, as though it came from a camel with
indigestion. All she could say for "milk that has slept" was
that it disturbed her own sleep.

She would eat one more section of her emergency

supply of chocolate, she decided, so she returned to the
room, pulling a bar from her duffel bag along with a bandanna for her hair. She broke off a rectangle of chocolate
and slipped back outside. The first bite she ate quickly, but
then she reminded herself to slow down, letting the next
portion soften in her mouth. She began walking aimlessly,
giving the chocolate time to revive her. Soon, she knew,
the women would rise to tend to pregnant goats, camels,
and cows, and men would head out with plastic containers
tucked under their arms to collect water from distant water
pans. But for now, the humans and their animals were not
quite awake and the nocturnal beasts had finally fallen into
slumber, and Mididima was embraced in a silence she'd
never heard elsewhere—dense and eternal, the same stillness, she imagined, that men and women here had listened
to forever.

She slipped past the thornbush fence that circled Mididima overnight, and that hadn't yet been taken down for
the day. She needed to think of Taban and the books; she
needed, even, to think of Kanika and the teaching—but
the chocolate and the fullness of the quiet somehow made
her think of Matani's wife. Jwahir, with her large eyes and
plump lips, seemed a woman well aware of her own beauty.
While the other women of the tribe wore their hair in
braids that ran along their scalps and then fell in the back,
Jwahir allowed one braid to lie across her forehead. Her
eyes were decorated, and she had designs tattooed around
her wrists, something Fi had not seen on the other women.
Jwahir seemed a woman accustomed to pampering, at least
as much as life in the bush would allow, and Fi wondered

for a second if Matani's wife was good enough for him, and then she shooed away the thought.

A shrieking noise shrill enough to make her jump jarred her from her musings. Instinctively, she dropped behind a bush and ducked her head. After a few seconds, she peeked out.

The sound came from her left, a dozen strides away. A group of monkeys were leaping around madly on a squat acacia tree. Their bodies were gray, their faces were black, and they had long, snowy eyebrows. At first, they struck her as cute and comical in their hyperactivity. Then, looking closer, she caught her breath.

Their ears sat to the back of their heads. A cloud of buzzing flies surrounded them. Most unsettling of all, their expressions seemed crazed, their high-pitched screeching demented.

She remained kneeling, watching. The monkeys, she finally realized, were hurling stones at some target behind her. By shifting her body and inching quietly to the left, she could see, sunk below the surrounding grass, a young cow. Its legs were splayed on the ground. It appeared to be relaxing, observing the world, except she saw that its widened eyes were glassy, as if in shock.

This calf was the monkeys' mark. But why? Why were the monkeys keeping their distance from the calf but throwing stones? And why did it allow itself to be attacked? Then she noticed its right front leg awkwardly bent—perhaps broken? Poor, injured beast, she thought. The entire scene seemed surreal.

She found a stick and hit it against first the ground and

then a bush as she rose and yelled. "Stop!" At the sound of her voice, the rioting creatures turned toward her, their screeching dying. They were about a third her size, but they stared with such small cold eyes that she felt a rush of apprehension. Some let their heads loll to one side. A couple bared their teeth. She had a sudden image of them pelting her, or hurtling themselves on her, biting, clawing, wrapping their long tails around her neck. "Shoo," she said, this time a little more weakly than she would have wished.

One, larger than the others, seemed to be the leader. He stayed on the tree, but jumped toward her on the branches, swung back, and then thrust himself toward her again in an aggressive way. The others circled him, giving him sideways glances, their noises softer now, more like hissing.

Fi took a step, a bit tentative, then another one, less so. "Back off," she said, addressing the larger monkey directly, trying to speak with more assurance than she felt. She banged her stick on the ground again and then waved it at him. "Go!"

The monkeys stopped moving entirely, almost in unison, except for their heads swinging back and forth between her and their leader. She felt blood pulsing at the base of her neck. She stepped forward, still holding the stick, so that now she was between the monkeys and the calf.

The light breeze of early morning had died away, and the air felt sucked clean of oxygen. She heard a single cricket, and then the largest monkey swung off the tree. He hit the ground in front of him twice with his fists.

His gaze was unfocused. She waited, unable to guess his next move.

Then he turned. He bounded away without a backward glance, and the others followed. Before leaving, one of the smaller monkeys reached over the top of the grass to wave a silent fist, as if to say, "A curse on your mother." And they were gone. It was over.

She took a deep breath and let her shoulders sink before approaching the calf, which seemed to become even more agitated now that the monkeys had left. It raised its hind legs as though to try to flee, but couldn't because of its broken front leg. It made a soft sound full of pain.

"Shhh, shhh, little one." Fi finally dropped the stick she'd been gripping all this time, and inched forward until she could reach out to pat the calf's neck. She tried to hum as she'd heard the young girls do while tending the herds. "Oh, lo lo. Oh, take it easy. Oh, lo lo. We'll get you home."

After a few minutes, the calf dropped its head against her knee—whether out of exhaustion or trust was impossible to tell, but she felt a rush of tenderness and decided not to leave the animal, even to seek help. Perhaps she could carry it. It was so scrawny that it probably weighed less than thirty pounds.

She tested the thickness of the stick she'd been carrying. It felt right: it wouldn't bend too easily; nor was it too stiff. Tugging her bandanna off her head and using her teeth to tear it into three strips, she made a splint to stabilize the calf's leg. In one guidebook, bandannas had been mentioned as important to "bring on your safari" because of their light weight and multiple uses. Fi never could have imagined this use, though.

Taking a deep breath and holding it, she slowly slipped

her hands under the calf's stomach. She slid one arm around its chest and another around its rump, pulling the animal close. Then she straightened her knees and lifted. The calf made a small mewing sound, but remained motionless in her arms. "Thank you, baby," Fi whispered. "Keep it up." The calf felt heavier than she'd expected, and holding it was awkward, but she could make it back to the houses. She hadn't come that far.

Concentrated on keeping the hurt animal as still as possible, Fi put her nose into its scratchy coat, inhaling its dank scent. Occasionally the calf shifted its gaze to look at her with watery eyes.

Reaching Mididima seemed to take a long time. Fi's lower back began to ache, and she considered sitting down to rest for a moment, but decided it would be too hard to get back up again. "You're tough, little baby," she murmured to the calf.

Fi had begun to get fully tired when she heard a shrill cry. It startled her; had the monkeys returned? No, it was a young woman who had seen her and was summoning the others. Soon, seven women surrounded her. They lifted the calf from her arms and examined it, their hands flying expertly over its muscles in a way she admired, talking to her all the while as though she could understand. Her legs felt weak, her head a little dizzy, and she sank to the ground.

"There were these monkeys, up in a tree." She raised her arms as though to mimic branches, and then realized how absurd she must look, speaking foreign words while gesturing to the sky. Two men joined the group and one of them hauled up the calf and carried it away. Fi was sorry to see it go; she'd grown attached to it. The women squatted around her and began stroking her arms and hair, talking to her, turning the attention to her that they'd been focusing on the calf. For a second she was startled by the sight of her own pallid skin that, next to their deep tones, looked undernourished. But she quickly relaxed under their touches, soothed by the dip and swell of their banter, amazed and comforted at once by the ease with which they swept her up and included her in their female community.

Then Matani was among them. The chattering young women quickly surrounded him. Fi smiled over their heads and he returned her smile, but they didn't speak—they wouldn't have been able to hear one another above the voices of the women. After several minutes the women helped Fi to her feet and pushed her and Matani toward one another, using their shoulders, smiling. This was the first time she'd felt fully accepted here, and their acceptance filled her with a longing for more. She reached out to squeeze one woman's hands and the woman giggled, and then others reached for her hand as well. A few men had joined the edges of the group by this time; she knew none of them, though. Except for Matani, she'd had little real contact with the men, who generally hovered just outside the circle, like sentries, when the library visited.

"They say to tell you thank you, first," Matani said. "And they want to know what happened."

"The calf will be fine, won't it?" she asked.

"They think so, yes."

She explained, then, about the monkeys. As she spoke, the incident lost its sinister aspect and struck her as funny again, the way it had for a second at first. She started to giggle, but her laughter died on her lips as she looked at Matani's face, which grew more stern as he listened. He translated her story for the group, and they began to murmur among themselves.

"What?" she asked. "What is it?"

Matani and the women talked for a few more minutes, and then he took Fi by the elbow and they began walking toward the acacia tree under which he held his classes. Two of the women trailed a couple of feet behind them. Matani seemed lost in his thoughts.

"What's worrying you?" she asked, putting a hand on his arm in an unconscious gesture, but then becoming very aware of her hand, its pale spill of light against his rich darkness, and the heat and angles of his forearm. She moved away.

"First, you could have been hurt," he said.

"But I'm fine."

"Also, when monkeys behave erratically like that, they are thirsty. Driven mad by thirst."

It took Fi a moment to understand the implications of his words. "They must have come from a dry area," she said. "Your water holes are still wet."

"For now."

"In another week, maybe two, it will be the long rainy season."

"If it comes," he said. "The rains have already failed many times." He shook his head. "The monkeys are a sign of what we already suspected. Not far beyond us, there is drought, and it is catching up with us."

"But it won't, it won't, because—" She broke off here, not sure how to end the sentence, how to find the words that would make a smile flood his face as it did when he'd seen her a few minutes ago. That's the word she thought—*flood*—and it occurred to her to wonder how many such words, used colloquially, came from images of an abundance of water.

"Don't look so serious," Matani said gently. "Don't carry this with you."

But how could she not? Because drought would bring the hardship of less food, maybe even famine. It might mean no more school. And, maybe, no more bookmobile for Mididima.

"I go to teach now," Matani said. "And the girls would like to spend the morning with you."

So that is what they wanted, these two girls still lingering nearby. Fi smiled at their obvious eagerness. Seeing her smile, they stepped forward, one on each side, taking Fi by her hands.

"I'll see you at midday," Fi said to Matani, who answered with a nod, the unlikely dimples in his long narrow cheeks deepening. And then the girls, giggling, pulled her away.

The Librarian

THE CAMEL BOOKMOBILE WAS ON THE MOVE, HEADED FOR its bimonthly visit with two tribes that, loosely put, neighbored each other. Mr. Abasi, astride Siti, led the way beneath a sky decorated with silky white filaments draped so far above the ground they seemed to belong to another world. Four weeks ago, he'd seen a herd of zebras grazing in this area. Now they were gone and the grass was browning from the bottom up. The earth was undeniably flexing its muscles, and without a respectable spell of the Millet Rains, it would reclaim its prominence on the plains. Then they'd see that Mr. Abasi had been right, these foreigners who didn't understand about drought and famine and nomads. Then the "villages" visited by the bookmobile would vanish like the water holes themselves, probably with a good portion of the country's store of books. And none more quickly than Mididima.

But he'd given up for good on trying to enlighten anyone. Word of the Camel Bookmobile had made a bit of a splash in the international press, from the Netherlands to Belorussia, thanks to media packets distributed by the American companies that were helping fund it. File photos of Miss

Sweeney had been dispatched, and Mr. Abasi's boss had been quoted. A photographer even flew in from London to shoot roll upon roll of the camels and the books. Siti was still adorned with the coins and tassels provided for the event.

Frankly, Mr. Abasi had other concerns. That was why he'd been looking forward to today's trip in a way he never did. He had worries to discuss, and no one with whom he could appropriately discuss them. But there was Siti. Since that day when he'd made his startling discovery, he'd grown to appreciate the reversal of fate that his ancestors handed him. He could talk to his mother now. And she couldn't talk back.

He glanced behind him and saw that he was far enough ahead of the others, so he bent forward, putting his mouth close to the camel's small but powerful ear.

"I know you liked your missionaries, Mother," Mr. Abasi said, speaking in a brusque whisper. "Especially the"—and here he snorted—"missionary food."

Siti's muscular nostrils flared as she groaned, a sliding four-toned call of warning. Mr. Abasi paid no attention. Such daring in his speech was permitted now.

"Yes, they helped pay for my stay in England, the bit that the scholarship didn't cover," he said, waving his hand dismissively. "But I cannot tolerate these foreigners any longer. At least, not unless they simply go quickly skipping off into the bush with their smorgasbord of cameras. Let them spend their time chasing migrating wildebeests, or floating in hot-air balloons, or skydiving, dear God—or only our dead ancestors know what. As long as they have nothing to do with me."

Siti's ears cocked back to show she was listening. Mr. Abasi found this gratifying.

"I've spent years—my whole life, really—observing these visitors. I admit I used to envy them their small, obscure privileges—complimentary perfumed shampoos provided by the game lodges, and drinks served in tents looking out at the sunset. I envied them, too, their self-satisfaction. By the end of their safari adventures, they always seemed to feel quite—*intrepid*, that's the word. They went home content that they'd weathered the African experience, and happy enough to leave the Africans behind."

Siti grumbled deep in her throat.

"I don't mind being left behind," Mr. Abasi said. "What I resent—what I always resented in people—is their insincerity."

Siti ducked her head, setting her dangling coins jangling and pitching Mr. Abasi forward. He managed not to fall off.

"Straighten up; I'm not talking about you, Mother," he said. "You were sincere—but way overblown. Anyway, don't get offended with me. It's Miss Sweeney I want to talk about. She's a different sort of foreigner. She couldn't be less interested in safaris or complimentary shampoos. And she doesn't even look like the others. It's as if she's just shuttled in after a long trip from a more primitive place, with her dark, frizzy hair flying. No camouflage colors for her—instead, it's that purple bag loaded with poetry books. She's sincere, all right. Also annoying. Now, go this way."

Mr. Abasi could tell from the angle of the sun that they had strayed a little too far east. As Siti turned slightly to get back on track, he rubbed his eyes, suddenly noticing that the glare of the day made them water. "I've been sleeping poorly, waking early every day," he said. "But what do you expect? I know that if anything happens, they'll blame me. Yes, me! Even though I've opposed this whole operation from the start. I'll be answerable."

Siti gave a cry that almost sounded sympathetic.

"What might happen? Too many possibilities to count," Mr. Abasi said. "She could be abducted by *shifta*. Mauled by a baboon. An irritable goat could gouge her. She could eat something poisonous or contract a mortal disease. An elder could put a fatal curse on her. She could be taken as a second wife."

Mr. Abasi felt his own shoulders sag under this recounting of potential disasters. For a while, man and camel— or mother—traveled in silence. At last, Mr. Abasi recovered enough to go on. "I'm not cut out for this," he said, "overseeing a white woman's misguided cultural rescue mission."

Siti stopped, looked back at him, winked, and bared her teeth. How well Mr. Abasi knew that false, knowing smile. His mother had warned him on many occasions that becoming a librarian was a mistake, involving too much needless pressure. She'd wanted him to sell small electronics instead. "But don't listen to me," she'd said more than once in an icy voice. "Better to be a man who talks only to himself. That way, you'll never be contradicted."

"Well, I admit it," he said now. "This part of the job is mad. Allowing her to trim a lion's mane would have been wiser."

But what did he mean by the word *allowing?* Women—all women, as it turned out, and not only his mother—were untamable. It would be best to simply disregard them. "I'm trying," he said aloud. "I'm trying to forget about her."

Siti tossed her head in a knowing way.

"No, Mother, nothing like that. She's only a responsibility," Mr. Abasi said. "I'll be perfectly happy when she's gone."

The camel gave a skeptical hiss, spitting a soft spray of saliva.

"Oh, be quiet," he said, irritably. And, remembering how much his mother hated silence, he refused to talk for the rest of the trip.

Scar Boy

TABAN LOOKED UP FROM HIS DRAWING AND COCKED HIS head, listening to the footsteps make a partial circle around his home and pause. The steps sounded light, so he doubted they belonged to a man. Man-steps worried him most right now. He could always peek through the holes in the wall and see who it was, of course. But he didn't want to be reduced to peering from his home like a cowering bush rat. He took four slow breaths before the steps shuffled, then moved away.

"They're hovering," he said softly.

Badru lifted his head from his bowl of millet and studied Taban questioningly.

"They've been hovering for the last two days. Haven't you noticed?"

Badru stared at him for another beat, then shrugged.

Taban knew his brother had no idea what he was talking about. Maybe Badru didn't even believe him. Badru hadn't developed a sixth sense about the footfalls. He'd never needed to—he didn't spend as much time within these walls, sensing what lay outside.

Taban had been studying the footsteps for years. He

could tell a person's size, sex, age, even mood. He was long accustomed to the usual pattern: the vibrations approached, picked up speed as they neared, and swerved slightly away as though his hut were barricaded by an invisible ring of poisonous knobthorn bushes.

The steps closest to his hut were always the shortest and quickest. Fear made feet move faster.

But lately, the footsteps had begun to follow a different path. They advanced toward his home, much nearer than before, and paused for as many as ten of Taban's breaths before reversing and moving away. Taban felt the clear warning in that pause. They wanted the books. The white woman's presence had made their desire more urgent. They thought Taban was useless, expendable, and maybe even evil. Eventually, the footsteps wouldn't hesitate; they wouldn't retreat.

Sometimes he thought he should simply leave before the situation became treacherous—not only for him, but for his father and Badru too. They weren't as watchful as he had become; they wouldn't even recognize the danger until too late. They shouldn't be sacrificed.

But where would he go? How would he survive, day to day?

And besides, what about Kanika?

Kanika's footsteps were what first attracted his attention. Her walk was light, almost tripping, and she always headed in his direction without pause. She'd never treated him with fear, never scurried away. His father's heavy steps spoke of sorrow and guilt; Badru's were short and controlled. Both reminded him of what he was. Of everyone in Mididima, it was Kanika who treated him like any other person. He couldn't resist that.

Now he heard footsteps again, a man, drawing near, stopping. This time Badru noticed too. He looked up and caught Taban's eye. They sat silently, staring at each other as they listened. It made Taban think of bush rats cowering while the hook-beaked martial eagle looped overhead; and as much as he hated the feeling, he knew Badru hated it more, because Badru was less used to it and felt he didn't deserve it.

Taban wished he could apologize, but he felt himself involuntarily harden against the blame he could see in his brother's eyes—not only for the books, not even mainly for the books. For the hyena. For being what the hyena made him. And for how that had affected Badru's life.

Badru waited until the steps walked away. Then, in one fluid movement, he stood, kicked the bowl he'd been eating from, turned, and pushed out the door.

Taban sat quietly in the empty hut. "I'm sorry," he said.

Then he bowed to his drawing again.

The Drum Maker

ABAYOMI WAS HEAVY-EYED AS HE WALKED BACK TO MIDI-dima. He'd been tired before, lie-down-on-the-ground, let-the-earth-take-him exhausted. But he'd always known that he had something to do next, and he'd known what it was, and that certainty had been like a drink of vigor. This time, when he thought of his next step, he lacked confidence. He changed his mind as easily as tall grass swayed in the wind.

He'd left the settlement at noon the day before and returned in the middle of the night to sit alone inside the *kilinge*. In houses around him, people slept—his sons, his friends, Jwahir. He'd watched the fire for hours, hoping his heart would calm, but the flames were mocking. "What do you want me to do?" he'd asked without any clear sense of who "you" was or what form an answer might take. No one replied.

He'd thought, unreasonable as it sounded, that someone would reply.

He'd left again before anyone had awakened, and walked in a widening spiral around Mididima until the muscles in his legs shivered with a desire for rest. He'd thought about staying away for another night. Hiding until decisions were made, until issues were resolved without him, and then coming back to find what fate had left him.

But he couldn't this time. He was heading back, within sight of his own home now. He had duties.

First, he had to speak with Taban about the missing books, and right away. It had already become too much a topic in Mididima. But he dreaded questioning Taban. He'd paid no attention to the books—for all he knew, his son had actually handed them over and was being accused without cause by those who'd never trusted him anyway. And besides, because Taban spent so much time inside, alone, he should be allowed his books if he did still have them. Abayomi didn't want to be the one to take them away.

Still, it wasn't fair to leave Badru, as spirited as he was, to defend his brother. Badru had long ago adopted the attitude of the attacking jackal, but it was feigned. Without Taban, Badru might now be learning to read with Matani. He would have been a thoughtful man, like Matani's father. As it was, the hyena's attack had disfigured Badru as well as his brother, though Badru's were scars of defiance. He disdained authority as Abayomi never had. Abayomi only hoped this wouldn't become his defining trait.

"Hello, Abayomi," one of the men called out as he entered the settlement. He nodded greetings. He didn't expect any questions about where or how he'd spent his night, and certainly not why. His neighbors, he knew, would accept and even honor his need for time apart; after all, no other man here had charge of children. As for his feelings for Jwahir, no one would guess. She'd already been taken, and he'd been unmarried so long he doubted that his maleness even occurred to anyone anymore. Besides, except when the Camel Bookmobile was visiting, he and Jwahir had been discreet.

Before he went home, he stopped to drink some of the water stored in plastic containers and kept under a small ramada. He shook several empty ones before he found one with water still inside. He'd been thirstier than he'd realized. He drank so quickly that a drop dribbled down his chin and dropped into the earth.

"The boys are fine?" he asked his cousin Chege.

"I saw Badru this morning," Chege answered. "All was well."

Abayomi felt only slightly reassured. Chege's observations of the boys were superficial, he knew. Chege had not been forced to become half-female as Abayomi had, so he wouldn't notice unless the stench of death emerged from Abayomi's home. Abayomi's sons needed their father. They always had, in different ways, and they would go on with that needing for three more years. Then, together, they would join their age group and leave him for month after month to herd cattle outside Mididima, and to form new, grown-up alliances. Already, Badru went to the dances that the young sometimes had beyond the settlement borders. Taban did not, but when the time came, he would follow tradition and go with those his age to herd cattle—he had to, if he hoped to become a man in Mididima.

That was a time Abayomi dreaded. He feared being alone—he could admit that to himself now. Of course he had a role among his people as the maker of drums, and a place in the procession of his ancestors. But after his boys left, no one would be next to his side when the sun rose. No voices in his hut, no arguing, no laughter, no shared meals.

No one his age slept alone. He should have married Jwahir long ago, before life got this complicated. Panic and a promise got in the way.

As he turned from the ramada, he saw the women walking past on their way to the crops. He averted his face, then glanced their direction, trying not to stare, hoping to appear casual. His eyes quickly found Jwahir. Her hips swung forward with each step, then rocked slightly back. His gaze slipped up to the beads around her neck, then to her face. Such a combination of silkiness and determination. She, too, was watching him, but out of the corner of her eye so as not to be obvious. Still, he felt the question in her sideways glance, in the way she moved. He gave her the slightest nod. Her face softened. Her lips curved.

Yes. After all the unsettled, pondering hours of night, it had been resolved that simply. In that nod, a commitment was made. He'd told her yes, even though he didn't know how he would bear the consequences.

Abayomi remembered first noticing Jwahir. She thought it was the day of the Camel Bookmobile's initial visit, and he hadn't told her otherwise. He didn't know how she'd react if she knew that his desire had begun more than a decade before.

It had been one morning a bit after sunrise. His wife, pregnant with their second child, had already milked the cattle and made breakfast for Badru. Abayomi had just risen and gone outside. There he'd seen Jwahir singing under a tree. She had her back to him; she'd thought herself alone. She was eleven. He couldn't imagine why she wasn't working with the rest of the young women. Later he would learn she had a knack for slipping away from work.

It wasn't her singing that drew him; her voice, in fact, lacked harmony to his ear, and the lyrics she'd invented were about picking mushrooms after a rain. But as she raised her arms, rotated her shoulders, and swayed her spread legs, the rhythm in her body ran through him like a gulp of palm wine. He was moved by her obvious self-confidence, and by the balanced flow of her body as she danced her feet together and then divided them again. He'd crouched in the shadow of his home, watching until she quit singing and wandered out of sight.

His wife had been fifteen when she'd married him, and from the start she'd been a shrewd woman, with none of the naïveté from which he himself suffered. It didn't take her long to sense Abayomi's attraction to this younger girl, though he never knew how she guessed, since he'd pushed it quickly from his mind. She made him pledge never to take another wife. He'd been embarrassed to have been so easily discovered, and readily agreed. She'd wanted the vow in blood, though, so he'd cut his finger. She'd sucked it, and had their older son, young Badru, do the same, though the toddler didn't know what he did or why.

At the time, of course, Abayomi hadn't anticipated being a widower—probably never, certainly not so soon.

Taban had been difficult for his wife from the womb. She'd continued to do all of a woman's work, but she complained of headaches, of blurred vision. Still, he wasn't prepared to lose her during childbirth. Though Jwahir delighted him, he still cared for his wife.

After her death, the village elders proposed that Abayomi remarry immediately so a new wife could help care for his sons. They suggested his wife's sister. He refused, citing his promise not to take another spouse and his desire to concentrate himself on the still sickly newborn Taban. What attention could he give to a woman now, anyway? The elders argued and cajoled, saying that a man was unfit to care for an infant, but they finally gave up, nevertheless still expecting that he'd change his mind soon enough, once faced with the work of rearing children.

And indeed, after nearly three years of being a widower, Abayomi found that his promise to his first wife no longer seemed to have meaning. He decided she would want him to have help with her children. He began thinking often of Jwahir, then almost fourteen. He rehearsed how he might propose himself to Jwahir's father, what he might offer. He was strong, a hard worker, and not a poor man.

One day, he'd walked far from the settlement, Taban on his shoulder and Badru running behind. He'd let the boys play in the bush while he paced a few steps away, thinking of Jwahir and rehearsing his proposal to a gray acacia tree. It was not the first time he'd practiced to a tree. In the beginning, he'd stumbled over his words, but eventually they'd found their way into his blood, and he could speak easily. In a few days, he thought, he would take his application to Jwahir's father. Then this handsome, confident, lively woman would come to live with him and his sons, and he could lie with his head against her shoulder.

He was so close to accomplishing his dream. The vividness of this image of the two of them together was intoxicating that day as he stood before the acacia. He lost himself in his vision, and he allowed his attention to wander from his boys. It wandered until Badru's high-pitched scream cut the air, and Abayomi turned, and he would never forget the horror of the sight that met him. Over his little boy, there leaned a humpbacked beast with saliva the color of sunset dripping from the corner of its mouth. Its eyes were small orange fires.

He sprang forward and killed the hyena—later, he couldn't even remember how—and then he ran as quickly as he could, Taban in his arms, the terrified Badru clinging to his leg. After he reached the settlement, Badru fled to their home to hide, while he took Taban to Matani's father.

Taban recovered, after a fashion. But they all three— father and both sons—bore scars, though Abayomi's and Badru's were less visible. Abayomi knew what the attack was meant to tell him. It was a warning: he was not to marry another. If he did, his boys would come to further harm, and next time he would be unable to save them.

He'd confided in Matani's father, who urged him to regard the tragedy as a condition of life in the bush, not an omen. He knew the sensibility of the advice, but he could dismiss neither his conviction nor his guilt. He waited for Jwahir to marry. That, he thought, would allow him to forget.

Jwahir, though, did not marry as quickly as the other women. She grew more beautiful and spurned the young men with whom she'd spent her childhood. Her father had two wives and eight children, but only one daughter. He allowed Jwahir her way. So Abayomi had carried a shred of private hope, mostly unacknowledged even to himself, until Matani returned and the two of them wed. Right before the wedding, Matani's father died, leaving no one to guess at Abayomi's despair.

Then not quite four years after her marriage came the day when she'd literally run into him. That physical touch, accidental though it had been, left him at once joyous and alarmed. Even more miraculously, she'd begun to talk to him. And she seemed to like their conversations; she seemed to take on a glow; she wanted more.

Only she was married to the son of the man who'd saved his son's life. So Abayomi had told himself to be content with the time the Camel Bookmobile allowed them. A gift to him from an unlikely source—a collection of books. He had managed to be satisfied, just managed, until the day she touched his cheek, ran her hand along his shoulder.

Then events began to move with the speed of a cheetah.

By now, Abayomi had reached home. He hesitated for just a moment outside the door. Matani would come to him today, he knew. Matani would come to discuss Taban and the missing books, but he would find another topic waiting. It would be difficult for Abayomi to discuss Jwahir with the man she'd married. He was good at creating drums, he knew. He spoke best with his hands. When making words, he floundered. Still, he understood that words were what he had just promised Jwahir. And he was, he reminded himself, a man of his promises.

Though the day was only beginning, he longed for it to be through.

The Teacher

THEY'D PUT A RED SMUDGE ACROSS HER CHEEKS AND three black ones on her forehead and now, though she was still wearing her faded jeans and a lavender T-shirt and her hair stood apart from her scalp, she looked transformed. Her wide-set eyes seemed to leap from her face. He was surprised he'd never before noticed how striking they were: blue in the middle ringed with the brown of the earth, as though they couldn't make up their mind about whether to be one color or the other. He was briefly distracted by her collarbone. Most of the women here covered their collarbones with beads. He forced himself to focus again on her face. She looked as though she'd shed many moons' worth of responsibility. "We had fun," she said.

"I can see." He handed her a cup of *chai* and a piece of bread. "Do you want to walk a bit after lunch, before we go to Scar Boy?"

She nodded. "How was the teaching?"

"They were"—he hesitated, hunting for the word— "unsettled this morning. The story of your confrontation with the monkeys has traveled."

She took a sip of the *chai* and looked down into her

cup. "Matani," she said. "Will you tell me about the Great Disaster?"

Matani raised his hands to the sky. "It's a brief story. For five years, our elders say, water no longer flowed from the sky. We call it the Time of Thorns. That's what people ate."

She watched him, silent.

"Half died," he said. "Mothers learned a lesson: a lullaby will not calm a hungry child."

She gave up sitting cross-legged and stretched out her legs, flexing her toes. "How long ago was this?"

"A generation ago. It is not in my living memory."

"A generation? Then it won't happen again," Miss Sweeney said. "Not that way. Today you have irrigation. There are international organizations, and relief centers, and towns you can reach if you need to."

Matani shook his head. "Ours is a contradictory people," he said. "Our elders would prefer drinking from an elephant's footprint to leading the tribe into a town or taking them again to a famine camp."

"If they had to?"

Matani considered how to explain without insulting Miss Sweeney. "Our elders will tell you the towns and feeding centers are filled with people who have failed." He added quickly, "No rudeness is meant."

Miss Sweeney touched Matani's fingertips lightly with her own, leaving behind a suggestion of warmth. "Please don't weigh each word with me," she said. "I'm not as fragile as that." Matani tried not to think about the touch, except to remind himself how vastly different were relations between men and women in Miss Sweeney's country.

"Anyway," Miss Sweeney went on, "couldn't you convince them that towns are not to be feared?"

"Me?"

"You've been to Nairobi. You're educated. You're kind and smart. You—" She stopped short, and a look he recognized as embarrassment flew across her face. That surprised him. She was usually brash, like Jwahir, who never seemed embarrassed. Between the two of them, he was the one given to self-consciousness.

"You misunderstand my importance to the tribe," he said gently.

She leaned forward, silent.

"You know about age-groups?" he asked.

"Every thirteen years, all the young men between— what is it? twelve and twenty-five?—become a sort of fraternity."

He nodded. "And each new age-group starts out by setting up camp outside the settlement to graze the cows. In this way they become a unit and their links are secured. When my group was being initiated, my father sent me away to study."

"That's not your fault."

"But as result, I'm seen as different. I lack the closeness many of the men share." He hesitated a moment. "Some question my loyalty. They say I favor the city over the tribe."

He'd made it sound as if the men made such accusations, but in fact this charge came directly from Jwahir. She'd told him the previous night that he must send the library away after recovering Scar Boy's books. Otherwise, she said, he was choosing the Distant City over her. As she spoke, he'd seen her father's face staring out at him, cold and judgmental. What he'd wanted was to hold his wife in his arms, but she'd turned into a village elder. He hadn't replied. He hadn't told her that he believed loyalty to her and to the tribe required, in fact, doing everything he could to keep the library coming. The passing of time, he hoped, would allow them to discuss this more easily.

Miss Sweeney waited for him to continue.

"Our tribe sees itself as survivors who share a pact with the land," he said. "The story is that we were slaves to another tribe—this is perhaps a thousand years ago. And then we escaped. We were without weapons, but the land protected us. It offered up food and hiding places. So the connection between our people and the land is strong. Not only this place where Mididima rests, but all of it. The earth, to us, is a living thing with thoughts and feelings. That's why, when my father first brought the irrigation buckets, there was great suspicion. Many felt we should not trick the soil."

"Your father was simply trying to make the most of what water you have."

Matani shrugged. "Maybe you'll understand better if I say that many here believe drought is not a natural phenomenon. They think it's something we call down upon ourselves."

"How?"

"Varied ways. The Great Disaster, for instance, occurred because a man of the tribe forced his will on a young woman."

"Rape, you mean," she said.

"I don't know your word," he said. Miss Sweeney took a bite of her bread, her face unreadable. "I've offended you."

"No. It's silly. Romantic of me, really, that I didn't think of you having those problems here." She stared at her left hand, then wiped it on her jeans. "What happened to the man?"

"Nothing for several weeks. The guilty man's closest friend was the woman's brother, so naturally, the brother struggled over what the Hundred-Legged One would want. Finally, the brother killed his friend."

"How?"

"A gun. The first our tribe had ever seen. He traded two cows for it. And today he's honored for this. He is among our sacred ancestors. He righted a wrong."

"If you believe the matter was set right, why would this lead to the drought?"

"The punishment came too late," Matani said. "By the time the man was dead, the drought had already bared its claws and taken hold."

"What happened to the woman?" Miss Sweeney asked after a pause.

"She was not held blameless. Her life, too, became misery. Eventually she offered herself to a passing tribe and left."

Miss Sweeney still had half of her bread left. She set it down on a square of cloth spread on the ground.

"And you," she said. "What do you think causes drought?"

Matani hesitated. "I'm a modern man," he said. "Still, I

struggle with this. I cannot fully discount the idea that our misdeeds can cause catastrophes of all sorts."

They sat in silence for a few moments. He watched Miss Sweeney push her fingers through her hair. She had so many questions, more questions than he ever knew one person could pose. The people of Mididima, it occurred to him, didn't have that much to ask about. Some had wanted to know of Nairobi—or the Distant City, as they insisted on calling it. But a sentence or two usually satisfied their curiosity. And in school, the children sometimes asked questions, although just as often, he got wandering eyes and silent tongues. In general, none of his neighbors seemed to dream of elsewhere. By adulthood, they were instilled with a confidence that there existed no important knowledge they didn't already have.

He was curious, though. He was curious, for instance, about Miss Sweeney.

"Of all the places you might have gone," he said, "why here? Why Africa?"

She didn't answer immediately. A mixture of expressions crossed her face at such speed that he wished to stop and freeze each one until he could decipher them. "I believed the bookmobile could change lives in settlements like this," she said finally. "I still believe that. But it was personal, too. I knew something existed beyond my world, something important. Like a flavor I had to taste if I wanted to be fully alive."

Her words stilled the breath within him. He thought he understood precisely what she meant. Matani had known, even as a boy, that he would follow his father's path and study in Nairobi as his father had done. He'd also known he would return home to help his tribe, as his father had done. But Nairobi had shown him that there was much to experience beyond Mididima. This was the dream he nurtured for his son. His son would study in Nairobi, too. But he'd made a private vow: his son would not return to the arid desert, where there was rarely enough food and never enough water, where a man could not rise in the middle of the night to turn on a light and sit in a comfortable chair and read. His son would stay beyond Mididima, and taste the world.

Miss Sweeney stood. "Scar Boy," she said.

So lost was he in his own thoughts about his own son that Matani felt momentarily confused.

"Let's walk first," she said. "And then we'll go reclaim those books."

Of course. She wasn't here to talk to him and rescue calves. She was here, this woman who listened so intently, for the library books. She was here and soon she would leave.

The Girl

BADRU GREETED HER AT THE DOOR. THAT TOOK HER ABACK.
Without thinking about it, she'd expected Scar Boy to
be alone. That's how she always saw Scar Boy—alone. But,
then, she'd never come during the day before.

"Kanika," Badru said. He breathed her name in a way
that irritated her. She felt as if flies covered her body or
mosquitoes hovered over her head.

She knew Badru, of course, but she'd never paid him
any attention. Now she saw he looked as Scar Boy might
have if a hyena hadn't attacked him. His skin was the shiny
warm brown of dampened soil. He had wide shoulders—in
fact, she thought they were the widest of anyone in the
tribe except Scar Boy. His cheekbones were high and defined, his eyes clear. His lips jutted forward, glossy as though
they'd been polished. She stared at them a moment, rotat-
ing her face a little to see if she could pick out her reflec-
tion the way she did in Miss Sweeney's mirror.

He shifted on his feet, waiting, unsmiling.

"I'm here to speak with your brother," she said.

He didn't move to the side. "My father told us no one
should come in while he was gone."

She laughed, to put Badru in his place. "He didn't mean me," she said.

Badru didn't contradict her, but he didn't move. Had she and Badru ever even spoken before? If so, she couldn't recall. Now she got the sense that he was as stingy with words as Scar Boy.

"Your brother would want to talk to me," she said.

"Let her in," came Scar Boy's voice.

Badru eyed her a moment more, searchingly, from head to foot, and then stepped aside. Kanika gave him a look that she'd give one of the kids who wasn't trying during school time—though they mostly tried with her.

Scar Boy was sitting on a grass mat, straight-backed. It startled her to realize she'd never been in his hut before— they always met outside. It was messy, she saw. Metal bowls tossed in one corner, clothes into another, nothing neat. The books could be under any pile. Abayomi should have remarried. Kanika couldn't think of another man who'd lost a wife and hadn't.

Scar Boy grinned at her and then, glancing at Badru, closed down his smile. "Hello," he said.

She sat before him. "I came as soon as I could get away. It's important."

"Badru," he said, dismissal in his voice. Kanika did not turn to look at Badru. She watched only Scar Boy's face.

"You need someone with you," Badru said. "Both of you do."

He was right, Kanika knew. It was taboo for a young couple to be alone together in a hut. Though she couldn't imagine that anyone would suspect Scar Boy of being part of a "couple," Badru was nevertheless trying to save his younger brother from any possible accusations. Badru's point was reasonable, so why did he make Kanika feel so prickly?

Scar Boy hesitated, then nodded. He turned his attention toward Kanika.

"They've begun wearing amulets for rain," she said. "Two of the elders are traveling to Mount Surina for special prayers."

"Superstition," Scar Boy said. "You don't believe that?"

"Don't you?" she asked. "But never mind. It doesn't matter what we believe. If it gets even a little drier, they are going to want to find something—someone—to blame."

Scar Boy looked at the wall to his left as if words were written there. "Maybe there *is* something that punishes," he said. "Something evil and half-alive that strikes down little children or pregnant mothers. But a specific human sin that blows away the rain clouds . . . " He paused, and shook his head.

"I don't want them to blame you," Kanika said. "You have to give back the books. Now it's not only for me."

He reached out his hand as though to touch hers, then pulled it away. "You think of me," he said softly.

"Of course I do," she said, letting her voice snap. There would be no show of warmth, not with Badru listening to every word. Besides, somehow Scar Boy had turned her kindness into permission to act ridiculous. "I think of you," she said, "and I think of me and I think of the whole tribe."

Scar Boy was looking at her with something soft and

aching in his gaze. Whatever it was, she didn't want it. She stood up and allowed her voice to go cold. "Give back the books." Then she turned to Badru. "That's all I wanted to say to your brother. I'll leave now. And you can go back to guarding the door."

Badru shifted. "You and I," he said. "We used to play together. When we were little."

"I don't remember," she said, her words clipped where his were slow.

"That's only because you were littler than me," he said. "You liked it. You liked playing with me."

She understood suddenly why Badru irritated her so. In his glance, his tone, he seemed to speak of intimacy between them. No one else dared look at her like that, not even Scar Boy.

"I don't remember," she repeated.

"You used to climb on my back," he said, "and I'd take you for rides. You squealed, I remember that. I bet if you think about it, you'll remember too."

"I don't think so."

"You will." He touched her arm lightly, his expression serious. And then, standing there facing the door with her back to Scar Boy, she felt something run between them, something she couldn't name because she'd never felt it before. It was elusive, like a blast of hot wind or grass brushing against her leg. It confused her.

She pushed it away, whatever it was, and half closed her eyes as she stepped out the door, so she didn't see him. She ran directly into Abayomi, her head bumping into his chest.

Abayomi looked even more startled than she. He opened his mouth, closed it, then opened it again. "Kanika," he said. "Are you fine? What scared you?"

Kanika didn't answer. Let Scar Boy and his brother say what they wanted. Before she left, though, she looked directly into his face. She wanted him to see there was no apology there. As she looked, she saw where Badru came from. Abayomi's lips had the same shape; his eyes had the same color and were just as wide. Only—and here came the unbidden thought—only he wasn't quite as beautiful.

She would not, she vowed silently, come back to see Scar Boy during the day again.

The American

THE WALK HAD STRETCHED ON. THEY'D BEEN TALKING almost as much as breathing, in fact, for most of the afternoon, a patchwork of overlapping topics. When they paused near the monkey tree, she asked him about his mother. She didn't know where the question came from, exactly, and he hesitated before answering. The heat that had been pressing down on their heads and shoulders was just beginning to lift.

"All I know about her is a green fabric with red flowers," he said.

Something in his face reminded her of the fleeting scent of honeysuckle. It made her want to take that moment and hold it. She stayed very still.

"When I was little," he said, "my father would pull out that material from where he kept it wrapped and stored in a corner. He would lay it on his lap and smooth it with his hands. Sometimes he would hold it to his face."

Then he grew silent, and she waited a long time; she waited until she was afraid he had stopped on this topic for good. "Did you ever find out . . . " She let her words trail off.

"It was my mother's, but more than that, he never told

me. I wanted more; I wanted a memory of my mother, since I had none of my own. But my father said memories made it harder."

"Harder," she said, "but sweeter at the same time."

"Yes?"

"Yes." She was thinking of her own mother and her father. Of the memories she had and the memories that, like Matani, she had been denied. She put her hand on the trunk of the monkey tree, which felt surprisingly cool despite the heat. "After today, I think I should carve 'I was here.'" He looked puzzled. "It's what people do sometimes. Graffiti, it's called. They make their mark on a special place, and it's the bridge that connects them to everyone else who comes by later."

"It's a nice custom."

She laughed. "They don't always think so in my country. There are laws against it."

He smoothed the tree trunk with his hand. "Come," he said finally. "I'm going to show you a plant that repels *mbu*. Juice-drainers. What you call mosquitoes. Kanika told me you brought a net."

He led her just beyond the huts to a group of small, grayish plants that grew close to the ground. The leaves were the size of thumbs, and nearly as fat. He pinched off half a dozen. "Put out your arm," he said, so she did, and he broke the leaves, one at a time, to release the liquid within, and stroked in long sweeps, his dark fingers moving from her shoulders to her wrists and back up again. She watched him while he worked, his concentrated face, the rhythm of his hands. The moisture from the leaves cooled her skin, made it tingle. He put some on her shoulders, and then her neck, moving her hair to one side.

"I smell like onion," she said, laughing.

"But now you won't need the net."

"I've learned something new."

"I've thought before," he said, smiling, "that the teaching must go both ways."

They walked to Scar Boy's hut, falling silent, a little awkwardly—the way people can, Fi thought, after they've shared some unexpected intimacy and aren't sure how it's changed them. But of course, this intimacy had changed nothing. Within an hour, Fi would have the books. Tomorrow morning she would watch Matani teach again, and maybe even help—she'd been imagining taking the kids through a rendition of "Head, Shoulders, Knees and Toes." Then the next day, she would leave.

Matani called out as they reached Scar Boy's hut. The man who greeted them at the door was surprisingly muscular; his arms were those of a laborer, and Fi realized she'd become accustomed to the typical lean Mididima body type.

"Taban's father, Abayomi," Matani told her. And then she heard Matani pronounce her own name.

As Matani spoke, Abayomi kept shifting, looking at his feet, then his hands, then up into Matani's face, then away again. First thing, Fi decided, she would tell him not to worry, that it was no one's fault, these things happened. That in America, patrons sometimes built up enormous fines before the library finally revoked their cards, only here the supply of books was so meager, the possibility of collecting fines so unlikely, that they'd decided on a stricter policy—too strict, in truth.

But when Matani paused in his speech for a moment, Abayomi blurted out a few words in a rush. Matani shook his head and gestured toward her. Abayomi spoke again and Fi, without knowing the meaning, could hear the insistence.

"He wants to speak with me alone a moment," Matani said. "I'm sorry. Our people are not accustomed to strangers. I'll be back quickly."

"Of course." Fi watched the two men walk away. Taban's older brother, the one who'd brought the news of the missing books on library day, stood just outside the door. She smiled, but got no response.

"Oh. Well," she said. She looked up at the darkening sky and then back to find the older brother still staring.

Fi wished she had Kanika to help her because at that moment, her mind seemed drained of Swahili words, and in the local dialect she knew so little. She knew how to say "How are you?" so she said it, threw it into the conversation a little late, but the brother didn't respond. She wished she could find a way for them to talk about the weather at least, or how quickly night fell once it made up its mind. Or the subtle scent of maize cooking around them. Or even the mosquitoes.

She truly felt like a *mzungu* now; that meant *foreigner* in Swahili, and she'd always liked the reckless sound of the word. *I might as well recite poetry*, she thought, and then she tried saying it aloud, directly to the older, phlegmatic brother, "I might as well recite poetry." His face remained still, so she repeated it, experimenting, spreading her arms and stressing the final word in the sentence. He watched without expression.

She lowered her voice and opened one hand. "I bring you, with reverent hands, the books of my numberless dreams." She cleared her throat and decided to pretend she was on a podium in a recital hall, reading Yeats's *A Poet to His Beloved* to an audience that was not impassive like this older brother, but instead hushed by the intensity of the lines. She widened her stance and raised her voice.

"White woman that passion has worn," she recited, "as the tide wears the dove-grey sands." For a moment, she felt as if she were floating above, looking down at the scene: a woman in the African bush theatrically delivering poetry to an uncomprehending audience of one, and she began to giggle. But if Taban's brother considered her behavior the slightest bit curious, he gave no sign. His look remained deadpan. She swallowed her laughter and went on. "White woman with numberless dreams," she recited, "I bring you my passionate rhyme."

She glanced behind her and felt relieved to see Matani returning—no more relieved, probably, than this young man watching this stranger-woman wave and exclaim and laugh. Thank God for Matani. He would chuckle once she explained.

But as he drew nearer, his expression quashed her gaiety for the second time that day. He looked deflated, shoulders sagging, eyes unfocused. Was this more about the drought? Or fear about the missing books? Immediately she thought, *Don't let it be the books that have caused this concern.* That would be too much.

Abayomi was not yet in sight. "Matani, what is it?" she asked.

"I must get you home." He sounded vague, ill, and he gestured with one hand for her to follow.

She glanced back at Taban's still indifferent older brother. "What's happened?"

Matani took about a dozen steps before he rushed away from the homes, pushing aside the thornbush fence the men stretched around Mididima each night. She followed to find him several feet away from the fence, bent over, throwing up.

"Matani." She put a hand on his forehead to support him, the way her mother used to do for them when they were sick—the one time all her brusqueness disappeared. His forehead felt clammy.

He didn't seem aware of her touch at first. He convulsed again. After a few minutes, he turned toward her slightly. He wore a look of surprise coupled with embarrassment. "Sorry," he mumbled.

"You should have ice chips." She put an arm around his shoulders. "It's the best when you've vomited. Of course, you can't have that here. Have they ever had ice, the people here?" She was babbling, she knew.

He nodded, then shook his head. "Sorry," he said again.

"Everyone gets sick," she said. "Don't worry about it. I'll help you home, where your wife can take care of you. Tomorrow is soon enough to deal with the books."

He turned away from her, gagging. His chest was still heaving when he spoke. "Not home," he said.

"What?" she said, certain she'd misunderstood.

He sank to the ground, knees to his chest, and she squatted next to him. "What?" she repeated.

"I can't."

"Yes, you can. I'll help you."

He looked away, and she waited. "Abayomi," he said after a moment, "says my wife, my wife—"

She caught a glimpse of something desperate in his face. "Matani, if you've had some fight, it doesn't matter now. When you're sick, you need—"

"Doesn't want me," Matani interrupted.

"—to get home, get rest, talk about it later—"

"Abayomi told me."

She didn't understand. "Is this about the books?"

"While the bookmobile was here, Abayomi and my wife . . ."

She shook her head, still confused, and then it dawned on her. "You mean—?" She felt stupid. And naive. From the outside, life in Mididima had seemed so clean and uncomplicated.

She touched his shoulder. "What did he say, exactly?"

He rubbed his eyes, then looked down. "It's a blur. I can't remember."

"Maybe you misunderstood. You were only gone five minutes. Too short for anything important."

"He said he was sorry," Matani began slowly, "and that he owed my father so much but that he'd always loved Jwahir and they'd been together during the bookmobile visits and she wanted to become mother to his two . . ." He broke off, looking ill again.

She hugged him awkwardly, patting him. "It doesn't

sound right," she said helplessly. "Maybe it's just a *thing* . . . temporary." God, she sounded lame. But what should she say? She didn't have magic tricks for this.

Matani stood and walked unsteadily a little farther away from the thornbush fence, and she followed. She took his arm at the elbow to support him. She didn't know if he would shake her off, but instead he leaned into her, seemingly unaware.

"I knew it," he said, and though he spoke in English, it was as if he spoke to himself. "Somewhere far inside, I knew it. That's why he didn't have to say much."

Fi felt a surge of anger. "Come. Stay at Kanika's," she said, though she knew he couldn't stay in that hut with three women.

He shook his head. He drew himself up. She could see what effort it took. "Let me walk you back," he said.

She took his hand at they walked. His palm was callused. His fingers were surprisingly long. She wondered what he would do now, tonight, but didn't want to ask. Once they'd reached the edge of gathered huts, she pulled him to a stop, struck by a sudden intuition. "Don't leave Mididima," she said.

Of course he wouldn't leave, she thought as soon as she said it. How could he leave, by foot? And where would he go?

But he didn't dismiss her comment. He stood, hands at his sides. He didn't answer at all.

"Don't leave," she repeated. And she reached up to kiss his cheek, inhaling the scent of him. It was a chaste peck but still totally improper, as she intended—as if her indiscretion could prevent him from deserting his village.

From deserting her.

The confidence she'd been feeling in Mididima, she realized, stemmed from Matani. He'd made it easy. So now she was going to be presumptuous. She was going to make a plea. "Go where you need to tonight," she said. "But be here tomorrow."

Part Five

Drought smites mosquito populations—but only for a season. Then, studies show, they return in great force. They are, in fact, unstoppable. Consider that they have two hundred offspring at once, and that they carry diseases that kill someone every twenty seconds. No wonder Aristotle composed a treatise about them, the Greeks wrote them into funereal songs, and the Egyptians cursed them in hieroglyphics.

—Professor Petri Jaaskela, lecture on mosquitoes
University of Helsinki, Finland,
Department of Forest Entomology

The Teacher's Wife

JWAHIR'S SHOULDERS BEGAN TO ROLL, HER FEET TO SLIDE. SHE closed her eyes, extended her arms, tossed back her head, and shook. She twisted and shimmied and flexed her fingers. Her necklaces pounded on her chest. Her earrings leaped at either side of her face as she chanted.

When I was born, I was warned—I will sing all night,
By my mother and my father—I will sing all night,
How the sun beats down—I will sing all night,
I'll survive the day—but I will sing all night,
In the morning I will go home.
Go home . . .

She echoed the men who, not forty broad strides away, were singing these same words within the *kilinge*. She loved the beat of the nighttime drumming, its thrust of life and heat and lust and promise.

At the same time, it infuriated her. It had become the sound of exclusion. She could dance and chant within her home, as she was doing now, or in Leta's home, or with one of the other women. But only there. Most evenings, women of the age to be mothers—even if they hadn't yet had their first child—were barred from the *kilinge*. Men, grandmothers, and children were allowed.

"Why?" she'd asked her father years ago, when she—still a girl—first become aware of the rule that would later apply to her. "Why shouldn't I be allowed to go?"

"Don't worry," he'd said, laughing. "It won't interest you then. The one who turns soil to food and dung to shelter needs sleep at night, not nectar. You'll see."

But it wasn't true. She needed nectar. And she still didn't understand why she and her sisters and cousins should be required to make the harmonies of the daytime—clattering dishes and slashing brush and stacking wood—and forbidden the more intoxicating music of the night.

She remembered the first time her father took her to the *kilinge*. She'd been five, perhaps six. She'd stood by her father's side, balancing on one foot, then the other, mesmerized by the singers' faces. They were people she knew, people she saw all day long, but at night, within the sacred enclosure, they'd turned profound. The men, who often seemed so stony-faced, became at once wise ancients penetrating the dusk and young hunters proudly carting home their first kills.

She quickly forgot, however, the shine in their eyes, the proud swelling of their chests. She forgot their presence entirely as she lost herself to the rhythm that wrapped around her like the dark. She felt the animal heartbeats, knew their animal sorrows. She felt herself joined even with creatures she'd never seen: colorful birds that flew above swollen rain clouds and big-eyed mice that drank from rivers below the earth's surface.

As she stood there, transformed, she began to dance. But

she wasn't aware that she was dancing. No one had ever shown her how to dance; she didn't even know the word. Had she tried to express it, she would have said that she became the music. Her feet, her waist, her legs, her head were all in motion. She would have twirled directly into the middle of the sacred hut, right next to the fire, if her father hadn't grabbed her arm.

"You are part of the circle," he'd said. "Not its center."

"But it's where I belong." Her feet were still stomping, still pulling her inward.

"Jwahir."

His voice allowed no room for argument. So she obeyed him then; she stuck to the edges, because she didn't want to lose the right to come again. What happened within the *kilinge* was nothing less than the truest part of a life; she realized that right away. It gave her a chance to convey what she normally held close. The drums, the chants, the flying bodies within the enclosure all combined to create a coupling of those now alive with those who'd come before. And when she joined in, she became larger than herself. She became part of that which would live forever.

She began to dream, that very evening, of being an old woman, old enough to lead the others in singing and swaying. Old enough so that all her brothers and sisters could hear her chanting and say, "Oh, yes," and, through her words and the beat of the drum, better understand the essence of their own lives.

If she were Matani, she would spend every night within the *kilinge*. The days, then, would leap forward like a jaguar instead of a crawling like a tortoise. But Matani was made of different cloth. Though his walk had a swing and a rhythm that struck her as a prelude to dance, he didn't hear the music calling his name. He always slipped away from the circle to return to her. In the first months of their marriage, his devotion had filled her with pride. She'd wedded an exceptional Mididima man. And then, in a reversal—she'd experienced so many reversals with Matani—she became embarrassed by the ways in which he differed from his neighbors.

Jwahir thought of all this as, alone in their home, she danced. The evening stretched on and Matani didn't return, and in this way she knew that Abayomi had spoken to him. She tried, still dancing, to imagine the conversation, what phrases Abayomi must have used, how Matani might have answered. She swung and jiggled and quaked until her legs trembled and her chest ached and sweat trickled down between her breasts. She heard the drumbeat growing faster, more insistent, and the sound of trilling emerge from the *kilinge* and she imagined a struggle, maybe even a murder. But that vision was fleeting. She knew Matani was too civilized to kill Abayomi for loving his wife. Matani was too much a part of the Distant City. This was, in fact, Jwahir's main complaint. "My main complaint," she chanted aloud as her hair and feet flew in time with the beat. Someday, she decided, she would make a song about Matani and Abayomi. Later, after it all was settled.

Jwahir danced until she was so tired that the pull of the earth taunted her, until she collapsed to her mat, until she could pull a skin over her body and sleep with no thought of the future. She slept hard and dreamless.

A noise outside the door awoke her. She pushed herself up, thinking perhaps it was Abayomi, whom she'd half expected all night; or Matani, who surely wouldn't simply give up. For a second, she didn't know which man she would rather it be.

"Jwa-jwa," a woman's voice called. "You ready?"

It was Leta, who nearly always came for Jwahir in the morning. But could it really be morning already?

Leta peeked her head around the door, her sleeping baby daughter strapped to her chest. "Matani's already busy?" she said. "You are lucky, my friend. None of the other men has risen yet. They were late last night at the *kilinge*."

Jwahir did not meet Leta's gaze as she rose. "We've time for milk?"

Leta studied her friend. "You slept poorly," she said. "Perhaps you have something small and warm within?" She touched Jwahir's belly and smiled.

Jwahir went out to the goats. Her body, which had been so fluid deep into the night, felt stiff now. Leta followed.

Jwahir hesitated in front of a goat. "I remember . . ." she said.

"What?"

"I remember loving Matani like a fire burning."

Leta said nothing, but gently pushed Jwahir aside with her shoulder and took over the job of milking the goat into a cup, her long arms moving gracefully despite the bundle attached to her chest.

"Every drop of blood in my body felt alive," Jwahir said. She squatted heavily. "I used to think I could die watching his face as he spoke. He had passion."

"He still does," Leta said evenly.

Jwahir rubbed sleep from her eyes. "Yes, but mostly about why we have to be educated in this other, trivial way."

"And about having a child, I believe." Leta finished with the milking and gave the cup to Jwahir. "Drink."

Jwahir took a deep swallow. "Even from the beginning, when his talk enchanted me," she said, "I wasn't sure I believed. At first I thought he wanted our people to gain this skill so they could get jobs that earned cash. A practical reason. I thought even my own father might grow to accept that idea."

"Your father!" Leta shook her head. She took the empty cup from Jwahir and drew more milk from a goat.

"But it wasn't for cash," Jwahir went on. "Matani wanted the books for their own sake. He insisted that this Camel Library come, Leta. Insisted. So what results is his own doing." She stared at her friend as if daring a contradiction, and then handed Leta the cup.

"It's not his fault that Scar Boy is as he is," Leta said. "Matani shouldn't be blamed for that."

"I'm not speaking of Taban."

Leta looked into her cup of milk. "Jwahir, I've meant to tell you. I've begun to learn to read."

"Leta, Matani didn't come home last night."

Leta glanced up sharply. "Well, even the great Matani chews too much *khat* one evening," she said after a moment. "Maybe we should go round him up."

"I didn't want him to come home."

Leta rocked the cup with a circular motion, making the milk rotate. "And what," she asked lightly, "has he done to annoy you?"

"Annoy!" Jwahir tossed her shoulders. "It's not such a light thing. I love—" Leta's baby began fussing and Jwahir's voice, which had started out strong, suddenly became quieter. "Someone else," she said, so softly she was sure Leta couldn't have heard over the infant's squall.

Leta rose, bouncing her baby. "She never wakes at this time," she said. "The mood in Mididima is odd today." She whispered to the baby, unintelligible words that Jwahir knew were a blessing from the ancestors.

Within a moment, the baby quieted again. Leta remained standing. "Jwahir," she said, "watch that you don't get tangled in your own nonsense."

Jwahir hated Leta's condescending tone. She wanted to shake her, to hurt her. "You can be so infuriating," she said.

"Me?"

Jwahir paced around the goat, her body suddenly full of excess passion. "You remember when I was pregnant, and I told you I felt something wrong with the babe."

"It was a hard quarrel between us."

"But you finally agreed to help me end it. You brought me the *anchi*." Jwahir remembered swallowing the ground tuber that the women gave cows that had just birthed calves. It helped the animals expel the placenta. She'd heard the women whisper that *anchi* would also end a pregnancy. None had whispered, though, about how much it would hurt—the cramps that doubled her over from one evening to the next afternoon, even after the unborn child inside her had fled.

Leta's face was downcast. "Why bring that up now?"

"I lied," Jwahir said, giving each word its own weight.

"I know." Leta looked unhappier. "I still wish you hadn't hidden your pregnancy from Matani."

"I don't mean to Matani. I lied to you."

"What?"

"I never thought anything was wrong with the baby," Jwahir said. "I just didn't want a baby. *Don't* want one."

"To me?" Leta turned abruptly and walked once around Jwahir's hut, eyes lowered, stroking her infant's head. When she returned, she stopped in front of Jwahir. She sighed, a heavy sound intended to show that she'd worked hard to regain her patience, and then she spoke. "Everyone fears motherhood," she said, her voice tight but resigned. "It's not so scary once it happens. In fact, your life feels—"

"Fear?" Jwahir snorted. "I'm not afraid. I don't want my breasts to lose their stuffing and grow flat, Leta. I don't want my face to wrinkle from worry. I don't want your intimacy with exhaustion."

Now that she had Leta's attention, now she would speak her full truth. She stomped her foot, an involuntary gesture that she immediately regretted because of its childishness. "I love Abayomi," she said loudly, relieved to have said it.

Leta's mouth fell open, and Jwahir was briefly gratified to see that her news brought surprise. Then Leta shook her head scornfully. "Abayomi? He's an old man."

"Your husband is only ten years younger."

"Abayomi is of another age group," Leta said. "He makes drums that talk, but he doesn't know how to talk himself. He will soon bore you. Why would you want him instead of Matani?"

"He talks to *me*."

"When have you even—?"

"When the Camel Bookmobile is here."

Leta took a step toward Jwahir, reached out a hand as though to shake her by the shoulder, and then let it drop to her side. "Do you really want to shame Matani in this way? Do you want to risk the penalty you will face for shaming Matani?" She shook her head. "I hope for your sake that whatever you have done can be reversed."

The two women stared at one another a moment. "We are the last of this, you know," Jwahir said. "Soon women will know it is not family that is sacred, but their own lives."

Leta made a low, scornful sound. "That which eats you up is in your own clothing, Jwahir. It's always been that way with you."

"No. I've grown up since I married Matani. Abayomi and I understand each other."

Leta laughed. "I can imagine the language you and Abayomi speak. The talk of honeyed rain."

Jwahir covered her ears. "I've been loyal to you forever. Why can't you do the same now?"

Leta pulled Jwahir's hands from her ears. "You favor tradition when it suits you to speak against the library, and oppose tradition when you think you want some other man."

"They are two different things."

"You've the heart of a chanter who loves one song at sunup and another at sundown," Leta said. "Don't you see that both are part of the same day?"

"No," Jwahir said. But her voice sounded flat, even to

her own ears. She was suddenly tired. So this is what she would face, just a taste of what would rain down on her. She turned away from Leta, putting the last of her energy into her voice. "I'm done with this discussion," she said. "The goats wait. Let's go."

Those, she vowed, would be the last words she would ever speak to her childhood friend.

The Girl

K ANIKA WOKE IN A FOG. THE SKY WAS CLOUDLESS, THE COLOR of ash, and her step felt less solid than it should, as if she might at any moment stumble. As if somehow during the night, she'd lost track of herself. *Kanika who?* That feeling stuck tight as she prepared a bowl of boiled maize and handed it to Miss Sweeney. It stayed as she felt Miss Sweeney's hand at her back, and even as Miss Sweeney began to speak, so it wasn't until a request had been made and repeated, until Miss Sweeney lingered, waiting for a reply, that Kanika became alert enough to try to remember what had just been said.

"But now? You don't want to wait for Matani?"

Miss Sweeney looked into her bowl with an indecipherable intensity. "I . . . " She hesitated before finishing. "I think he's busy this morning."

"Oh, no, Miss Sweeney. He'd want to go with you." Kanika stopped, knowing the implication was that she did not. "I'll find him," she said after a moment, and turned eagerly to search for Matani, so that she wouldn't need to visit Scar Boy's home today.

"Wait, Kanika."

There was a curious urgency in Miss Sweeney's voice that caused Kanika to stop. For the first time, it occurred to her that perhaps Neema was right. Maybe there were cultural differences that were not translatable, that were in fact irresolvable. Maybe she shouldn't go to the Distant City after all—the strength of that unexpected thought surprised her.

"He was—he was ill last night," Miss Sweeney said. "Perhaps he sleeps in today. So I'd rather—won't you take me?"

Kanika looked at the cooking fire and imagined pieces of herself drifting away with the smoke. What could she say except yes?

"You'll finish eating first?" she asked. Miss Sweeney nodded, leaving Kanika relieved to have even a brief respite.

Kanika went back inside, ran her fingers over the hair braided close to her scalp, and straightened the necklaces that rested on her collarbone. She picked up Miss Sweeney's gift, the mirror, and studied her eyes—one, then the other. She had never examined herself like this before. Instead of looking to see what she would find in herself, she was trying to catch a glimpse of what someone else would see.

She heard her grandmother behind her. "I'm glad you go with Miss Sweeney," Neema said. "A fly with no one to advise it follows the corpse into the grave. But you'll be able to talk with Scar Boy. You'll get the books from the boy."

The unnatural shine in her grandmother's stare surprised her. "He's not a boy anymore," Kanika said lightly.

"Truer than you know. And the right word from you will be sharper than a razor." Neema pushed Kanika out the door. "Go," she said. "Swallow nothing from him."

When Kanika and Miss Sweeney got to Scar Boy's home, no one greeted them at the door. That meant that Badru was not home. Scar Boy was alone. Kanika felt instantly more relaxed. "Ayayaalaa," she sang out playfully as they entered, letting her voice roll over the sounds as if she were chanting within the sacred enclosure.

Scar Boy did not look lighthearted. He didn't even greet them. He sat on his mat, eyes downcast, hands limp in his lap. He must have heard them coming and guessed their purpose. How could he not? Kanika had warned him over and again that he had to turn in the books. She looked around, imagining for a second that the books would be sitting somewhere, one stacked atop the other, waiting. What were they again, these books Scar Boy was so reluctant to relinquish? One about other peoples' religions, she thought, though she couldn't recall for sure. At any rate, there was no sign of them.

"We're here, Taban," she said unnecessarily, and though she was irritated, she felt sorry for him too, because he'd let himself be cornered, he couldn't stop playing this game even when the moment had become serious, when a foreign woman had come all the way to Mididima and the elders had made it clear to Abayomi—and Abayomi had surely made it clear to his son—that the books had to be returned.

When Scar Boy finally looked up, though, the last of her sympathy evaporated. His gaze was remote and cold and held not shame, but an accusation. One she couldn't interpret, except to understand that it was aimed at her—maybe because she was the one, in the end, to bring the white woman.

"It would have been Matani," Kanika said, "but we couldn't find him. Miss Sweeney can't wait any longer. She asked me to come and translate her request, so she can go back and this can finish." Scar Boy continued to stare at her, his glance heavy with a meaning she did not understand. "This is not my fault. I warned you over and over." He didn't move. "Please," she said. "Tomorrow you may again be as talkative as a grain of sand. Today, it's time to speak. Tell her where the books are, and then I'll take her away."

Scar Boy cleared his throat. "My brother," he said slowly, "is handsome. Isn't he?"

Kanika's heart thrust into her throat. Her fingers began dancing nervously on the beads around her neck. "The books. Where are they?"

He touched the outside corner of his scarred eye. "My brother Badru," he said.

Why was he doing this? Maybe he had a reason. Had he seen something in her that she was refusing to see in herself? Maybe they could talk about it, alone together at the edge of the settlement, but not here, not now. Now he was violating everything between them by throwing out these words in front of a stranger—even one who didn't understand their language.

"You're a man," she said. "You're almost a man. You're not a child."

He rotated his left shoulder. "Do you . . . " He broke off, settled his shoulders, and lengthened his neck. "You like him?"

"Why are you saying this?" Kanika cried. "What's happened to you, Scar Boy?"

A raw look came over his face. He stared for a long hot beat, and she stared back, just as angry. "What did you call me?" he asked.

It wasn't until then that she realized what she'd said. Her eyes widened and she took in a quick breath of air but she didn't answer.

"You've been the one," he said, each word measured, "the only one I've counted on never to call me that. I believed that you wouldn't call me that even in your mind. I believed that in your thoughts, you had other words for me."

"It's today," she said. "I've been——"

But he wasn't listening. He turned toward Miss Sweeney, who still lingered by the door. Kanika had practically forgotten her. "I will speak with her alone," he said, lifting his chin.

"You can't. You need me for that. You share no language," Kanika said. She said it softly, as a mother might speak to a child she has punished too severely. *OK now. Let's go on.*

Scar Boy gestured to Miss Sweeney, urging her to come closer, to sit. "Leave us," he said.

"This is foolish." But Kanika knew he would not bend. Scar Boy had a powerful determination. She'd always known that about him.

Miss Sweeney, sitting now, looked at Kanika with a face full of questions. But Kanika couldn't think of what words to use to explain in English—in any language, it occurred to her—so she said nothing. She raised her shoulders, let them fall, and left.

Scar Boy

THE MINUTE KANIKA WAS GONE, TABAN COULDN'T HELP wondering at what he'd done. He, who had always avoided people, had insisted now on being alone with someone—a woman, and a stranger—who spoke a language he could not begin to understand. He stared at this foreigner without knowing what to do. He stared until the moment grew unbearably long, and then he stared more.

At last she reached into a bag that she'd worn in on her back, and she pulled out a book, and she held it up as if to show it to him. The cover was a wonderful color—red, but not a shade he knew, not rich as the earth could be, or raw like a cow's severed flesh. It was a deep red, full of promises and unexpectedly shiny. He wondered if he could find a way to re-create that color. He could have uses for it.

And she was talking in a voice he didn't mind. He could almost visualize it, dense and textured and a little hoarse. Of course, it lacked the light music of his Kanika's voice— but here he corrected himself quickly, not *his* Kanika. And he was about to begin thinking of that, and of the pit in his chest that was flooded with his own bitterness, when she surprised him, this foreign woman, by opening the book and extending it toward him, talking all the while.

She'd opened it to a page that showed a sketch of a human-like figure clasping its chest. In pain, or in passion—he was left to wonder. It was a simple drawing, but like food for the starving. He wanted to stare at it, to study each line, see how it had been done.

But, too quickly, she pulled the book away again and opened to a page and began to read, her own hand at her neck. And as he watched her, following the movement of her voice, he began to understand that books meant to her what his drawings did to him. They were (he struggled to put it into words in his mind) an escape—no, more—a place to hold that mystifying rush of human emotions, from his gratitude at being alive to his frustration at the hardship of life—no, more—an expression of the need to separate from his own narrowness and join with the Hundred-Legged One, the rays of the sun.

And so he reached behind him and pushed aside a straw mat. He decided, and in a single second. He didn't have the words to explain to this woman that it was wrong, what they'd done. How uncivilized it was to bring an unsolicited gift from their world and then dictate how it must or must not be used.

Lacking those words, he would instead reveal what he'd earlier intended to show only to Kanika. The pages and pages of precise and vivid images that had flowed from his center, through his limbs, out his fingertips and that had allowed him—a mutilated, solitary island of a boy—to speak of his dreams.

He'd show her what had become of the Camel Bookmobile's overdue books.

The Teacher

MATANI WOKE TO THE SOUND OF BOYS LAUGHING. NOW HE would never have a boy; that was his first thought. Not to cradle, not to guide, not to set on his father's path of bringing the modern world, little by little, to Mididima. His ambitions had not been so grand, after all. But now it would end as badly for him as it had for the pearl diver in the book Miss Sweeney gave him. Without a son, he would be shamed before his people. Even more: he would never be remembered as a son remembers, never a particular man's sacred ancestor. And so he would die more thoroughly than men with sons. He would pass more quickly into the void of nothingness.

But before that recognition could sicken him again, he had a second one. He shouldn't be hearing boys laughing. It wasn't midday yet—he could tell by the angle at which the sun shone through the gaps in the walls that enclosed him. Those boys should be in school. They weren't, of course, because he was here. Lying within the *kilinge* in a heap, his tongue hairy and his head swollen.

He'd been here the previous night when the men began to gather, their voices surprised as they greeted him. The chanting started, and over the noise of the drums, someone—he couldn't recall who right now—passed him leaves to chew. Although he generally had little use for *khat*, he took them. That first taste was so bitter he almost spit it out. He shifted the wad to one side of his mouth and put a cup to the other, drinking milk that has slept. Softening the bitterness. Slowly, he stopped noticing the flavor. The *khat* distracted him, for a while.

Now he untwisted his tangled body. He rubbed his cheeks where the skin felt rough and dirty and massaged his scalp with both hands as if to return circulation to his brain. And he remembered Miss Sweeney: her cool hand as she'd held his forehead, her serious eyes as he tried to explain something he didn't yet understand himself. He remembered her lips, definite as they touched his face. It had taken every bit of his willpower not to open his arms and fall into hers.

But she came from such an unimaginable place. Who knew if her sympathy was only an act of kindness expected in her country? He didn't want to guess about anything anymore. He was beginning to understand the fragility of the heart.

The worst that had ever happened to him, before this, was his father's death. It had come a week before his wedding to Jwahir, and he'd barely allowed himself to feel the punch to the chest, and the hollowness that followed. He told himself the timing was meant to make him and Jwahir love each other more. They'd share her father, she'd said; they'd be husband and wife and brother and sister at once. And he'd believed. How he wished he had that time back, to mourn the way he should have mourned, instead of rushing on with his life.

He shook his hands as though to free himself from

thinking of both Jwahir and Miss Sweeney in unexpected ways, ways that seemed all wrong. Miss Sweeney had come to get the books, only that, and enough ineffectual days had passed. She'd probably heard that he was sleeping it off in the *kilinge* when he should have been up and taking her to Scar Boy. He'd have to steel himself to do that, even if it meant looking past Abayomi.

And what had Jwahir heard? He needed to go to her, but he didn't want to go sad. He didn't want to go while he still might cry.

He pulled himself from the sacred enclosure and splashed water on his face. The two laughing boys were Nadif and his younger cousin.

"Boys!" He coughed, trying to clear the hoarseness from his throat.

They were crouched on the ground, playing a game with stones. Nadif lifted his head.

"Round everyone up. We'll have school, even if a little late."

"We had school," Nadif said.

"In your dreams, perhaps, but not this morning."

"No, we did. With Kanika and Miss Sweeney."

"With—" Matani looked away from the boys, toward the houses huddled beyond them. "What did you do?"

"Miss Sweeney taught us some of her magic," Nadif's cousin said.

"Not only that," said Nadif. "We worked on reading, and then we taught Miss Sweeney."

"Taught Miss Sweeney?" Matani said. "Boys, Mididima is too small for fibbing."

"It's true. We taught her how to say, 'The leaves in the tree have driven the monkeys crazy,'" Nadif's cousin said.

Matani narrowed his eyes at the boys. "Where is she?"

"She walked that way, Teacher," Nadif said, pointing the direction.

"Enough of your game for now," he said. "Gather the others. Yes, I know you've read. But we have more to do."

He walked to where the crops grew, and then to the area where Miss Sweeney had seen the monkeys, but it wasn't until he reached the first watering hole that he found her. He was glad to see she was alone, though girls and goats were within shouting distance.

"*Jambo*," he called. He felt undeniably better just seeing her, and he could hear it in his voice.

She turned to him with her serious smile and waited for him to reach her. "I wanted to see how much water you have," she said.

"When we see the bottom, we get worried," Matani said. "Can you see it yet?"

She shook her head.

"Then no need to worry." He reached spontaneously for her shoulder and squeezed it.

"I'm glad to see you," she said.

He wished he knew how to understand comments like this. He touched his cheek where, last night, she had kissed him. Then he brushed her cheek with the back of one hand. "You've gotten burned while you've been here."

"I'm fine," she said.

"You are," he said softly. And then he added: "You taught

the children this morning. I'm sorry. I spent too long with the stars last night."

"I loved it. They're so bright." She reached down and dipped her fingers into the water. "How did your evening pass?"

He didn't want to tell her about the blur of his evening. He recalled now that at one point he rose and began to chant. "My love," he'd sung, and the men had echoed him. "My love."

"Is a black-fronted purple-throated mosquito-eater," he'd sung, and they'd echoed.

"It's fallen from the sky," he'd continued. "And landed at my feet."

One or two, he was sure, had been laughing. And he couldn't blame them. He would have laughed, too, if he weren't in his own skin, his own wife about to be taken, not by death, which would be less shameful, but by her lack of love.

Someone had grabbed him by the arm—though he couldn't clearly recall who it had been. "This is what your books would take from us," the man had said. "Our sacred chants. Our traditions."

Another man added: "See the bad spirits that enter Mididima because the white woman is here, where she doesn't belong? She must go."

That angered him, he remembered. He'd said something about Miss Sweeney being good and pure, and then there had been some snickering and Jwahir's father had stepped between him and the others and someone had called, "If you think that world is so much better, then go. Go, with your books and your white woman."

Now Miss Sweeney stood quietly waiting, her hands shoved into her jeans pockets.

"Thank you," he said, "for helping me last night. I'm sorry about it."

"I'm sorry about—" She broke off.

He squatted, and she knelt too, and he looked into the water at their reflections, light and dark, and beyond them a pale sky. He thought about telling her that, in some ways, he'd never been as intimate or as open with a woman as he'd already been with her.

"You know what Abayomi told me?" he said instead. "That his heart leaps up to the sky with Jwahir, and that hers does the same with him." It hurt to say aloud, but it was also like washing out a wound. "He said because he honored my father, he would offer himself to me. He stretched himself on the ground and handed me a gun that he had taken from the *kilinge*."

Miss Sweeney lifted her eyebrows. "You can't be serious?"

He laughed at her tone and the way she put it. Seen through her eyes, it did seem crazy: Abayomi on the ground, Matani holding the gun in his drooping left hand, the barrel pointed at his own feet.

"Thank you," he said. "I'm glad you're here." And he wished, for a moment, that he could touch Miss Sweeney, and talk to her whenever he wanted to about whatever he felt like, and he wondered what it would be like to be married to someone like her. But there were no women like her in his village. Maybe no women anywhere like her, who could so quickly become an indelible part of a foreign place.

Then he touched his head, because he remembered why
Miss Sweeney actually was here. "The children are waiting
for me now," he said. "But afterward, I haven't forgotten, we
will go to Scar Boy."

"I've already been."

"You have?" He looked away from her, because he was
ashamed that he'd let her down, and then he looked directly at her because he wanted to know. "You got them?"

Some girls with goats were coming closer. Miss Sweeney stood and waved at them. "It's complicated. Could we
talk tonight, after dinner?"

So Scar Boy was still holding out. Sitting in a corner
of his hut, dizzy from his own moment of power, making
Miss Sweeney wait, threatening the library's future. A rush
of anger surged through Matani's arms, up his neck, and into
his cheeks. "May the sand clog his windpipe," he muttered.

"Don't worry. It'll be all right."

Matani knew the anger that his heart spilled on Scar
Boy came from other places too, but he didn't care to sort
it out right now. "Yes," he said. "It will."

"So we'll talk tonight?"

This was enough. Matani had let his father's love for
Scar Boy protect him too long.

"Matani?"

"Yes, yes, tonight," he said. Now he'd go directly to
Jwahir's father, and never mind the consequences. He
wanted the whole of Mididima to know what Abayomi's
son was doing, how he'd refused to give back the books.
"Tonight."

The Grandmother

NEEMA DID NOT SEE HER GRANDDAUGHTER UNTIL WELL after the morning's work. She'd given herself the job of making sure two small ones spent the afternoon at the crops, scaring birds away. Already, some of their precious plants had been pecked because of inattention, and they all knew it was not a year to lose even a mouthful of food.

But small ones were not easy to find. Mididima's children had vanished like Egyptians gulped into the Red Sea. The whole settlement, in fact, felt on the edge of disarray, as though a wind were about to gust, the kind that tears threads loose from fabric and sends flatbread flying. No one had followed the rules. The goats had been taken out late, and what happened with school? Women were scattered in the distance, their bright clothes like markers, as though none had maize to cook or mats to weave. Men's voices seeped from the *kilinge*, normally left deserted during the day. She knew they had lit the fire and would keep it burning to appeal to the Hundred-Legged One to bring rain, and that the oldest among them had begun to gather themselves for a trek to the mountains to beg for water to fall from the sky.

But the disquiet had another cause, too; she whispered a name to herself, and hoped Kanika had resolved it.

She finally found two girls playing a game with sticks, and told them to come, and bring their library books. "Don't spend the whole time chattering," she said. "One can practice reading while the other watches for birds."

Then she began circling the settlement, searching with growing urgency for Kanika. No one seemed to know where her granddaughter was; and this only heightened her own sense of bubbling uneasiness.

Kanika must have reclaimed the overdue books, Neema told herself. Not only was Kanika determined and persuasive, but Scar Boy would listen to her. Even if no one else noticed, Neema had seen what his face revealed, those few times he'd emerged into daylight to visit the Camel Bookmobile. She saw what he felt for her granddaughter.

At last she spotted Kanika at a distance, laughing with Wakonyo and Thegoya. That was unusual—Kanika generally had little to do with those girls. They weren't being raised as her granddaughter was. Wakonyo had even been circumcised.

"Kanika," she called. Kanika turned, waved, and bent her head close to the girls, talking one more minute before loping toward Neema.

"Peace on you, *Nyanya*," Kanika said cheerfully.

So then, all was well. Neema stroked her granddaughter's cheek. "You and Miss Sweeney got the books."

Kanika squatted and poured dried millet from a bowl onto a cloth.

"You should let everyone know that the lion's dry breath is no longer on our necks," Neema said.

Kanika didn't answer, didn't even look at Neema.

"Was Scar Boy sorry? Did he say why he kept them?"

Kanika used both hands to sift through the millet, removing pebbles as though it were a job that demanded full focus.

"Kanika?"

"Yes?"

"Miss Sweeney has the books?" Neema put her hand to her stomach, feeling it contract now that she'd been forced to turn it into a question. "Doesn't she?"

Kanika didn't reply.

Neema put both hands to her head and sank down on her heels. "What did Scar Boy tell you?"

"Sc—" Kanika broke off. "Taban sent me away," she said. "He and Miss Sweeney talked alone."

"They can't talk alone," Neema said reasonably. "He can't send you away."

Kanika shrugged—where had that shrug come from? Neema didn't think she'd ever seen her granddaughter make that gesture before.

"So *she* got the books," Neema said.

"I didn't talk to Miss Sweeney about that. Matani was gone this morning, and when Miss Sweeney came back, she helped me teach."

"She didn't say anything?"

"She taught us songs—one about a spider, another about our ears hanging down, and tying them in a knot." Kanika looked up at the sky and giggled.

"But she would have told you, if she didn't get the books," Neema said. Kanika lowered her head back into her task. After a moment, Neema added, "Why would Scar Boy send you away?"

Kanika threw aside a handful of pebbles and stood. "*Nyanya*, I will finish this later, with your blessing. I told Wakonyo I would help her gather firewood."

"Wakonyo?" For the first time, Neema wondered if Kanika spoke the truth. She remembered her daughter Dahira slipping away to meet the man who would later become her husband, using some story about fetching water. Neema hadn't doubted Dahira for a moment because she'd always been so obedient. More obedient than Kanika.

But Kanika didn't want these boys. Hadn't she said that, not two nights ago? And Neema wanted Kanika to be out in that larger world; she knew it was right despite the ache she felt in her own chest when she thought of growing nearer to death in the void left by Kanika's absence.

"You and Wakonyo are friends now?"

Kanika shrugged again. "We're getting firewood."

As she strode away, Neema noticed her granddaughter's legs—they had become so long that the span of her steps might already equal Neema's. In another year, Kanika would be the age that Dahira was when she'd married. Time couldn't be restrained. Nothing should be hastened; nothing ever could be slowed.

Neema sat and picked up Kanika's job with the millet. She liked the feel of the warm grains shifting in her palms, and the pebbles, irregular and slightly cooler. Usually she could sort millet with her eyes closed—in fact, that's how she preferred to do it.

Now, though, she couldn't settle her mind. It leaped from one worry to the next. She covered the millet and rose.

A white woman should not be so difficult to find in Mididima; she should stick out like a pile of glowing beach sand. But Neema wandered everywhere unsuccessfully. When she asked about Miss Sweeney, many gave her odd looks that made her uneasy and left her certain that the people of Mididima were running out of patience—but not with Scar Boy, as it should be. With the bookmobile. With Miss Sweeney.

"The white woman should leave," one woman, Chicha, said outright. Neema waved her hand to dismiss the remark, but finally gave up the search and returned home. And there in front of the hut was Miss Sweeney, leaning back on the bag she'd brought, eyes closed.

That wouldn't do. Neema had already stretched her patience farther than it would go, waiting to find out what happened with the books. She picked up a tin bowl and spooned *ugali* into it, allowing the spoon to bang noisily against the metal. When she turned back, Miss Sweeney's eyes were open. "Eat now." She handed Miss Sweeney the bowl. "Food skirted your mouth this morning."

Miss Sweeney took the bowl without speaking and sat up. Neema squatted across from her. She waited for as long as she could. Miss Sweeney still had not taken a bite. But Neema had to speak. "The books," she said.

Miss Sweeney looked into the bowl, then set it on the ground.

"I'll go to him," Neema said, suddenly loud, unable to

contain her frustration. "He is not a handful of water that can't be grasped."

"It won't help."

There were words Neema knew in English, but didn't quite understand as they came from Miss Sweeney's lips. So the camels wouldn't come again? Even with Scar Boy's books returned? No more of the books that had saved her life, that would advance her granddaughter to another, more modern place?

But why?

"Maybe the council of elders can find a way to show Mr. Abasi that we are a people of light and not darkness," Neema said, knowing the elders would not stoop to try to persuade Mr. Abasi of anything.

"Or maybe I can convince him."

To doubt Miss Sweeney would be rude. But Miss Sweeney had already told them that Mr. Abasi had more power than she. Mididima's fate would lie with the librarian from Garissa, and he didn't strike Neema as merciful.

Miss Sweeney lifted her water bottle and held it against the blue sky. She took a long sip before speaking. "Don't worry, Neema," she said.

More words that didn't quite make sense.

Perhaps, at least, Neema could ease the way for her granddaughter before it was too late. "You and Kanika taught today," she began tentatively. "You can see that she will have much to offer in the Distant City."

Miss Sweeney said nothing. Her eyes were closed and she looked pale. She was useless right now.

"Eat," Neema said, gently shaking Miss Sweeney's arm. "Eat while I watch."

Miss Sweeney opened her eyes. Neema waited until Miss Sweeney took a bite. She watched the white woman hold the pasty mixture in her mouth and then swallow it.

"More," said Neema.

Miss Sweeney smiled. "Will you talk while I eat?"

"Of what?"

"Your life." Miss Sweeney stirred her *ugali*. "Kanika's mother was your only child?" she said slowly.

"No. I lost two before that," Neema said. "Both in childbirth. It was a curse that came from sitting on a rock." The rock her cousin sent her to, the one that did not change her enough to avoid circumcision but made it so she had trouble giving birth.

"I'm sorry," Miss Sweeney said.

Neema waved a hand. "It was difficult then, but it's long since I've thought of those two small ones. Dahira, I still miss. It comes to pass that the one who fetches water with thee is more difficult to lose than the ones who are but possibilities," she said.

Miss Sweeney put down the bowl, but Neema lifted it and handed it to her again. She waited until Miss Sweeney took another bite. "My daughter was my mother reborn," she said. "Both more gentle than I. I lost my mother a second time when Dahira was killed."

Miss Sweeney took another bite and put the bowl aside. "What happened exactly?"

Neema looked away for a moment. "I don't speak of it," she said.

"I'm sorry."

"It's not to spare me that I'm silent. It's to spare Kanika."

"Then you may be wrong." Miss Sweeney reached out to touch Neema's hands, as though to soften her words. She looked even wearier. "My mother kept her secrets, too, and I didn't feel it as a gift," she said. "I'd rather have known. It was my history as well as hers."

Neema tipped her head and considered this pale woman before her. "Why should I burden Kanika with a sadness that doesn't belong to her? She'll have enough sadness of her own, finally. She doesn't need mine." Then Neema gestured toward the food. "Eat more."

Miss Sweeney tipped her bowl, showing Neema that it was empty.

Neema rose, stood behind Miss Sweeney, and began to run her fingers through the white woman's brown, curly hair. "I'm going to braid thee," she said. Let one thing be set to order on this day of anarchy.

Miss Sweeney leaned her head back a little. "Talk while you do it? Please?"

Neema gathered the hair from the scalp, feeling its texture. It was a strain to speak English. On the other hand, the stories she'd read of others' lives over these last few months had left her with a greater appreciation for the thread of her own life: a childhood spent at the ocean, then, as a young woman, bewitched by a man traveling from the desert, a man of beautiful skin and gleaming eyes who brought her to live among his tribe and left her too soon a widow. Through her own will, Neema had become the only widow in Mididima to manage a family herd. She'd cared alone for her daughter and then her granddaughter. Now she was setting Kanika on a path that would gain her many stories of her own.

But soon, Neema would be leaving this place. Sudden recognition of that fact shot through her. Without the bookmobile, her time would come near again, she felt sure.

If she didn't tell her stories now, she never would.

"A discord over water rights," she began, speaking slowly. These were more words in English than had been required of her before. "That's why my daughter and her husband were killed at a water pan. Our men vowed revenge. They swelled to the settlement of the other tribe. But once there, they fell weak in the face of judgment. They settled for eight cattle and four goats for my son-in-law, three cows for my daughter. Since I was caring for Kanika, I got all the animals. Not much for a daughter's life."

Neema had never worked with hair the texture of Miss Sweeney's. The strands were fine; the braids slipped out easily. She would use less hair, she decided, and make the braids narrower. She moistened her fingers on her tongue and gathered the wispy curls near Miss Sweeney's right temple.

"I did not agree with what our men did," she said. "Compromise does not bring peace to the heart. A year after Dahira was killed, I fed one of my cows the poisonous root of the *chuchi* plant and then slaughtered it right away, so the poison would hold in the meat."

She paused, remembering how she'd led the cow away from the settlement one early evening; drained a potful of blood from its neck; and then, as the weakened animal lay breathing heavily, sawed beneath its chin. She remembered the immediate rush of relief that came from the act of taking another's life, and how that release taught her something she never forgot.

Miss Sweeney stirred, tipping her head to look up at Neema. "Keep still," Neema said, and waited for Miss Sweeney to settle herself again.

"The men wanted to know why I squandered the cow," she went on, "but I told them what I did was within mine own basket. I went to the well where they killed my daughter, and there I gathered firewood and roasted the meat. The young girls of the tribe that slew Dahira came to fetch water, and, seeing a stranger, they fetched the young men instead."

She'd developed a rhythm now. Her hands were moving across Miss Sweeney's scalp like hips swaying to music, making neat rows where before there'd been a tangle. Miss Sweeney's head was tipped back, her eyes closed.

"The men came with their ugly tones," Neema said. "I spoke in my dead daughter's docile voice. I said, 'I've come to leave meat for a child I lost, and with your permission, I would place the offering by the well so my child could drink while eating.' They were young. By the way I spoke the word 'child,' they thought I meant a little one, and they imagined they would gain more than they would lose to such a small spirit. They laughed at me, and they agreed."

The braids were wrapped around Miss Sweeney's head now. Neema worked on the hair that remained at the back of Miss Sweeney's head.

"I made the meat as delicious-smelling as I could," she said, "and then I left. It took the passing of one full moon before I heard two of them died of poisoning."

Miss Sweeney put her hands on Neema's to stop their movement. "But didn't it just continue then?" she asked. "Didn't they take revenge in return?"

"They couldn't," Neema said, "even if they guessed the source of the poison. They had stolen the meat from a spirit."

Neema began braiding again and after a moment, Miss Sweeney spoke. "But what if the ones who died were not directly responsible for your daughter's death?"

Neema heard the doubt in Miss Sweeney's voice. Clearly Miss Sweeney came from a place where despite—or maybe because of—all its modern magic, men were less resolute.

"Whenever an oath is broken or someone is shamed, the evil spirits are drawn to our people," Neema said firmly. "The penalty against the offender—or whoever stands in for the offender—must be strong. Otherwise, the evil spirits will turn on us."

She stepped back to inspect Miss Sweeney. The white woman's face was laid bare to the day, her hair finally calmed. Though her worried expression was harder to miss now, Neema had nevertheless done a beautiful job. She placed her thumbs at the center of Miss Sweeney's forehead and moved each toward the temple as if to smooth the skin's surface.

"Now thou art my daughter," she said. "Thou art of us. And so do not be troubled. We will watch over each other."

The American

AFTER NEEMA'S *UGALI* AND NEEMA'S WORDS, FI SLEPT HEAVily, with dreams of water. Water for bathing, water running over dirty dinner plates and flushing down toilets and dampening lawns and sloshing in buckets for scrubbing floors. Treated water in swimming pools and galvanized steel tanks, dentists' water picks, water from drinking fountains. Stagnant puddles with mosquitoes darting above them and water in outdoor fountains with coins at the bottom. Water shooting up through artesian wells and cascading down mountainsides. And mostly, water from the sky: big drops like pigeon peas, little drops like millet, windblown rain that falls sideways, and downpours that wash dust off cars and people.

She woke, perhaps an hour later, with a parched throat and a mind full of scraps of poetry: *My bones drank water; water fell through all my doors, you're a better man than I am, Gunga Din.* A dark-skinned water carrier, an ignorant white soldier from afar.

Still partly asleep, the poetry running through her mind, she lifted her water bottle to her chapped lips, parting them to let the liquid fall in. Was it the power of suggestion, or was the air drier than it had been four days ago? She opened the Irish poetry book she'd brought from home and read familiar lines as she drank. She felt drained. She rarely slept during the day. But the conversations with Matani, and then Scar Boy, had worn her down, and besides, time here had turned fluid. She couldn't measure it at all on cloudy afternoons like this one. When the light refused to clearly signal morning or afternoon, the hours merged, and the pattern she'd clung to—now she would eat, then sleep, then rise—became an overgrown trail, impossible to follow, and eventually pointless. She'd been surprised when Kanika had reminded her that tomorrow was the day the camels would return for her.

As she read, she became fully human again. A line of poetry was a perfect moment, a spray of words daring and loud enough to take her somewhere unexpected. Just one line, the right line, could immerse her in something larger, crucial. Wasn't that why she'd come to Africa, too? To be absorbed into something beyond herself, more meaningful.

She picked up Kanika's mirror and was startled by how different she looked with her hair braided back, every strand captured and corralled. Her eyes had always been her best feature, wide and of an indefinable color. But now they seemed deeper. Tomorrow night, back in Garissa, she would take out the braids and wash her hair with ginger shampoo and let it dry in the air, frizzing away from her head. But for tonight she was someone else. Someone exotic and intuitive and full of possibilities.

She heard Neema outside. For the first time since arriving in Mididima, she wasn't eager to be among people.

She wanted to save her talking for Matani. That conversation might be difficult. So she stayed inside, watching a tiny spider move casually up and down the wall, swinging from side to side, legs fluttering, no web in sight. It looked daring as it plunged down on its invisible thread, more certain as it climbed up, but then it would plummet again.

As Fi studied the spider, it occurred to her that this might be the right time for prayers. She might, if she knew how, ask for mercy for Scar Boy, understanding from Matani or for herself, wings on her tongue. But she'd never learned to pray, not in a way that felt real or natural. She did know how to kneel or how to receive Holy Communion. Her mother used to dress up the four children and take them by subway to St. Patrick's Old Cathedral at the corner of Prince and Mott, full of incense for holiday services. From the way her mother gathered her lips as soon as they entered, though, and the way her eyes got smaller and tighter, her children knew these visits were only for show. Something had driven belief straight out of their mother, something she wouldn't discuss, and by the time Fi was about ten, they no longer attended St. Pat's, even for the holidays. So now, instead of prayer, she watched as the spider hung itself over and over on a rope of its own making, purely for the thrill, the grace, the risk.

At last she heard Matani's voice. His anguish of a night ago was imperceptible. In fact, he sounded lighthearted, as if he were telling Neema a joke. Or perhaps a riddle. "Catch a riddle," she'd heard him direct the children when he was about to test them orally. Kanika had translated for her. Another phrase of local slang. When his students did well, he awarded them imaginary cows. That was as much as they knew about grades.

She came out of the hut and he turned to her. "Ready?"

"Yes," she said.

He walked with swinging strides away from Mididima, as if he wanted to be rid of it, and she kept up, acting as if she knew where they were going, though she had no idea and decided not to ask.

They walked for nearly half an hour, barely speaking, sometimes side by side, sometimes with him leading, until they reached the shallow water pan that Neema had mentioned to her, and a hut, and a beautiful green patch—a pocket-size oasis.

"How can you think of drought when this lies so close to you?"

"It's already shrunk from a month ago," Matani said. "It's where the young ones take the goats and cattle, though no more than once a week. You can't tell it now, but Mididima itself used to be greener and wetter than this little spot. A permanent settlement drains the water supply."

He squatted on his heels outside the hut. She sat facing him, cross-legged.

"This is as far as we go, because of the *shifta*," he said. "Except for the young men, who take the cattle away for longer periods."

"It's lovely."

He looked around as if seeing it for the first time. "Yes," he said. "It is." Then he turned to her. "It's also where couples come to be together."

She laughed. "Like a drive-in movie in the bush?"

He shrugged, puzzled. "Here, men and women stay the night. They get to know each other better. For us, it is very accepted."

He was staring at her so directly that she had to look away.

"You haven't asked me," she said, "about Taban."

"But I know," Matani said. "He wouldn't give up the books, not even to you. He will, though. The men have been discussing how to force him. Let's leave it in their hands."

"Matani." Fi put both her palms on the ground, feeling the warmth from the soil move up her arms. "They can't recover the books."

"They can. They'll pressure his father, and then—"

"He *used* the books."

Matani spread his hands. "By this you mean?"

"He tore out their pages."

Matani stood. Anger flared in his face. "We will repair them," he said hopelessly.

Fi rose too. "He's drawn on them."

"Drawn?"

"In *The Iliad and the Odyssey*, there were sketches. Bodies of warriors and women. He traced them. Over and over, Matani. Teaching himself. And on the white spaces in the book of meditations, he also drew pictures."

"Drawings." Matani circled the outdoor fire pit, muttering. "We'll sell a cow. We'll pay the cost—"

"And he had others. I think even before this, he was tearing pages out of books, and we didn't notice. He hid them in a hole in his hut."

Matani put a hand to his forehead.

Fi slowed her words, willing Matani to listen. "He's incredible, Matani. The raw talent. He sees in remarkable ways."

Matani didn't seem to hear. "How did he hide this from us?" he said.

"I'm not angry about—"

"And why didn't his father—?"

"He needs to go to the city," Fi said. "Listen to me. I want to help him. He should be given lessons. But in a way that won't interfere with his basic impulse. His work should be developed."

"Work?" Matani looked at her, incredulous. "You want to reward him?"

"The rule about missing books is too strict, don't you think?"

Matani shook his head. "Even if I were to agree, the council would refuse. They will say Mididima can't spare a young man to go away and draw pictures."

"What does he do now, that he can't be spared?" Fi said. "I haven't seen him outside his home yet."

"There's another objection. How would he survive in a city?"

"If Kanika went with him . . . "

"Kanika?"

"She wants to become a teacher."

"You amaze me," Matani said. "Again."

She grinned at him. "It would only be for a while," she said. "In two years, they'd be back. And then, Kanika would be trained."

"How would this be paid for?"

"Let me worry about that," Fi said. "I have an idea or two."

He looked at her and shook his head. "You've been planning," he said. "You would take two from us?"

"I'd rather make it three." Her own words, uttered unthinkingly and insistently, surprised her. But when he looked into her face, she refused to take them back.

"You mean me?" he asked in a tone so vulnerable that it touched her.

After all, it occurred to her, wouldn't it be good for him to leave now? Without a wife, what held him here? "You could escort them, Matani, help them get settled," she said. "And maybe stay a while. Further your own education."

Matani gave a rueful smile. "The education from out there has not helped me much here," he said.

"You could travel. New places, foods, people."

"Miss Sweeney—"

"Fi," she corrected.

"Fi." At last, he called her by her first name. "I can't answer you," he said, "about Kanika and Scar Boy. If you are serious, others will have to decide. But I wouldn't—"

She waved to stop him. "Let's just see." She put her hands on her hips. "And now, about the bookmobile."

"Let's not talk of it," he said quickly.

"The books were not lost through carelessness," she said. "I'll bring some drawing paper next time. Everything will be fine."

He shook his head. "It is too late for fine. But it's not what I want to speak of now—not Scar Boy or the books or the thirsty air or— "

Fi put one finger to his lips to silence him. "OK, you're right," she said. "No more. Not now."

When she took her hand away, he touched his own lips with his long, slender fingers and remained silent for a moment. "Tomorrow afternoon," he said at last, and he looked at the ground and back at her. "So soon."

She was conscious of the charcoal color of his eyes, and the night air on her neck. "Matani," she said, "I want to thank you for everything. Last night, when I asked you to stay, I realized—" She hesitated.

"I wish—" he said. Then he bent over and straightened the rocks that circled the fire pit, and walked to the door of the hut. She followed.

"Is that how you've gotten to know women?" she asked, gesturing toward the hut.

He shook his head. "I've never spent a night here."

"Why not?"

"By the time I got back from the city, I was already older than most of the unmarried men, so I went directly to a wedding."

She peeked into the hut. It held a large grass mat covered with three or four hides.

"Couples lie together until morning," Matani said at her side. "They have time to talk."

"Only talk?" She was teasing him and she thought he might squirm, but he didn't.

"Not only talk," he agreed. "But the woman keeps her skirt tied between her legs, so there will not be an unexpected child. And after that, they are—how should I say it?—not ordinary friends."

"No, I'd imagine not." She laughed.

"Like you and me," he said, speaking slowly, studying her. "It is the way of our people," he added after a moment. "Everything is so uncertain and fleeting for us. Will it rain next week? Will we have food next month? When we are here, we forget all that. We say we are drinking honeyed rain."

She caught her breath. "Honeyed rain," she said. "A perfect poetic phrase."

His eyes widened as he looked at her. "Fi . . . " he said. He broke off. He brushed his fingers against hers, and then gestured toward the hut's door.

It was a confusing moment. Fi understood what he was asking, even without the words. But she wondered if he was asking because she seemed exotic, or because his wife had been unfaithful, or because he felt something for Fi. She wondered if it mattered. She tried to think clearly, but it was difficult, and it occurred to her that such decisions are rarely made with a clear head.

Then her mind flashed on an image of him grinning in welcome when she arrived at Mididima.

And another of him learning to do a cartwheel.

And another of him listening to her talk about the monkeys.

And it seemed, for one impossible moment, that she'd come to Mididima not only to bring books and encourage literacy, but for this, to learn about drinking honeyed rain from this African man in the bush, and to take that learning away with her.

Hovering at the door of the hut, she answered him with one step forward.

Part Six

Beware the mosquitoes; they swarm at finales. They are present at deaths, when blood is free-flowing. They flourish at the finish of summer. They will remain, the final taunting life form hovering above the final water puddle, after the last misguided human is gone and the world has ended.

—Black preacher from Heaven's End cult
Corner of Bourbon and Conti,
New Orleans, June 2003

The Girl

"GERTRUDE BELL WAS A GREAT WOMAN." KANIKA SPIT onto her hand and wiped it beneath her arm before turning the page. "She went everywhere and met everyone. She climbed mountains, visited ruins, gave advice to leaders. She was a *spy*." Kanika gave special emphasis to the last word, although she had only the vaguest idea what it meant. "There are many ways for a woman to be powerful," she said, tapping one finger on the page. That had been a discovery. Before, she'd thought Neema's was the only method.

Wakonyo, sitting across from Kanika, shifted impatiently. "You read so much, Kanika," she said. After a moment she added: "But maybe that is good. It takes your attention away from here. It has not felt right here since the white woman arrived."

Kanika shook her head. Miss Sweeney was not causing the tension in the air. Scar Boy was the problem—Scar Boy disrupting schedules, souring everyone's mood, dominating grim talks among the elders. Kanika thought everyone in Mididima knew that by now. But she didn't want to discuss it with Wakonyo. She sighed. "You should read this book," she said. "A paragraph or two at a time."

Wakonyo played with one of the braids at the back of her head. "All I want to learn to read are the signs in the Distant City."

Kanika looked at her sharply. "You want to go there?"

"I doubt it, but I want to be able to read the signs." Wakonyo laughed. After a moment, she added, "They say the camels will not come anymore, anyway."

Wakonyo was fine for some conversations, and she knew how to swing her hips and extend her arms when she walked. She had a flair that Kanika lacked. Sometimes she wore her necklaces long in the back, a style that she said she'd invented and that the boys found alluring.

Some discussions, though, just weren't worth it. Kanika stuck her face more deeply into her book. Miss Sweeney was like Gertrude Bell, a little at least. She would find a way to continue the Camel Bookmobile. And next time, Kanika had already decided, she would borrow a book about the ocean, any ocean as long as it was like the one Neema had grown up next to, one that was large enough to encompass an entire world. She wanted to read about the creatures that stuck to rocks or faded into seaweed, revealing themselves only when a swimmer got too near. She wanted to read about the currents that brought things close and then took them away again.

Wakonyo began chatting nonsense rhymes to the goats, so Kanika had to concentrate hard on the words in the book. By the time she realized someone was speaking her name, she knew it had been said more than once. She looked over her shoulder.

"What are you doing?" said Badru.

Wakonyo giggled, winked, and moved farther away.

Kanika stood up hurriedly. Why was he here, outside his home? She'd thought that if she didn't go to Scar Boy's hut, she wouldn't see Badru.

But that had been a silly idea. Scar Boy was the one who stayed indoors.

He was smiling, and that startled her. She wasn't sure she'd ever seen him smile. His teeth were white and small. She was determined to speak before he did, to hide her confusion. "The men are angry with your brother," she said.

"I heard."

"With all of you."

He nodded.

"I don't know what they'll do." Her voice, to her ears, sounded too concerned. She took a step backwards. "Probably not much, in the end," she added with exaggerated indifference. "That's what Neema says." She didn't mention that Neema disapproved of leniency toward Scar Boy, that Neema favored a stern punishment and "repentance."

Kanika tucked her book under her arm in a gesture of finality. She turned slightly, but didn't walk away. Badru looked at his feet, giving her a second to study him. His skin reflected the light, making its darkness richer and deeper. It was the same color as the ocean's depth, Kanika thought.

"How's your brother?" she asked, mainly because nothing else came to mind.

"You've not been to see him," Badru said.

Kanika felt her cheeks grow hot. She knew Scar Boy

had been drawing pictures of her. Miss Sweeney told her. Kanika wondered if Badru knew, if he'd seen the sketches.

"Is that why you came?" she asked. "To tell me to go see him?"

"No," he said, his tone surprised, but she'd already begun walking then, not away from Mididima, not toward it, but parallel to the cluster of homes and people, the core of what she knew. She moved quickly. Badru caught up with her in two long steps. He matched his pace to hers.

"I heard from Wakonyo that you might go away."

"I might," she said, wondering when Wakonyo had spoken of this to Badru.

"What would you do?"

"Learn to teach."

"You already know how to do that." She looked quickly to see if he teased her. "Will you teach me to read?" he asked.

"Me?"

"I can't learn from Matani."

She walked a few more steps, conscious of the sensation of mosquitoes buzzing in her stomach, exactly what she felt before the bookmobile came. "If you want," she said.

"Would you come back?" he said. "Like Matani did?"

She stopped and faced him. "It's too early for these questions. I'm not even sure I'll go yet."

He smiled. "Kanika," he said after a moment, "why don't you ever come to the dances? Whoever walks can dance; whoever talks can sing. You know about the dances, don't you?"

Of course she knew. Some evenings she'd even imagined what it would be like to slip outside the thornbushes that wrapped around Mididima and join his peers as they pounded on drums borrowed from the *kilinge* and sang their own songs, different from the grown-up songs, and danced as long as the moon floated across the sky. Why hadn't she ever gone? Because Neema didn't want her to be ordinary? Unfair. She hadn't wanted that, either.

"They're fun," he said. "Wakonyo goes."

She knew they danced at the farthest water pan, where the children sometimes took the goats. There was a fire pit, and a hut. She thought about Badru there. The adults were a little afraid of him, because he was Scar Boy's brother, and because he carried a kind of fierceness about him. But he was popular among the young. He was probably one who led the chants, in fact. She imagined the flames playing off Badru's face, and Wakonyo watching him sing, Wakonyo swaying with her necklaces down her back. It gave her a strange feeling, as if something inside her were unraveling, or as if she'd thought she had finished a chore and had then discovered it undone.

"I have to go," she said. "Miss Sweeney is leaving today. I've made a goats' hair bracelet to give her and the children are—" She broke off, then started again. "I have to go." She turned away.

"I'll come to you tomorrow," he called.

That stopped her. "What for?" she asked.

He pointed at the book still clamped beneath her arm. "To begin to learn to read."

The Teacher

THE SURPRISE OF IT, THE UNEXPECTEDNESS, THE SHOCK, actually, like a rare cold morning. He hadn't planned on any of it.

And the magic, each framed by the other: dark on light on dark. The sweetness that freed something that he'd been holding tight for weeks, months, maybe longer. For a moment, he was afraid he might weep.

She saw it, and touched the bone beneath his right eye. *What?*

He shook his head without answering.

But she wouldn't let him stay silent. Nothing, in fact, could have prepared him for how she made him speak. With Jwahir, all had been restrained, reined in, even his breathing; he hadn't known any other way. With Miss Sweeney, the words came spilling out even as their bodies neared and merged, making everything that happened between them exotic, slower, more intense. The words took on a dreamlike quality, blending and then leaking through the walls of the hut. He imagined those words rolling over in the dust, traveling in every direction until they met again in her country, on the other side of the world.

When you touch me there . . . She sucked in her breath, then stopped and traced his eyebrows with a finger.

He stroked her neck, diving below the collarbone. *And there.* She kissed his fingers. *Why do you like to teach?*

He stared at her, making himself focus for a heartbeat. "The speed of their minds." His own mind was slowing.

She met his rib cage. *Your mouth, your tongue.* She arched away, then stretched forward to murmur in his ear. *What made your father brave enough to leave here?*

"His grandfather's spirit told him to go."

Their feet entwined, and the sight of them joined startled him anew. Before he could get used to it, she had another question. *And if you could go anywhere, where?*

He hesitated longer over this answer. "Perhaps your America." He raked his spread fingers down toward her thighs and then up again.

Then, as she inhaled in musical gasps, *Will you sing for me? One of your songs.*

"Sing? Now?"

Yes.

"I need," he said, the words halting. He concentrated. "I need someone to echo."

Shuddering slightly, she pushed him away, slowing her own breath so speech could come, her tone determined. *Do it in English. I'll echo.*

His laughter came out large and loose, as unfamiliar to his own ears as weeping would have been. "Many of ours are made up on the spot. Let me see if I can do it." He shook his head to clear it and then used his thigh as a drum.

"Gather, people, and listen to me," he sang, and she echoed.

We met beneath an unlikely sky; let the sun stay down.
The earth divided to make a path; let the sun stay down.
Now the taste of honeyed rain; let the sun stay down.
Will linger always on our tongues; keep the sun down.

When he got to the last line, she held still a moment, then started touching him from the top again, his eyelashes, his cheeks, his shoulders. This time, she was silent until he rose above and parted her. Then her words were jagged.

Drinking honeyed rain.

In all the topics they touched on, before and during and afterward, they did not speak of the future. Not any part of it. Neither of them asked or offered what would happen next—to the Camel Bookmobile, to Mididima, to them. Matani was glad for that. He didn't want to try to explain how the fear of coming drought made his tribe harsher. In other places, places not so far away, people spoke about the weather in casual tones. Rain came, or it didn't; an event was delayed; a man took off a garment, or maybe added one. In Mididima, after too many cloudless seasons people began to droop with the certainty that they were being punished. The old men set out on long treks across the bush and up into the mountains to get closer to the Hundred-Legged One and beg forgiveness, while those who stayed behind tried to settle on what precisely had to be forgiven. The books, Scar Boy, Matani himself—who knew when the suspicions would end this time, or where the blame would finally land? And while they debated, Matani knew, the ground as far as one could see would relentlessly turn the washed-out color of a white man's skin, and the animals would be the first to die.

How could he talk to her about that? Not now, when they were squeezing the last bit of preciousness from the day.

Then he didn't even think of it anymore. It disappeared—the dry dust, the vacant sky, the ruined books, the son he'd wanted. All of Mididima. He found that he didn't miss it.

The Hundred-Legged One betrayed him, bringing morning's rays too soon, the light buzzing with warning. He held her hands in his, kissed each palm. On the way back, they paused at the monkey tree. He took her arm to stop her, and touched the center of her chest above her heart. "I was here," he said.

Then she went to Neema's hut, he to the *kilinge*. He heard no noise from within, so he was startled to find Jwahir's father there. He wasn't ready for this, not yet. But he had nowhere else to go. He steeled himself for the lengthy greeting.

But Jwahir's father simply looked at Matani's feet, his legs, and then his eyes. "Scar Boy's books," he said.

"Yes, they're gone." Matani sat to rest his legs and arms. Before, he wouldn't have said it so baldly. He would have found a way to soften it.

Jwahir's father paced. "I didn't want to believe until I heard it from you," he said, and Matani could tell by the iciness of his gaze that he was trying to decide where to place blame. "Gone forever?"

Matani nodded. "Scar Boy tore out some pages, drew on others."

"Did you tell him the rules?" Jwahir's father asked.

"Of course," Matani said.

"Then, what—"

"None of us could have known what he was doing." Matani hesitated, making Jwahir's father wait, wanting to appear more reluctant than he was. "None except his father," he said.

"Abayomi." After a moment, Jwahir's father turned toward the fire. "The elders have gone, but I don't think they will be able to persuade the rains to come this time," he said. "The foreign woman leaves today. After that, we have work to do."

"Of course."

"Now I'm sure your wife awaits you."

Matani was not in the mood to be dismissed from the *kilinge*. If ever he needed the grace of the ancestors who gathered there, it was now. He sat without moving.

Jwahir's father's opened his mouth as if he might say more, but did not. He backed out.

Matani rose and held his hands before the fire that the men kept burning now, that they would burn for a full three days as part of their plea for rain while the elders made their trip. Three goats also would be sacrificed, he knew, beginning tonight. It would be another late evening. But he didn't think of that now.

After a few minutes he sat again, resting his back against a drum. He wondered about a different life for himself somewhere far away. For a man such as he, an African raised to try to help his people, was it possible to simply choose to move away? He had no idea, and he waited to see if an answer would come. As he waited, he sank into the copper and gold spikes of flame, and as his gaze softened and he drifted, the hiss of the fire transformed itself into the sound of a shower, then a cloudburst, then a storm, and finally a pounding of thunder as though the ground itself were a stretched hide played by a master who demanded too much of his dancers, too light and quick a step, but rewarded them with floods from the sky.

"Teacher! Wake up!" It was Nadif, tugging at his arm, practically pulling it from the socket. Matani, who never slept during the day, had now done so for the second time in a row. "She's ready to leave."

Matani shook his head to clear it, but weariness clung to him. Outside, he expected to find that finally, miraculously, rain had come. It was dry; the water had been only in his sleep.

He heard the children's voices rise and loop with excitement. They were gathered under the acacia tree, chanting a farewell song. He stood at a short distance, watching. One of the older girls led the chant, and the others danced, kicking up red dust with their heels.

She was sitting cross-legged beneath the tree. She didn't look like someone who had stayed awake through the night; her skin was fresh and translucent as water. She was glancing around, hunting with her eyes, and she smiled when she saw him.

He wondered what this must look like to her, the natives in their send-off dance, and he wondered if she wished she had a camera to take a picture, to tell her friends back in America about her foray into a primitive African settlement. He was surprised by his own bitterness. But what else could he expect from this moment, with its loud deceptiveness, after a taste of the other?

She would leave, and they would be left with this, with Scar Boy's destruction, and it would creep up around them and enclose them like the walls of a hut they should have long ago abandoned. Was he glad that the Camel Bookmobile had come, bringing the books and this woman to Mididima? Of course. Yes, he was glad. But he also knew it had brought more problems than it had solved. Scar Boy's tattered sketches could never be turned back into pages of a library book. Abayomi's words could never be taken away.

In the distance, he saw the camels approaching. She followed his gaze and saw them, too. And she looked back at him with a startled expression, almost as if she hadn't expected them. And something else in her face. Loss.

That's what caught his breath and twisted it. As though she already knew something he didn't. But she didn't know; whatever she thought she knew might be wrong. He tried to remember the whole of what she'd told him about her life away from here, and he wondered what it would be like to live with her up a set of stairs in a city where everything could begin with the present moment, where the pressure of the before and the after would not be reflected in every face he saw.

She was hugging and kissing Kanika and Neema and some of the others.

"Teacher, Teacher, go say good-bye," the children said, pushing from behind.

She turned toward him, but neither spoke. And then she turned back to the children and gestured them to stand to one side, and in the space they left her, she did it. A cartwheel. A quick, graceful flip of her body.

The children, thinking it had been another trick for them, laughed and pointed, but she paid them no attention. She faced him, waiting wordlessly. He knew what she waited for. But he would not perform a trick, not now. He neither moved nor spoke.

After a few moments, the children crowded gaily into the space between them, and she leaned over their heads. "I'll be back," she said. "Very soon."

He needed to reply. He needed to say *Good, come back*; or better, *Don't go*; or better still, *I'll join you*. He wanted to say, *Your neck is beautiful*. He wanted to say, *I never ever thought my life would hold this, and if your leaving is what I must give for what I was given, then it was worth it*.

But the children were all around and Mr. Abasi was calling out and motioning for her to come, and anyway, he knew now, if he hadn't known before, that there were limitations to words—words in the air or on a page.

He reached forward, brushed her fingers with his. She looked down at the hand that he'd touched. Then she got on the camel and she waved. Glancing at him. At Kanika. At Neema. At the children. At him.

The Drum Maker

WHAT HAD COME FROM THE HAND OF HIS SON STUNNED Abayomi. Sketches of Mididima, seen from a distance at night, a sense of light emerging from the *kilinge*. Others of women working the crops, framed by the open door of his home. One of Abayomi himself, from the back, bent over a drum. And Kanika. Kanika from various distances and angles, the lines of her chin and shadows of her cheekbones, the arch of her eyebrows, her hair adorned. Each portrait real enough to embrace and yet containing a tiny invention, some fantasy. Flowers where none existed, a cloud of an impossible shape. Images inserted, often, to incorporate and hide the writing on the page.

Abayomi knew the art of making a drum. He thought of it as the act of forgetting himself, or perhaps—he wasn't sure about this—remembering himself. He knew how to mold the drum's body, to give birth to it, to make it open and balanced. He knew how to scrape and stretch the skin so that a drop of water could roll across it without sinking, and then how to attach the skin to the body, taut but with enough give so that the sweet spot could be as generous as a long rain or a tender woman.

He knew, too, how to test the finished drum, how to place his palm, then press gently, then tap with growing force, then pound to make sure that the drum was up to the task, that it could pulsate with the moments that transform a life, that devastate or thrill.

He knew how it was to begin building a drum at sunup, finish what seemed an hour later, and find it to be sundown.

He knew nothing, though, of what could be built by taking up a pencil and sliding it along a page.

Despite his ignorance, it was impossible not to see the power in what Taban had made. Abayomi felt pride and a longing for everyone to see the drawings—but this was coupled with the recognition that the work was as personal as a thought, especially the drawings of Kanika.

His son should be spared this public exhibition.

But his son would not be spared. He knew that the moment Jwahir's father appeared at his hut to collect the pictures.

Within the *kilinge*, Taban's sketches orbited the fire, illuminated by the flames. Some were held longer in a viewer's hands; others passed more quickly. Abayomi heard murmured exclamations, the occasional deep sigh. But the drawings themselves were not the focus. No one said, as people sometimes said of Abayomi—and should have said of Taban—that he'd been touched by the sacred ancestors.

"Cane him?" One voice.

"Not punishment enough," argued another.

Far too much, in Abayomi's view. But it was not yet his turn.

"Three cows?"

"That is as if taking from ourselves."

"And, besides, to whom should we give? The white woman? The thin-nosed man from the Distant City? Neither has use for them."

"We share some blame for allowing the books to come at all."

"So we should punish ourselves?"

"If we do nothing, we will be reduced to nothing." That was Neema, the only woman present. "If we do not extract punishment from him, the Hundred-Legged One will extract a harsher punishment from us all."

"What do you recommend, Neema? That he be killed?"

Now Abayomi lifted his head from his hands. There, at last—uttered as a challenge—was the question that had been skirting around the edges of this meeting and of Mididima since the ruined books were found. Did they think Taban had not heard it?

"Killed?" Neema stared directly at Abayomi, hesitating before answering. She looked slowly around the circle, staring into each face. "No," she said finally, though her tone sounded unconvincing to Abayomi's ears. "But whatever you think of the books and of the world that sends them—whatever this traveling library has meant to you—there is no denying that Abayomi's son is guilty of a transgression. And because of it, I think we all know what will be brought onto our heads."

Abayomi recognized Neema as a wise woman who had endured many losses. But he also knew she was schooled on the mercilessness of the first book ever to enter Mididima: the Bible her mother had given her.

"Say it plainly, Neema," someone murmured.

"The boy must be sent away," Neema said. "And then he must be—"

"Isn't banishment more than enough?" The voice that interrupted belonged to Matani.

One of the elders raised a hand, silencing them both. "Abayomi." The elder pronounced the drum maker's name in such a way that he knew it was, at last, his turn to speak. The moment he'd waited for, yet now he felt stricken by a strange panic.

He had to save his son this time, because he hadn't saved the boy before. He hadn't been alert enough to spy the hyena in the bushes and drive the beast away before it attacked Taban.

But what should he say? He wished he could take a drum from along the wall of the *kilinge* and beat out his petition. He'd be far better at that than at making speeches.

He looked at Matani, who sat at the outskirts of the circle. Once, he would have sought Matani's help, Matani's eloquence. Glancing away, he caught the eyes of Jwahir's father, who watched him intently. In the man's glance, there was a coldness that made him suspect it might already be too late for his words to do much good. But he had to try. This was his last chance.

"My son," Abayomi began haltingly, "Taban, you know him." His voice shook slightly. He took a breath, hoping to still it. "He lives with us. Yet he doesn't, through no fault of his own. The days pass and he is—by your choice as much as his—unseen."

He felt the heat of the fire caressing his cheeks, and the

warm blood in the tips of his fingers. His strength, he knew, lay in his hands, in what they could create. He wished their vigor would extend to his speech. "Who can live like that," he asked, "his life ignored? In refusing to become nothing, and in turning sheets of paper into fragments of himself—in daring to be visible through his drawings—it may be that Taban has been, above all else, brave."

He took a breath, not knowing if he was pausing or finished until he opened his mouth again and found no other words. For a few minutes, no one spoke. Then one of the elders nodded, dismissing him. They would talk in private now. He would be summoned again to hear their decision, but not soon. Their discussion of honor and duty and blame was likely to last through the night.

Before he left, though, Abayomi had one remaining obligation. He moved around the circle until he reached Matani, and then he dropped his chin so that his words would be heard only by the one for whom they were intended. "This is my punishment, what's happened to Taban. I know that," he said. "You must return yourself to Jwahir. She is yours. She will recognize it herself, soon. And once the books stop coming, it will be easier."

Matani listened silently. He did not look angry. Nor did he seem bewildered and hurt as he had that first night. Instead, his face was closed, and at the same time more complex, as though it held secrets of its own. It was a face, Abayomi recognized, that Jwahir would find perceptibly more interesting than the one she'd married. More intriguing, eventually, than Abayomi's own straightforward gaze. Even if he didn't give Jwahir back to Matani, even if he said nothing, she would wander back to him on her own.

"I will not interfere further with you and Jwahir," Abayomi said. "I'll never speak of this again."

He squared his shoulders and left. Outside the sacred enclosure, he sagged a moment before heading home. His insides felt like torn flesh. The wound would leave scars, but he knew from experience that it would heal. It was possible, after all—and he would help his son Taban learn this too—to live with a love that could not be returned.

The Librarian

THEY WERE IN THE MEETING ROOM AT THE LIBRARY SEATED around three gleaming white tables set in triangular fashion, three people on each side, windows surrounding them, a box fan on the floor, a card table in the corner replete with locally grown coffee, Assam tea, puffy air-filled pastry. Brightly lit angles everywhere. Mr. Abasi sat at one corner next to his boss, Mr. Munyes, up from Nairobi. To his right were three other regional library officials, and then the three foreign corporate sponsors, dressed in nearly identical dark suits and ties. Next came Miss Sweeney, then back to Mr. Abasi's boss again and it started all over. Mr. Abasi had never seen Miss Sweeney in anything except jeans; now she wore a dark, sedate skirt that seemed incongruous with how he'd come to view her. But in that outfit, she looked like a tall blade of elephant grass: vulnerable, yes, and yet strong.

The representatives from the investing corporation had oohed over wildlife viewed through binoculars and tasted *nyama choma*, barbecued goat meat, and now they wanted, above all else, to see the worth of their company's money in quantifiable black and white. Books to the bush. Improved literacy. Where was the proof?

Mr. Abasi's boss was running through various columns of figures, most of which Mr. Abasi himself had compiled. He hated numbers. He hated thinking about them, assembling them, typing them into spreadsheets. He watched Miss Sweeney jotting notes on a yellow pad, and thought back to a few days ago when he'd picked her up at Mididima.

As soon as he'd seen her, he'd made a quick visual inspection of her limbs. Nothing broken. No lacerations that he could see. He turned his face skyward to thank the ancestors for his good fortune, and then looked back at her. On second glance, he noticed there was something different about her. He decided it must be the sunburn.

"So you had a jolly good time?" he'd asked as they left Mididima.

"I did."

"And the two books are none the worse for wear."

"Ah. The books," she'd said.

He should have stopped then; he should have known they weren't stuffed into that purple bag of hers; but he'd prattled on a bit more, so relieved that she was alive and whole. "Your Camel Bookmobile project made the news while you were gone. There's a stack of clips waiting for you. You'll want to extend your stay, now that you've become quite the—" Only then had he broken off. "The books," he'd said.

So she'd told him as they rode back, and color sat high in her cheeks and she said she planned to use this meeting to propose a revision in the rules, a broadening of the program's goals, but he'd been barely listening because he'd been feeling smug, undeniably self-satisfied; it was exactly as he'd warned, lost is lost, but at the same time he was sorry for her, because somehow she'd become quite attached to this forsaken, camel dung of a . . .

"Mr. Abasi."

"Yes?"

"What's *your* take on this?" One of the foreigners was talking to him. "These are *your* people, after all." Perhaps it was Mr. Jackson or Mr. Beller—they all seemed interchangeable. They looked toward him.

Mr. Abasi cleared his throat. About what, precisely, did they want his "take"?

After a pause that lasted only a beat, the man—yes, it was Beller—looked back toward Miss Sweeney. "I don't care what you do about fines for missing books, Fi. Handle that as you see fit. But this other proposal of yours—well, the board of directors agreed to a onetime grant for a Camel Bookmobile. Not to anything else."

Miss Sweeney leaned both arms on the table. "The bottom line is, this is too good a cause to ignore."

Beller grunted. "Frankly, Fi, there are a shitload of good causes. What this one *had* going for it was that it was well conceived, reasonably priced, and politically attractive." Beller took a sip of water before continuing. "This other request—well, the list of what might go wrong could fill pages." He raised one hand to show he had more to say. "I remember our initial meetings, back in New York, Fi. You were clear then on a number of things."

"I was operating in a vacuum."

"You understood the perimeter of this program. Books for people who never had them before, to encourage literacy in backward places. A novel plan for how to get those books into the bush and one that would make use of a natural community resource—camels. It was a precisely defined concept, a grabber. I mean, it's philanthropy, and there's a feel-good component, but we want a little bit of a return for our goodwill dollar, and with the publicity we counted on, we knew we'd get that. Now, though, you're suggesting"—he ruffled through some papers in front of him—"that we locate worthy nomads, transport them to the city, put them up, educate them, cross our fingers that it all goes well. It's messier, more costly, and a lot less sexy." He sighed. "Look, I'm not saying no. What I suggest is that you write up a proposal for next year, and see how it goes."

"I don't want to wait. Two of them, maybe three, are ready to go now."

"Yes, I see. A boy who can draw."

Miss Sweeney sat very straight. "I want to make a difference in his life," she said. "We need to help patrons of the Camel Bookmobile become part of the larger world. That, after all, is the point of making them literate, isn't it?"

"Way beyond our mandate," Beller said again.

"So expand it."

She was, Mr. Abasi realized, the most audacious woman he could ever hope to know.

Beller loosened his tie. "We're at a bit of an impasse here, I'd say. Mr. Abasi? We still haven't heard from you."

Heads swiveled, once again, in his direction. Mr. Abasi rubbed his hands nervously under the table. He looked first toward his boss, who lifted his shoulders in the slightest of shrugs. He glanced at Miss Sweeney, expecting to find a plea in her face, but there was none. Her jaw was set in the determination he recognized; her eyes were merely curious.

Mr. Abasi felt something unfamiliar move through him and settle in his gut. A sense of power. Oh, he'd flexed a few muscles with his mother, in the form of Siti, but this— men scooted toward the edges of their seats, waiting—was something different.

He recognized that the power was limited. He wouldn't decide the fate of the Camel Bookmobile. Still, he could go on record, make the points he'd rehearsed so often and so articulately, explain that though the concept seemed gen- erous on the surface, it was actually naive. Trying to bring Western literacy to people in a place like Mididima might even be harmful. The intrusion, in fact, could throw life dangerously out of whack.

This was his moment. They were waiting.

Mr. Abasi cleared his throat. Miss Sweeney was staring directly at him. He felt drawn into her eyes. He had the sense of speaking only to her.

"The facts you have in front of you—the number of patrons reached, the titles of the most popular books, the cost per patron—do very little to reflect the human costs of bringing a library on the backs of camels to people like this," he said. "These people live hard lives by ancient values, and they're proud of that. They've developed a philosophy to deal with drought and death. When we arrive from the outside and insist that they learn to read—books that, as it turns out, are mostly about very different places and con- cerns—we confuse them. Possibly even undermine them.

I think Miss Sweeney will tell you that their young are as sharp as any. And their elders may be wiser. Compared with them, after all, we of the settled, literate society have a kind of inflexibility. So your project raises questions. Do they want to be part of what you call the 'larger world'? And who should be teaching whom?"

Mr. Abasi's boss, clearly anticipating fireworks, examined his fingernails with interest. Beller stroked his chin. Under the table, Mr. Abasi pinched one hand with the other and made a decision.

"Of course, some of them do want to join us, as Miss Sweeney has found. Besides, I don't think you've donated your funds in return for such a theoretical discussion," he said, addressing Beller directly then. "If I understand correctly, idealism is not what your company is paying for. Your project, because it is unusual and catchy as you've said, has already gained public attention. What you want are more newspaper articles, maybe even gold plaques to hang in your board of directors' room." He paused, scratching his head. "What you *don't* want is headlines about rich American corporations rejecting an opportunity to help the Camel Bookmobile readers for what amounts to the cost of, say, three plane tickets, business class, from New York to here."

He raised his chin, wishing briefly that Siti were in the room to hear him. He glanced at Miss Sweeney with her head bowed, the hint of a smile dancing at her lips. Then he leaned back into the silence.

Scar Boy

HE DREW. OBSESSIVELY, WITHOUT STOPPING; WHAT OTHER choice had he? Should he sit and wait like his father, heavy and silent? His own body, fueled by nervous energy, would refuse that, and what would be the point, anyway? Those within the *kilinge* would arrive at their decision in their own time; nothing could prevent that now, nor could anything hurry them up. Should he hurl himself away from the hut each dawn, determined to escape by working all day and dancing through the night as hard as the body would allow? Should he, in short, become his brother? He could not, of course.

He was certain now of something they did not realize in the white woman's world: a boy cannot alter the path of his destiny. From the moment of the hyena's attack, the future had borne down, unstoppable and predetermined, and it didn't matter whether or not he learned to read, or fell in love, or simply waited silently like his father. Even drawing would not revise fate, but he could not stop himself from that. So he drew.

The sketches were smaller now; paper had become even more precious. But the work was exciting. He was calling forth every second of all those hours of practice to portray Badru. Only it wasn't exactly Badru. It was part Badru: Badru marked by one of Taban's scars. Nothing major. No limp. No misshapen eyes. Just the drag to the mouth, the smear that tugged the lips toward the ground, that controlled the expression, and that would affect each kiss.

Taban saw, after he penciled the face, that a single scar—though it made an impact—would have been so much less, and would have allowed him much more. But he couldn't change what had happened, not with the hyena, not with Kanika, not with the white woman's books. So he drew Badru in the hut, Badru at the door of the hut with the white woman, Badru beyond the hut with a girl Taban could sketch in his sleep, although in these drawings she had no face.

A sound: short, rapid footsteps that grew strident before halting at his door. "Abayomi."

Taban watched a *mbu* land on the back of his hand. He remained motionless, successfully willing it away as Abayomi rose and went to meet his cousin Chege. What brought Chege? Taban knew there'd been no decision yet. When it was over, he would hear the tribe's drums, like the drone from a swarm of mosquitoes. The thirstiest and most determined insects of the bush.

He was not curious enough to try to listen to the voices of his father and his father's cousin. He concentrated, instead, on the legs of his Badru figure. Strong legs in movement. He wanted to show the power and the possibility in those legs, to define each muscle.

"Taban."

He knew he could do it, if he practiced enough. And then he would be so close to Badru that perhaps he would experience some of what Badru lived through.

"Taban, I'm talking to you."

He looked up. His father's face was above him. In it, he noticed what he never had before. The contours of Abayomi's cheeks made arrows that pointed to his eyes. His eyebrows were part of a frame, and within the eyes themselves—that's where Abayomi held all his emotions. And they were immense. Such passions Taban had thought his father didn't have.

"Chege has come to give us the news early. So quickly now. Take what you can carry on your back," Abayomi said.

First among his father's feelings right now, Taban saw, was fear.

"We will go east."

There was much to draw in his father's face. Much he had overlooked.

"I've heard of water there, at the foot of a great mountain."

Now, at last, Taban heard the words. So that, then, must be the decision. He would be sent away. He wondered if it was better than death, which was the verdict he realized he'd been unconsciously expecting.

But perhaps it was death they'd been sentenced to, in fact. After all, how would they survive?

"Your step is not fast. But don't forget that no one is quieter," Abayomi said, as if he could read his son's mind. "They are giving us one of the tribe's three guns. And your aim will improve. We will be safe." He looked over his shoulder, then back at his son. "Whatever they intend, we'll be safe."

A question remained, of course. Taban waited, but Abayomi turned away without saying more. Taban let his palm fall to his drawing. "Badru?" he asked.

Abayomi spread a cloth and put three bags of maize and a pot in the middle before he spoke. "He's better with the others," he said.

Of course, Abayomi was right. Badru already had been moving away. Besides, Abayomi and Taban were to blame for the hyena. Now Abayomi and Taban would do the moving.

Taban needed to get up, to help his father prepare. But he couldn't, not quite yet. He bent again before the page with the Badru-Taban figure, and in another corner, he drew the inside of this hut, the hut that had held his whole life, the spaces in the walls that let in dust and light, the holes through which Kanika poked her sticks, the mats where the three of them had lain, his father's drum-making tools in the corner, and Abayomi on his heels before the cloth that would travel with them.

He drew it all, so that he could hold it one more time before he let it go.

The American

THE CAMELS' STATELY, ROLLING PACE HAD NEVER BOTHERED Fi before, but now it strained her patience to the breaking point. She wanted a car, a train, a helicopter, some modern metallic machine that could bring speed; she wanted to burn the ground beneath her. She imagined parachuting in, supplies strapped to her belly. "*Jambo, jambo!* I'm here."

Instead she was part of this crawling caravan: three camels, a driver, a bodyguard, Mr. Abasi, and her. Plus boxes of library books and, in her duffel bag, a school application, a pile of cream-colored drawing paper, pencils, and a sharpener. She imagined Kanika's ample smile, Taban's steady stare. She wanted Taban to know that she returned the confidence he'd put in her by showing her his sketches.

"What a difference this will make to his life," she'd gushed to Mr. Abasi during a weak moment when anticipation got the best of her, and then she'd steeled herself for a sarcastic comment, something about uncultivated nomads. He'd shaken his head, but said nothing.

And Matani. She touched her lips, then her neck, and thought of the small of his back, where a garden patch of hair bloomed. She couldn't imagine the logistics and didn't care to try; she knew only that she wanted his hands at her waist, her face buried somewhere in the hollow between his shoulder and his neck.

"AIDS," Devi had said in a phone conversation a few days earlier, that single acronym standing in for a whole sentence, a rambling question, an hour-long lecture.

"No. Not there. Not him."

"You sure?"

"Sure," she said, flicking away doubt.

"Well, then," Devi said and took an audible breath. "Then it's great. It's perfect, sweetie. Memorable, an adventure, none of the potential permanence of someone solid and reliable like Chris, and not the kind of affair where you're going to get your heart broken." A few beats later, into the silence of the phone, she added, "Right?"

Right. Absolutely. This was drinking honeyed rain; that's what it was.

And yet sometimes the unexpected happened; there could be a joining that looked so unlikely from the outside, and obstacles enough to fill an encylopedia, and still, a swoop of emotion would end up dictating the future.

Not that she expected it this time.

"I might spend an extra night," she'd told Mr. Abasi. "Just in case I don't have a chance to go over the application with Kanika. She'll need help filling it out."

He raised an eyebrow. "And how will you get back?"

"Someone from Mididima will accompany me."

He stared at her a long moment, then waved his hand and turned away. His knowing look made her uncomfortable, but she appreciated that he didn't raise any objections. Mr. Abasi had grown on her.

It was hot, a day scorching enough to darken the boldest tips of grass. From her seat on the camel, she poured water into her cupped hand, then rubbed it on the back of her neck and into her hair. Where was Mididima? Shouldn't they see it popping up on the horizon? It was past lunchtime, after all. Now a watch might be useful, so she could keep track of how long they'd been traveling.

"Mr. A."

He glanced over his shoulder.

"Are we lost?"

He shook his head.

"But shouldn't we . . . "

"This place is at the end of our lives," he said. "Have you forgotten? But we're getting there."

She wasn't even sure the passing scenery looked familiar. It had grown more tan in just a week. She wondered if she recognized that bunch of grayish bushes.

And just as she thought she'd have to ask again, highlighting her blistering impatience, there it was in the distance: that grand, elegant woman, the soaring acacia tree. She closed her eyes for a second to hold close the anticipation. Almost there, almost there.

Then she opened them, hungry for the sight of smoke from the *kilinge*, the scattering of colorful clothes.

The camels moved forward, step by lumbering step. But the huts were not springing into view. Could it be the wrong acacia? She ran her eyes over it. No, it was the one.

"What—" She let the start of her question hang in the

air. The three camels slowed as they approached the tree, snorting, underlining the silence.

Mididima. It was gone. The ground looked slightly swept where Mididima had been, but a solitary black bird with a purple ring around its neck was the only sign of life. It hopped boldly toward them, and then turned to take flight.

"Miss Sweeney," Mr. Abasi began, and something resigned in his voice stirred Fi to action. She put her arms around the neck of her camel and tried to steer him to the left. She knew where she needed to go. The camel refused to budge; it didn't want to break from the bunch.

A lumpy beast wouldn't outdo her in stubbornness. She slid down and took off, walking briskly.

"Miss Sweeney?"

"Be right back, Mr. A."

After a few minutes, out of sight of the others, she began jogging. She ran until she reached the hut in which she and Matani had spent their night. She paused before the door. The skins that had covered the grass mat were gone, but otherwise it was the same, streaks of light sliding through gaps in the walls, clinging to the shadows. She went inside and walked once in a circle along the walls, looking for a trace of something she couldn't name. She closed her eyes and lifted her hair, dropping her head to one side, trying to feel the leaf juice Matani had smoothed on her skin. Her breath came short and shallow.

Outside, the fire pit sat cold. But the water pan still had water—that brought a sense of relief. They wouldn't leave precious water. And they wouldn't leave her, not like this.

Matani wouldn't leave. They must be somewhere hiding. A game, a magic trick to answer her own, yes, that was it.

She strode back to the monkey tree and searched the branches, half expecting a clue that would send her to the next place, and the next, a scavenger hunt, until finally she found them. She put her hand on the tree trunk. It felt thin, loose, and dry, like the skin of an ancient man.

The crops. Of course. That must be where they were. They were surely huddled together, waiting, giggling at her wild search. She trotted, focused, keeping her mind clear until she reached the rise. The plants had been pulled; the soil had been torn like a victim of violent crime; the irrigation buckets were gone. She stared off in the direction where she'd seen the giraffes and the zebra. "Where are you, Matani?" she whispered.

Her walk back to the acacia was slow. Mr. Abasi and the others were shifting awkwardly, talking among themselves.

"Something's happened," she said. "I was just here with them. There was no—"

"Sometimes it's like that."

"No. That doesn't make sense."

Mr. Abasi was silent.

"They were so worried about those missing books. They wouldn't—"

"They didn't." He pointed.

And there under the acacia tree, she saw the piles. Three neat rectangular plateaus, dozens of colorful spines. She felt a painful hollowness in her stomach as she knelt and picked through the books. *Project for Winter.* The math textbooks. *Baby's First Five Years.* She knew without counting: except for the Bible and the two Taban had used, it was every book that had been in Mididima.

She swallowed, waiting for the ability to speak, trying to ignore the tight feeling between her eyes. "Where have they gone?" she said over her shoulder after a minute.

Mr. Abasi raised his hands. "Who can say?"

"But they can't have gone far, and they need water. We'll look for them." She hated the tremulous quality to her voice.

"Miss Sweeney." Mr. Abasi squatted next to her. "Your project has gotten big. Books, books everywhere. Now we have a dozen other godforsaken places waiting for a library, and not enough days in the week." He shook his head. "In the end," he said, "your Camel Bookmobile is greater than one tiny tribe."

"Just like that?"

"Sometimes."

She turned back to the books, letting her arms drape over the piles. She tried to list in her mind the other places the library visited, and to remember the names of the tribes that were waiting. Behind her, Mr. Abasi stood and said something to the driver and the bodyguard, and she heard them move off. A mosquito landed on her forearm and she smashed it, viciously. As if it would steady her mind, she tried to list the parts of a mosquito's body: the thorax, the proboscis, the banded abdomen.

"I'm going to take a stroll," Mr. Abasi said. "For a few minutes. And then we will get back on the camels, Miss Sweeney."

Fi heard his footsteps move away. She began to go

through the books, restacking them, randomly lifting some
to smell. *The Cat in the Hat.* The biography of Gertrude
Bell. *The Pearl.* She paused over that one. She'd forgotten
she'd given it to Matani. She had no idea whether he'd read
it or not; they'd never spoken of it. Something else they
hadn't had time to discuss.

She flipped through the thin book. It opened somewhere near the end; a piece of paper served as a bookmark.
She read idly.

"Will they follow us?' she asked. "Do you think they
will try to find us?"

"They will try," said Kino. "Whoever finds us will
take the pearl. Oh, they will try."

The bookmark, she noticed now, was a page folded in
half. One of Taban's pages, ripped from a library book? She
opened it up to words written in black ink. Matani's name
stood at the end. For half a second, she felt the uncertainty
of the thirsty man: to gulp or to savor the last sip of water?
And then she read.

Dear Fi,
*   I wish now for a telephone so I could tell you in my*
own voice. My people decided it was time to touch other
sands. They look for a place favored by more rainfall, and
besides, they do not want the young to forget how to tear
down and set up a house. In the end, this is the knowl-
edge they believe is too important to be lost. But I will try
to teach the reading too, when I can.

*Some of the children are practicing your magic, trying
to make a stick disappear in their hands. They, and I, will
never forget you.*

*Thank you in your language sounds so unfilled. We
have a better saying. Fresh water on your cheeks, Fi
Sweeney.*

Yours always, Matani

Fresh water on your cheeks. Was this the fifth local expression she had learned? If so—what was it Mr. Abasi had told her?—Matani could not deny her food, water, or shelter.

But of course, he could deny her. Of course he could, because he was gone.

And if this was right, if this was the only and best way for Mididima, for Matani, for her and Matani, she couldn't acknowledge that yet. Later, she would review every moment of her drink of honeyed rain. She would wonder about Kanika and Neema and especially Taban, whom she'd intended to help perhaps most of all. Later, she would ask herself, and ask herself again, who had given in that arid settlement of Mididima, and who had received; who had learned and who had taught.

But it wasn't the time for that now. She heard Mr. Abasi clear his throat somewhere behind her. Soon he would approach. Soon he would ask if she was all right, if she was ready now, and she would answer, a little curtly, "Of course, Mr. A." She would stand and wipe her hands on her jeans and they would pack up Mididima's books. The camels would protest at being turned around so quickly, but they would go. And soon Mr. Abasi would pencil in a tribe to

take the place of Mididima in the bookmobile's schedule and Fi would board a plane and fly back to New York
and hug Devi and see Chris and return to her library in
Brooklyn and look for another project to capture her heart
and trigger her imagination. And soon either it would rain
here, refilling the water pans, or it wouldn't, and the ground
would crack in protest.

  Knowing this, Fi sat under the acacia tree while she still
could. She stared from the note with Matani's handwrit-
ing to the plot of ground that so recently had been Mididima, and back again. "I was here," she said aloud. And then
she couldn't speak for a moment; her throat constricted as
Matani's fresh water dampened her cheeks before evaporat-
ing in the merciless, thirsty air.

Acknowledgments

To early and generous readers Dan Gilmore, Arra Hamilton, Susan Ito, David Orr, Jennifer Stewart, Nancy Wall, and Amanda Eyre Ward for their valuable suggestions.

To my editor, Claire Wachtel, for her keen eye and fierce dedication.

To my incomparable agent, Marly Rusoff, and her team for believing in this story from its inception, for shepherding it forward each step of the way, and for . . . well, just about everything.

To all the exceptional librarians who have infused me from childhood with their passion for reading.

To Rupert and Arra Hamilton, for unwavering love and encouragement, for supporting the unconventional, and for always making me think I could do it, whatever "it" was at the moment.

To Briana, for first telling me about the Camel Library.

And to David, Briana, Cheney, and Daylon for pausing to listen to ragged drafts of this story as it unfolded, for forgiving me the chores undone and meals uncooked because I was writing, and for filling my days with love and meaning.

Thank you.

Book donations to the Camel Library can be sent to:

> Garissa Provincial Library
> For Camel Library
> Provincial Librarian
> Rashid M. Farah
> P.O. Box 245-70100
> Garissa, Kenya

Book donations for small libraries throughout Africa can be sent via:

> African Library Project
> www.africanlibraryproject.org

To learn more about The Camel Bookmobile and Masha Hamilton please visit:

> www.mashahamilton.com

About the author

About the book

Read on

Insights,
Interviews
& More...

Meet Masha Hamilton

I GREW UP running barefoot and shirtless through the Arizona desert. From early childhood, I learned how to steer clear of rattlers and scorpions and how to manipulate two sticks to yank cactus needles out of my own feet and legs. I read about Native Americans who sprinted through the dry heat with a sip of water in their mouths and spit it out at the end of their run to develop willpower, so I practiced doing the same. I became strongly linked to the arid landscape, as well as the people: I made friendships in first grade that have lasted until today. Somehow this remarkably stable upbringing left me with a nomadic soul and the sense that some risks are worth taking.

After high school, I left Arizona to attend Brown University. There I learned that thick coats help when you live someplace colder than the desert. After college, I was fortunate enough to get a job with the Associated Press in Maine—someplace even colder. Later the AP transferred me to Indianapolis and then to New York City, where I studied French and lobbied for a position in East Africa. When the AP offered Israel, it seemed too good a story to pass up.

In Israel, I learned how dangerous intolerance could be and what it feels like to be deeply afraid. I was tear-gassed and shot at and arrested in a refugee camp outside Bethlehem. I was on a bus full of Israeli settlers that was attacked in the West Bank, and fled on foot with Palestinian "radicals" running from Israeli tanks late one night. Sometimes the stories people told me made me cry, but I tried to do so alone in the shower. I knew what they were enduring was more important than what I felt.

While on assignment in Finland, I met some Soviet journalists, followed their fingers as they pointed across the water to the Soviet Union, and was filled with longing. As soon as I got back to Israel, I began taking Russian lessons. I was sent to Moscow on temporary assignment and, despite the lack of decent food—or really any food I recognized except ramen noodles and green hot mustard—became enamored of the country. Somewhere in here, I went to Cyprus to marry a television editor, and seven weeks after the first of our three children was born, we moved to Russia.

In Moscow, I witnessed the end of Soviet Communism and the collapse of the USSR and learned how tightly people hold on to their dreams. I also learned to speak Russian much better than I'd ever spoken Hebrew ▶

> " I was on a bus full of Israeli settlers that was attacked in the West Bank, and fled on foot with Palestinian 'radicals' running from Israeli tanks late one night. "

or Arabic or French. I covered the Communist coup against Gorbachev, the long queues for bread, the collapse of Communism. Late one night, I tried to talk my way past a cordon of anti-Communist troops to enter the grounds of the Russian Parliament when it was occupied by pro-Communists (mostly old men and women holding on to their dreams). When an armed, belligerent, vodka-breathed soldier hoisted me into the air and began yelling threats, I learned my persuasive techniques were not adequate to the task, so I promised to leave. Instead, I leapt over a fence and got inside the compound to interview some people who were soon to die. Somewhere in the midst of this intense news story, I began to dream fictional stories in such detail and with such frequency that I realized I had reached a fork in my own personal path. I quit journalism to return to the United States and write fiction as truly and authentically as I could.

My first novel, *Staircase of a Thousand Steps*, was published in 2001 and won acclaim from booksellers. My second novel, *The Distance Between Us*, was named one of the best books of 2004 by the *Library Journal*. Although I strongly believe that fiction holds the ultimate truth, I learned that I am not able to completely give up journalism. In 2004, I traveled around Afghanistan, meeting women prisoners, interviewing child brides, and practicing shiatsu on women villagers. In 2006, in Kenya to research *The Camel Bookmobile*, I also interviewed street kids in Nairobi and victims of drought and famine in the north. I feel lucky to be able to spend so much of my time writing stories. ❧

> 66 Although I strongly believe that fiction holds the ultimate truth, I learned that I am not able to completely give up journalism. In 2004, I traveled around Afghanistan. 99

Visiting the Real Camel Bookmobile

WE HAD NOT SEEN a single building since leaving Garissa, Kenya—nor, in fact, any infrastructure of any sort. It was February, but as scorching and arid as a summer afternoon in Arizona's desert. We had been walking for two hours when, at last, a solitary one-room schoolhouse appeared on the horizon, signaling our destination. Under a nearby acacia tree, the camels halted, grunting and weary from our trip through the African bush.

"Toh! Toh!" the herders cried, whipping the beasts' knees to force them to kneel so their cargo could be unloaded. Barefoot children appeared as if out of nowhere, sinewy and dusty, leaning against one another as they watched the traveling librarians open a wooden box to reveal its cache: fairy tales, novels, atlases, biographies, and more, in English and Swahili. The librarians unrolled grass mats and spread out the books while the children waited for the moment when they could sit on the ground and hold a volume in their own hands.

Garissa, along the murky Tana River not far from the border with Somalia, is home to the camel-borne bookmobile, which travels deep into the bush to bring books to a semi-nomadic people known as pastoralists who have spent generations roaming in search of water for themselves and their camels, cows, and goats. Though they live in Kenya, most are ethnic Somalis; borders on maps are of little meaning here. Homes are built of grass so as to be easily transportable, paper and pencil are rare, ▶

> ❝ Barefoot children appeared as if out of nowhere, sinewy and dusty, leaning against one another as they watched the traveling librarians open a wooden box to reveal its cache. ❞

Visiting the Real Camel Bookmobile
(continued)

and illiteracy has hovered above eighty-five percent in this proud, isolated region where many have a strong attachment to the nomadic lifestyle and a suspicion of the modern world.

When the camel library began operating in October 1996, "checking out a book was not a clear concept," Garissa's head librarian, Rashid Farah, explained as we walked through the bush behind the lumbering camels. Mr. Farah chose camels to introduce his service in part because the bush is otherwise impassable and in part because he wanted to find a way to make the foreign familiar. These ships of the desert, after all, are as trusted as one's own grandmother here. Still, adaptation took time. "Parents would say to me, 'I didn't ask you to give my child this book. Why should I have to return it?'" Some also worried that the books might bring with them the corruption of the modern world—and especially AIDS, or "the slim disease," as it is called there.

But Mr. Farah persisted in his efforts to bring literacy to the bush, and now twelve camels accompanied by librarians trudge through the bush to four settlements per day four days a week, despite temperatures that linger around 100 degrees in a parched, undeveloped landscape. It may seem an oversized effort to try to spread a love of literature, but a single trip proves it's worth it. Those who live with chronic poverty in a world almost inconceivably different from our own turn the pages of books with something nearing devotion. These librarians are heroes in

> ❝ Some also worried that the books might bring with them the corruption of the modern world—and especially AIDS, or 'the slim disease,' as it is called there. ❞

their commitment to education and reading.

I first heard about the project from my daughter one autumn afternoon as I drove my three children to our local library. One detail in particular piqued my interest. Because books were rare and precious in the reaches of Africa far from the safari vacationers, the camel-powered library initiated a severe fine. If even one person lost a book, the bookmobile would boycott that entire village, choosing another to visit instead.

The fine was intended both to protect books so literacy could spread and to encourage a wandering people to adopt the practices of a more settled world. But reality, as always, would be more complex than theory, I knew.

As I listened, the entire arc of a story came to me in one gulp. I imagined an American librarian who travels to Africa to give meaning to her own life and ends up losing a piece of her heart. I saw a scarred African boy, once mauled nearly to death by a hyena, who finds an extraordinary way to enlarge his narrow world. I saw a huddle of mud and dung huts where a few books go missing, and where people who fear for their way of life turn their anger on the disfigured boy.

Through it all, I envisioned books—Dr. Seuss, Homer, vegetarian cookbooks, *Tom Sawyer*, Hemingway novels, Zen meditations, short stories about modern love—traveling through the remote desert on the arched backs of camels, like notes ▶

B I envisioned books—Dr. Seuss, Homer, vegetarian cookbooks, *Tom Sawyer,* Hemingway novels, Zen meditations, short stories about modern love—traveling through the remote desert on the arched backs of camels, like notes from another world sealed in a bottle and tossed into a sea. c

Visiting the Real Camel Bookmobile
(continued)

from another world sealed in a bottle and tossed into a sea.

It was the first time I've experienced a story in that way, and it was intoxicating. I began to share parts of it with my children, my voice rising as we pulled into the library parking lot. But then I stopped abruptly. I didn't want to spend the story's energy yet, I told them.

It was years later, in 2006, with my novel mostly finished, that I went to see the camel library for myself. Although I researched and interviewed by phone and Internet as I wrote the novel, I waited until *The Camel Bookmobile* was in the final editing stages to actually visit because I wanted my fictional story to be fully realized before my reporting tendencies kicked in. My daughter, who initially told me of the camel library, joined me in the trip. Visiting in the midst of drought and famine, we gave away maize and cooking oil wherever we stopped. Grown-ups gathered for the food, the women sometimes squatting under a tree and motioning for me to join them. Giggling children, too, were briefly interested in the appearance of a blonde foreigner and her daughter, but soon they forgot us and became consumed by the books, often reading to themselves in slow, hushed voices. I found myself as moved by the real camel bookmobile as I had been by the very idea itself.

Eighteen-year-old Ismael told me he has been checking out books from the camel library for three years, and he credits it with helping him improve the English he needs for exams he hopes will allow him to continue his education in a city. The books also aided in his understanding of scientific and mathematical concepts that he needs for the same exams. "I'm grateful for that. But I like the stories best," he said with a smile.

To continue their work, the camel library needed more books. The bush is hard on volumes, and sometimes in these semi-nomadic communities, those who have checked out books move on before the library can return. So, with help of two author friends, I began a camel book drive, with a Web site, www.camelbook drive.wordpress.com, for information that donors might need.

Though *The Camel Bookmobile* is fictional, some of the gray areas explored here do exist in fact. The region is in transition, the camel bookmobile is part of that evolution, and not all of the pastoralists are happy to see their lifestyle change. Nevertheless, the bookmobile continues to awe and inspire by its demonstration of the lengths people will go to share a love of reading, and the connection that books provide. ∾

> " With help of two author friends, I began a camel book drive, with a Web site, www .camelbookdrive .wordpress.com, for information that donors might need. "

Excerpt: *The Distance Between Us*

Following is an excerpt from Masha Hamilton's second novel, The Distance Between Us, *published by Unbridled Books in 2004.*

THE WHOLE OF HEAVEN is off-balance as they rumble out of the city: clouds one moment, darting sunlight the next. A dust shroud swirling around the Land Rover prevents Caddie from seeing where they are going or where they've been. Far behind them, a mosque wails its hellfire summons to those who believe. It's noon, then, and men of conviction are submitting their foreheads to the ground in a graceful wave, while she barrels forward into the formless, blind middle of a day.

The Land Rover rattles like a tin roof in a storm. Her shoulders ache, she's inhaling cupfuls of powdered dirt, and they have at least another ninety minutes to go. But those are only irritants. Her real worry is the driver, a complete unknown. Rob and the hotel concierge rounded him up when the regular chauffeur, the one Rob assured her was "the best in Beirut," didn't show. A driver is their lifeline in dusty, uncharted territory. This guy, well—she catches her breath as he swerves sharply and clips a roadside bush, aiming directly for half a dozen desert larks. The birds scatter and arc overhead, their fury sharp enough to be heard above the thrash of the engine.

"Christ," Caddie mumbles. In the rearview mirror, the driver gives her a squinty glare. Cobwebs form at the outer

> 66 The Land Rover rattles like a tin roof in a storm. Her shoulders ache, she's inhaling cupfuls of powdered dirt. . . . 99

corners of his eyes, and dried grime thick enough to scrape off with a fingernail is caked behind his right ear. "Who the hell *is* he?" Caddie mutters to Marcus, next to her in the backseat. "Should we really be—?"

"Cautious Caddie," Marcus says. "He's okay. Rob wouldn't use him otherwise." He leans over Caddie to address Rob, who's on her left. "Right-o, Rob?"

"He's fine. Told you. Checked him out." Rob is focused on adjusting his tape recorder's input level. With his scruffy hair and taut energy, he looks like a street tough instead of a network radio reporter. Here, that aura serves him well.

"See?" Marcus says to Caddie. "Anyway, what's our choice? Sit on our bums all day?"

They pull up short before a barrier of razor wire and man-sized chunks of concrete spray-painted black with Arabic graffiti. A Yaladi roadblock. She didn't expect it this soon. The driver cuts the engine and the air grows defiantly still. The dust finally gives up and sinks.

A slouching man with a knife tucked into his belt separates himself from a concrete slab, sticks out a hand to collect their press cards, and then, self-important on squat legs, strides into a hut. A second roadside militiaman, baby face and pear belly, plants himself next to their Land Rover, machine gun cradled in his arms.

Caddie brushes the dust from her hair. She wishes again that she were more familiar with this route from Beirut to the south. They are probably twenty miles from the border with Israel, twenty miles from the Mediterranean Sea. The land is scraped and stingy, abandoned even by ▶

> " A second roadside militiaman, baby face and pear belly, plants himself next to their Land Rover, machine gun cradled in his arms. "

animals and insects, left to these imprudent men with their weapons.

"One-two-'twas brillig and the slithy toves . . ." Rob intones into his microphone.

"You're going to drain the battery before we get there," Sven says.

"Something's wrong with the goddamned pinch roller," Rob says. "If I don't get the interview on tape, I might as well have slept in, saved myself this cowboy ride." Incessant worrying over the equipment, Caddie knows, is part of his routine. She has habits of her own. During interviews, she often makes up a ridiculous question or two that she would never actually ask, then imagines her subject's response. It's oddly soothing.

"You worry too much," Marcus says. "If the pitch is off, it's so slight no one will notice."

"Hey, bud, I don't worry enough," Rob says. "Otherwise I wouldn't be in the middle of fucking East Jesus letting some monkey point his gun at me."

Their guard has begun shifting gently from foot to foot, swinging his weapon as if in time to music. Watching him, Caddie almost hears her ballet teacher's shrill military voice: "One, two, on your toes, lift your head." She'd been, what? Eight, maybe nine years old, and remarkably clumsy, all clashing elbows and difficult knees. "Again, from the top. Let's plié . . ." She pictures this bulky militiaman, with his unexpected Santa Claus face, wearing a pink tutu. As he sways next to the hunks of ruined concrete, she is struck by a single, distinct wave she can identify only as elation.

How could she ever explain to someone back home what it is to cover a conflict? At least one like this that crisscrosses through the region, its front line changing daily, so that she can find herself unexpectedly *in it* at a moment's notice. Everyone with a television set observes the violence and horror. But, sitting on their couches, can they imagine the delight of unexpected absurdities? The rush of ecstasy, even, when the exotic intersects with the familiar? Or the way that seeing all this, up close, elevates a common life?

The driver slows again to about five miles an hour. Except for scrawny gray bushes hugging the roadside, the area seems forsaken. "Enough delays," Rob calls, bouncing his right leg. "Let's get the show rolling."

"Don't worry." Sven half-turns in his seat. "We must be almost there. Isn't that right?" he asks the driver in loud Arabic. "We are there?"

Their driver doesn't answer—in fact, Caddie realizes she's never heard him speak. She has no idea what his voice sounds like, and that suddenly registers as odd.

Before she can ask another question and wait him out until he's forced to reply, she catches sight of a bush up ahead to the right, jerking in a way it shouldn't. The air hisses and loses pressure like a deflating balloon. "Hold it," Caddie says, but she doubts anyone hears because right then a passing shrub rises and makes an inexplicable *ping*. "Hey—" Marcus exclaims, and he half-stands, faces her ▶

<blockquote>❝ Their driver doesn't answer—in fact, Caddie realizes she's never heard him speak. She has no idea what his voice sounds like, and that suddenly registers as odd. ❞</blockquote>

and raises his hands as though to block her from the bush, and then he leans on her, shoving her down, and Caddie is dimly aware of a *crack* and grayish smoke as she hears Sven in the front yelling, "Gas, hit the gas you idiot, go, go, go for Christ's sake!" It occurs to her that their situation must be serious for cordial Sven to call someone an idiot, and Rob sinks to his knees on the floor of the jeep, pulling her toward him, saying, "Oh Jesus oh fuck oh Jesus," so she's sandwiched between the two of them, Rob and Marcus, and she's aware of a peppery scent, and then, at last, she feels the jeep plunge forward and she tastes the dust that has settled on the leather seats but she sees nothing since her head is near her knees and Marcus is slumped over, protecting her, and the air becomes too dense to breathe, as though she's underwater, and they seem to be turning because she falls to her left in slow motion and she realizes she should definitely be afraid right now, very afraid, yet she feels separate from it, in it but apart, like she's that dirt caked behind the driver's ear, and they spin to their right and Marcus, who is still covering her body with his own—God, he's heavy—half falls off and at that same moment she feels something sticky like tree sap on her cheek and she touches it and it's blood. "I guess I've been hit," she says, shifting her body toward Marcus, keeping her voice light because she's already been flighty today about the woman and her toddler so hysteria now is impermissible, and then she knows, she knows right away and without any doubt. The blood is his and he's gone. ✍

Don't miss the next book by your favorite author. Sign up now for AuthorTracker by visiting www.AuthorTracker.com.